P

DAISIES FOR INNOCEN

"Cattrell, who also authors the Magical Bakery Mystery series under the name Bailey Cates, once again casts a spell over readers with this charming mystery filled with likable characters and funny dialogue." —Kings River Life Magazine

"Elliana is easy to like. She's one of those characters you would enjoy chatting with in real life . . . The killer confrontation is tense and well done. The wrap-up puts a smile on your face and leaves you disappointed to leave Poppyville and Elliana's mesmerizing garden. Rating: near perfect—couldn't put it down. Buy two copies, one for you and one for a friend." —Mysteries and My Musings

"Bailey Cattrell has planted all the seeds to get this series off to a blooming start."
—Escape with Dollycas into a Good Book

Praise for Bailey Cattrell writing as Bailey Cates
and the *New York Times* bestselling
Magical Bakery Mysteries

"Katie is a charming amateur sleuth, baking her way through murder and magic set against the enchanting backdrop of Savannah, Georgia."
—Jenn McKinlay, *New York Times* bestselling author

"A smooth, accomplished writer who combines a compelling plot with a cast of interesting characters that are diverse and engaging . . . while the story's magical elements bring a fun, intriguing dimension to the genre." —*Kirkus Reviews*

"[A] promising series." —*Library Journal*

NIGHTSHADE
FOR
WARNING

An Enchanted
Garden Mystery

BAILEY CATTRELL

BERKLEY PRIME CRIME
New York

BERKLEY PRIME CRIME
Published by Berkley
An imprint of Penguin Random House LLC
375 Hudson Street, New York, New York 10014

ISBN 9780451476890

First Edition: May 2017

Printed in the United States of America
1 3 5 7 9 10 8 6 4 2

Book design by Laura K. Corless

This book is dedicated to librarians everywhere

ACKNOWLEDGMENTS

I am grateful to everyone who lent their expertise and support to this book. Among them are my agent, Kim Lionetti, and the extraordinary team at Berkley Prime Crime. They include my insightful and wise editor, Jessica Wade, as well as Miranda Hill, Roxanne Jones, and Karen Haywood. There are numerous others that proof and polish and format and sell my books, not to mention the artist who created this enticing cover. I am also lucky to have so many talented writers in my life who critique, advise, encourage, and push me. Just a few are Laura Pritchett, Laura Resau, Mark Figlozzi, and Bob Trott. Then there are the dear friends who keep me going, including Mindy Ireland, Amy Lockwood, Barbara Clark, JoAnn Manzanares, Natasha Wing, Teresa Funke, and Jody Ivy. And finally, there's Kevin Brookfield, who has been putting up my writerly habits for ten years. Love you so.

CHAPTER 1

THE honeyed, floral scent of sun-drenched zinnias curled into the air from the half-barrel planters in front of the Poppyville Library. It was subtle, likely unnoticed by most passersby, but tantalized my senses with possibility. Distilled to its essence, the fragrance would deepen, become richer and multilayered. Inhaling deeply, I paused to consider how I might use it in a custom perfume. My corgi, Dash, immediately plopped down on the walkway, watching me. His foxy ears swiveled, and his head tipped to one side as if he was wondering what I was up to now.

Scarlet zinnias for constancy. White zinnias for goodness.

In the Victorian language of flowers, the dark, bird's-foot ivy that spilled around the edges of the barrels represented fidelity and friendship. In combination with the zinnias, the planters sent good vibes all the way down the block.

My stomach growled. Glancing up, I saw the enormous round clock at the top of the library building read nearly one o'clock, and I hadn't eaten lunch yet. Dash and I had already stopped by the stables at the other end of town to drop off a big bottle of lemon eucalyptus insect repellent. The black flies were biting in August, and Gessie King preferred to use the essential oil blend I'd developed rather than commercial chemicals to protect her horses. Then we'd picked up Dash's favorite peanut butter treats at Doggone Gourmet. Finally, I'd snagged two bags of hazelnut-shell mulch and a rosemary topiary from my friend Thea Nelson at Terra Green Nursery. Those were the last items I needed to add to my gardens before the photo shoot the next day.

Photo shoot.

I wanted everything to be perfect when Blake Sontag came to interview me for his piece in *Conscience Magazine* on the tiny house movement and small-scale, green living. Of course, nothing is ever perfect. But after spending every spare moment of the last three days cleaning and organizing, planting and deadheading, I felt confident my tiny house and the elaborate garden between it and my store would make a good showing.

Now, if only I could say the same about myself. The whole idea of being featured in a magazine article made me quake in my muck boots every time I thought about it.

Remember to mention Scents & Nonsense a few times— but don't be too obvious.

The women's business group I belonged to, the Greenstockings, had emphasized that in the flurry of e-mails that erupted after I'd told them about the interview. Unfortunately, Sontag's assistant hadn't expressed interest in my custom perfume shop when she'd contacted me, but it was sure to come up. The other Greenstockings had also urged me to publicize their businesses if the opportunity arose. Our charming little town buttered its bread with tourism, so naturally we wanted to get the word out about it any way we could.

Ha. As if I'll be thinking straight enough to remember all the things they told me.

I'd be lucky if I didn't pass out.

Shaking my head, I pushed into the library and breezed over to the online catalog with a brisk sense of purpose. My nose filled with the age-old aroma of ink on paper, flavored with a metallic soupçon of modern electricity and a hint of Pine-Sol. Dash trotted at my heel, his corgi eyes bright. He'd just had a treat, but there were always more behind the checkout counter, so he kept right on going when I sat down at the keyboard.

"Hello, Dash," I heard Maria Canto say. "Sit. Good boy." And then the sound of a dog cookie crunching between his teeth.

"Ellie," she said, and I looked up.

"Hey! Sorry I'm in such a hurry. Have to get back to the shop. Maggie's there, but she has to get to the Roux soon." My part-time employee also tended bar at the Roux Grill, the restaurant I'd owned with my husband until I'd discovered him shtupping Wanda Simmons in the walk-in cooler. Then he'd become my *ex*-husband. More than a year later he still managed to be a pain in the backside, though.

"Dios mío." Maria raised her eyes toward the ceiling in exaggerated supplication. "Always so busy. Still, I had a feeling you might come in today. I set aside a few things for you."

I hesitated, but only for a second. The book on botanical drawing I wanted could wait. I jumped up and joined Dash in front of the counter.

Maria perched on a tall stool. A crocheted headband in the same eye-popping lime green as her blouse held a wave of luscious black hair away from her face. Nearly as height-challenged as I was and comfortably padded, the librarian exuded calm and the scent of orange blossoms. I instantly felt my blood pressure drop a few points. She scanned my face with quick, intelligent eyes and reached beneath the counter. Retrieving a selection of magazines and books, she slid them across to me.

One book was a guide to preparing for an interview, and the other was on how to interview someone else. The periodicals were mostly back issues of *Conscience*. There were also a couple of issues of architectural magazines that showcased tiny houses.

But Maria wasn't a member of the Greenstockings, and I hadn't told her about Sontag's article. A smile broke out on my face.

"You know, Astrid would say this is evidence of your superpower," I said. Astrid Moneypenny was my best friend.

Maria's eyes widened. "My what?"

"We were talking about how so many of our friends seems to have unique, er, *gifts*."

She nodded knowingly. "Like your sense of smell."

I shrugged. "I guess. Or how Gessie can calm a horse with a simple touch."

"Astrid has her own way with animals," Maria pointed out. "Doc Ericcson says she usually knows right away what's wrong with the pets that people bring into the vet clinic, before the owners say a single word."

"Right. And *you* have the uncanny ability to know exactly what book someone might need." I leaned forward.

She matched my conspiratorial gesture until our heads were nearly touching.

"How do you do it?" I asked in a low voice.

Though in truth, if she'd asked me the same question about my olfactory skills, I'd have been hard-pressed to explain. I'd always had a fine-honed, even freakish sense of smell, which was linked to a weirdly empathic ability to sense what aromas might benefit another person— sometimes physically, sometimes mentally, and sometimes simply by tapping into memories via the oldest and most primitive sense humans possessed. I'd taken my talent for granted most of my life. Then, more than a year ago, I'd divorced Harris, sold him my half of the Roux Grill, and opened my dream business. In the course of getting Scents & Nonsense up and running, I'd realized I had a real gift, one that could change someone's day if not their life, and that I loved using it to help people. My custom perfume and aromatherapy shop had blossomed as a result.

There was more to my gift than I'd realized, however. A few months later, an encounter with a mind-bending plant oil had revealed hidden memories of my mother and grandmother, both of whom had passed away when I was a child. As a result, I was only beginning to explore the depths of my true connection to plants, their essences, and the ancient language of flowers.

Maria leaned even closer, her eyes darting around the library as if to see whether anyone was listening. "You really want to know my secret?"

Catching my breath, I nodded.

She spoke in a low voice. "Cynthia Beck came in to return some books this morning and told me all about the journalist from *Conscience*"—she pointed at the stack of magazines—"who's coming to do the piece on your tiny house." She straightened and sat back on her stool with a grin. "I thought you might want to bone up, if you haven't already. The interview's tomorrow, isn't it?"

I laughed. Cynthia Beck had started the Greenstockings a few years before. The other members were Thea, Gessie, Astrid, and myself, though other local businesswomen sometimes attended our meetings.

"Small-town gossip wins again," I said. "I can't believe Blake Sontag is coming all the way back to Poppyville to talk to me about my little house. I bet he hasn't been back more than half a dozen times since he left for Princeton years ago."

Not that I'd necessarily know if he'd visited his hometown. Poppyville was small, but not that small. However, Blake was a local boy who'd made good, and the rumor mill was always in fine working order.

A half smile lifted Maria's lips. "Cynthia seems to think he might be coming back to see her, as well as doing the article on you."

I blinked. "Oh?"

"You didn't know? That's how he found out about your house."

"*She* told him? I wonder why she didn't mention that at our last meeting. I thought maybe his sister had told him."

Maria quirked an eyebrow. "So you know the family? I moved here after Blake had already left to start his career as a big environmental journalist, so I only know Joyous." She gave a little snort before her hand flew to cover her mouth. She couldn't keep the laughter out of her eyes, though.

A smile tugged at my own lips. Joyous Sontag was one of the most militantly unhappy people I'd ever encountered. Like nicknaming a big lunk of a guy "Tiny," it was as if the elder Sontags had taken one look at their pinch-faced daughter and chosen irony over accuracy.

I shrugged. "Sort of. Joyous was a year ahead of me in school, but Mr. and Mrs. Sontag were friends of my dad and stepmother back in the day. Then they moved to Arizona, and Dad and Wynn moved to Florida. I wonder if they're still in touch."

"What about Blake?" she asked. "Were you friends?"

"Not really. He's four years older than me, which is a lot in high school." I paused. "Huh. I bet Ritter knew him. I'll have to ask him next time I talk to him." *Which had better be sooner rather than later.*

Ritter Nelson was my boyfriend. Of the long-distance variety, unfortunately. When he'd come back to town to stay with Thea a few months before, the old crush I'd had on her older brother as a teenager flared like a rocket. Lucky me, it turned out he felt the same way. Unlucky me, he'd left a month ago to resume his botanical research project in the Alaskan tundra.

A *six-month* project.

We'd known it was coming, and tried to keep things as casual as possible. It hadn't worked. The night before he left, he told me he was torn about leaving. He'd actually considered dropping out of the research team and staying in Poppyville. But I knew how much he loved his work and urged him to go. No way could I be responsible for him giving it up.

I knew that his team would be using an expensive satellite connection for phone and Internet, and personal time on it would be very limited. We'd spoken on our cell phones a lot as the group prepared in Fairbanks for the trek up to the research site by the Beaufort Sea, but in the last two weeks they'd been setting up in the wild, and I hadn't heard a single word from Alaska. Not a call, not an e-mail, nada.

My stomach twisted, and I pushed the thought away.

Maria hadn't noticed my distraction. Her forefinger trailed along one of the magazine covers. "Blake has certainly made a name for himself. *National Geographic*, *Esquire*. Not bad for someone who focuses on the environment."

I handed her my library card. "Maybe I should ask Cynthia for the skinny, so I know what to expect."

"All I know is that she and Blake were engaged for a brief time and have remained on what she called 'friendly' terms." Maria's eyes danced again.

I was surprised, but only mildly. Cynthia went through husbands like her employees at Foxy Locksies Hair Studio went through shampoo. Two so far, and she was shopping for a third. That she might have had a few spare fiancés didn't stretch the imagination much.

The door opened and a mother led two preschoolers in. I scooped up the books and magazines and turned to go. "Thanks, Maria."

"Hang on," she said. "I put this aside for you, too." She handed me a book on botanical drawing.

I stared at it, then up at her. Her mouth curved up in a slow smile.

"This is why I stopped by in the first place," I said. "How did you know?"

She shrugged. "I had a feeling."

DASH and I stepped onto the covered boardwalk, which ran in front of many of the businesses on Poppyville's six-block-long main drag. My footsteps echoed hollowly on the worn planks, reminiscent of the Old West sounds of the California gold rush that had formed the town in the 1840s. Within moments we'd reached my old, battered Wrangler.

"Come on, big guy." I boosted Dash into the passenger seat and went around the back to the driver's side. As I stepped out to the street, a squeal pierced the air. My head jerked up, and I whirled to see an SUV headed straight for me.

Big. Black.

And coming *way* too fast.

My mouth dropped open in disbelief. Dash barked, frantic and loud, teeth bared. For a split second, a distant sliver of my brain hoped he wouldn't follow his canine instinct to herd the monstrous chunk of metal away from me. Then the roar of the engine blocked out all sound and thoughts.

Including my common sense. At the last moment, I leaped back between my vehicle and the one next to it. Pain jabbed through my knee where I'd banged it on the fender. Tires screeched by on the pavement, and the driver honked.

Honked. At *me.*

My hand flew up, middle finger extended. The windows were tinted, but I caught a flash of light hair and dark, wraparound sunglasses in the passenger-side mirror before the Cadillac—it was an Escalade, I saw now— raced through the empty crosswalk leading to the playground in Raven Creek Park and veered onto the winding road that led south of town. It had a California plate, and I made out a six and a five in the number. It wasn't a vehicle I'd seen around town, though.

Tourists.

"That's the kind of visitor we can definitely do without," I said to Dash, my voice quavering from the flood of adrenaline. He gazed in the direction of River Road with worried eyes.

Rubbing my knee with a shaking hand, I frowned. There was only one stoplight on Corona Street, and that was at the other end where it intersected the county road that went out to the highway. The speed limit downtown was a tame twenty miles an hour, and hatched crosswalks guided the frequent foot traffic from corner to corner. The Cadillac would have picked off at least a few of the milling pedestrians if it had barreled down the entire length of Corona like that. Luckily, it had turned onto the main drag less than a block away. Amazing how it had picked up so much speed so quickly.

I could have died.

The thought popped unbidden into my mind. With a deep breath, I shook it off, hauled my four-foot-ten frame behind the wheel of the Wrangler, and started the engine.

Scents & Nonsense was at the very end of Corona, just before the park with its fitness trail, picnic areas, river access, and playground. I parked in the lot across the street so as not to take up one of the spaces in front of the boardwalk and reached into the back for the bags of hazelnut mulch. Over the seat back, I saw an old Volkswagen Westfalia camping van complete with a pop-up top parked in front of Flyrite Kites next door to my shop. It reminded me of the one my brother, Colby, drove.

Thinking of Colby—who was actually my half brother—made me smile. We were closer to each other than either of us was to my half sister, Darcy. Still, I hadn't seen him much after he'd ditched his degree in economics and the world of high finance to take to the open road at the age of twenty-three. He'd found his bliss wandering from town to town across the United States, supporting himself with odd jobs and custom woodworking. Three years later, we stayed in touch mostly by e-mail, text, and frequent phone calls. It was high time he planned a visit home.

The thought had no more flitted through my brain than I saw the bumper stickers on the van. The THIS IS HOW I ROLL decal was right next to a stylized picture of a phoenix with POPPYVILLE SUNBIRDS underneath.

The van didn't just look like his. It *was* his. Colby was back!

I dropped the mulch and jumped out of the Wrangler. Dash at my heel, I ran across the street to my shop, flung the door open, and stood on the threshold with a grin so big it almost hurt.

My brother turned from where he was standing in front of the register, a devilish grin spreading across his sweet face. "Surprise."

I launched myself at him. He caught me in a warm bear hug, lifting me easily off the floor and swinging me around. Dash ran in excited circles, while Nabokov hissed feline disapproval of such antics from the windowsill.

"Careful of that candle display, you two," Maggie Clement admonished with a happy smile. She was well padded, pushing sixty, and mothered everyone around her. "I'd hate to see your family reunion break the merchandise."

Colby set me down but kept his hands on my shoulders. "Hey, you. I probably should have called first, but I wanted to surprise you." His eyes flashed beneath the brim of his baseball cap. A fringe of dark hair poked out around his ears.

"Hey, yourself." He smelled of wood shavings and peppermint. I reached up and jabbed at his brown beard. "What's this thing?"

He rolled his eyes. "Of course that's the first thing you'd notice." He stepped back, and it registered for the first time that he had a companion. "This is part of my surprise. Ellie, meet Larken Meadows. Larken, this is my weirdo big sis, Elliana Allbright, aka Ellie."

I felt myself color. "Oh, my gosh. I'm so sorry. It's just

that I haven't seen Colby for such a long time, and this is so unexpected . . ." I trailed off.

Her serious gaze met mine, hazel eyes flecked with gold and framed by long lashes. She smelled of tender new shoots of green and rich soil warmed by sunshine. Her hair was the color of peanut butter, long and straight and parted in the middle. Her tanned skin was flawless without any hint of makeup. She looked at me for a few beats—probing, assessing—before a brilliant, crooked grin bloomed on her face, creating an off-center dimple and revealing a slight overbite.

"Hi, Ellie. Nice to meet you. Colby's told me a lot about you."

Her sudden smile was so contagious that I felt my own grin widening. But when I spoke, I sounded like I was just learning to speak English. "I, uh, nice to meet you, too."

Colby laughed and leaned toward Larken. "She doesn't know how to say that I never told her about you."

"Stop that," I protested, and held out a hand to Larken. "Welcome to Poppyville. I'm only sorry that you had to make your first visit with my very rude brother here."

"I'm not," she said, and the look she gave Colby was so adoring I almost didn't take it seriously. But she was earnest, very earnest. I had a feeling gravitas was Larken's default mode. However, I sensed it came from being grounded, not staid, from a position of quiet dignity rather than sternness.

God knew she'd have no luck being stern with my brother. And grounded? He could definitely use some of that in his life.

"Maggie here was saying you have a big interview tomorrow," Colby said, ambling over to the coffee urn. He helped himself to a cup of dark roast and one of the lavender short-bread cookies Astrid had brought over that morning.

"Oh, no. Oh, Colby, Larken, I'm so sorry! He's going to be here at nine in the morning, and there's going to be a photographer, and my house is so little, and—"

He held up his hand. "Relax. I might be your rude little brother, but I never intended to impose on your hospitality like that."

"Are you staying in the van?" I asked, unable to keep the skepticism out of my voice.

Larken laughed, a lovely sparkling sound. "Believe me, we've spent plenty of time in that van. And I love it!" she added pointedly as she took the steaming mug Colby offered her. "But we're indulging ourselves and staying at the Hotel California."

My shoulders relaxed. "Nice! How long will you be in town?"

The two lovebirds exchanged a significant look. Finally, Colby said, "To be determined."

I frowned, but before I could pursue it, Maggie reached under the counter and grabbed her tote bag. "Sorry, Ellie, but I've got to run. See you day after tomorrow?"

I nodded. "Sounds great." Maggie was taking the next day off to spend with her grandkids, but luckily Astrid would be able to woman the shop while I was busy with Blake Sontag. Heaven knew my assistant deserved a day off from both of her jobs, as hard as she worked.

Colby drained his coffee. "We're going to get out of your hair, too. I want to show Lark the house we grew up in."

"But you just got here," I protested. "Have you had a chance to go out to the Enchanted Garden?" I cultivated a garden behind my shop, which my customers and friends loved to sit in.

Larken shook her head.

"You're in for a treat," Maggie said as she headed for the front door, already gathering her bleached blond hair into a practical bun for her shift at the Roux Grill.

I followed her and flipped the sign in the front window from OPEN to CLOSED.

"Oh, now, I don't want you losing business," Colby said. "Not on my account."

I waved away his objection. "It won't take long to show you around, but I don't want to be disturbed." Quickly, I wrote a note that said I'd be back in fifteen minutes and stuck it on the door.

CHAPTER 2

❧

I LED them past the locked display case of perfumes, where LED under-shelf lighting lent a warm glow to the collection of intricate, colored glass bottles. We wound around tables piled with scented soaps and bath salts, soy candles, and drawer sachets. Larken paused to finger a sample of ginger-spiced body whip and remarked on the scented play clay in the children's section.

"Mmm. Citrusy."

"There's no age limit for aromatherapy," I said. "Pink grapefruit boosts self-esteem and helps with concentration, so I use it in a lot of my products for kids."

My brother rolled his eyes.

Larken punched him lightly on the arm. "Behave."

"I guess it does sound kind of *la-di-da* when I put it that way." I laughed and opened the glass door to the patio in the back of the shop.

"Bah. He's the same way about my interest in wild-crafting," she said. Wildcrafting was the practice of gathering plants from their natural habitat, for food or for medicinal purposes.

When my eyes cut toward Larken, Colby grinned. "That piqued your interest, didn't it? I knew you two would get along."

We stepped outside, skirted the grouping of comfy rocking chairs and the porch swing hanging from the pergola, and paused where the flagstones met a blanket of luxuriant moss beneath the stained glass birdbath.

"Holy moly," Larken breathed.

Her eyes raked over the space between where we stood and my tiny house nestled at the back of the lot. Terraced beds marched above and below a mosaic retaining wall, overflowing with herbs and scented flowers. Nabokov—Nabby—the Russian blue shorthair who had come with the storefront, followed us out and made a graceful beeline for his favorite perch atop the wall. A blowsy Don Juan rose tumbled over the north fence, a tiny sparrow's nest firmly clasped among the thorns. A narrow path wound among thriving beds of jasmine, larkspur, and butterfly weed circled a small grassy area where a round table and wicker chairs invited visitors to sit with a cool drink and take in the verdant surroundings, and ultimately ended at an asymmetrical boulder hunched in the center of the space.

The words ENCHANTED GARDEN were etched into its rugged face.

Larken stepped off the patio with an expression of awe, trailing her fingers along the birdbath and smiling at the collection of finches, wrens, blue jays, and one intrepid woodpecker gathered at the many feeders. Then her gaze lowered. Her eyes widened, and her breath caught.

"Ah. You found the fairies," I said.

Colby frowned.

"Don't worry, little bro. I have yet to see any actual pixies out here." Though after some of the things I'd experienced in the garden, I probably wouldn't have been surprised if one suddenly popped up and waved at me. I pointed at the whimsical miniature garden tableau Larken had spied. It was landscaped with ferns for trees, baby tears as ground cover, and bordered with sweet woodruff that extended to a lichen-covered rock with an eight-inch door set into the side. A tiny wooden bench invited the wee folk to sit and rest a bit, and a diminutive tire swing swayed temptingly. "I do like to provide them accommodations, though."

"There are more of these?" she asked, moving farther away.

"All over. See that path?" I pointed to a tiny winding track I'd created from smoothed shards of sea glass. "If you follow it through the lavender and around that stand of delphinium, it will take you to a gnome door in the apple tree."

There were similar doors, some only five inches high, a few twice that size, set into rocks, the fence I shared with Flyrite Kites, and the stone edging of the mint patch. And near them were tiny gardens that I'd carefully crafted, containing more ferns trimmed into teensy trees, juniper starts towering above dollhouse-size Adirondack chairs, low-growing woolly thyme, dwarf mondo grass, and English boxwood bonsai. I had planted the first diminutive scene under the hummingbird feeder, but it ended up being so adorable and had been so much fun that I just kept creating more throughout the Enchanted Garden.

Larken followed my directions, Dash trotting ahead of her, and stopped next to the ancient gnarled trunk of the fruit tree.

"Why didn't you tell me you had a girlfriend?" I quietly hissed at my brother. It wasn't as if he hadn't had the chance. We talked at least once a week.

She looked over. I smiled and waved. Hands clasped, she gazed down, a small smile on her lips. I could sense the earthiness of her soul, and imagined the smells of rich, wet soil and pine straw.

"It has to be serious if she'll put up with traveling in that van of yours," I continued.

Next to me, Colby shook his head. "It's . . . complicated. We've known each other for a while, but only recently decided to take it to the next level."

Ritter's face passed across my mental movie screen.

"Ellie, this is adorable!" Larken called.

"Girls," my brother muttered.

I nodded. "The kids love it."

"I wasn't talking about the kids."

I grinned up at him. "Okay, maybe a lot of us don't grow out of a love for dolls and miniatures, but don't try to tell me you're not a twelve-year-old boy at heart. A twelve-year-old boy on a perpetual camping trip."

He laughed. "You got me there."

But Larken had turned to look at us, and I saw immediately that she'd heard—and my words had cast a pall. A sudden empathetic light-headedness made me sway on my feet. With an effort, I steadied myself.

She loves my brother, but she's unmoored. She needs roots. Deep roots.

Without warning, a breeze caught up a shimmering whirlwind of pink hydrangea petals. They swirled around her, caught in her hair, gently buffeted her cheeks, and then settled back down to the ground. Her mouth opened in an O of surprise.

I smiled. Since creating it, I'd learned the Enchanted Garden was more than just a few words etched into a rock. It was a place alive with possibility and rich with botanical intelligence that went beyond heliotropism.

And Larken was an earth-soul who had instantly connected with that energy.

Colby was oblivious, of course. That was just as well. I went over and broke off a calendula flower, then stepped briskly toward the apple tree. Crushing it slightly between my fingertips, I sniffed its light perfume. My dizziness abated, and I knew the scent would help comfort Larken.

Handing it to her, I said, "Take a whiff."

Eyes wide, she obeyed. Her shoulders relaxed, and I, too, felt more solidly connected to the ground beneath my feet.

"Boy, you weren't kidding when you said your house was tiny," Colby said, looking past us.

My home was covered with hand-hewn cedar shingles, and the door had been crafted of scraps from a demolished barn. On each side of the door were neat, four-paned windows. Old-fashioned geraniums trailed from the window boxes beneath them.

I turned toward him. "You're the one who gave me the idea, you know. It's three hundred twenty square feet, but that's plenty for Dash and me." The tiny house movement was about living simply in a small space. The small, green footprint had appealed to my environmental side, and since starting Scents & Nonsense hadn't left me with much money after the divorce, the price was right.

We went in, and I gave them a quick tour.

"Here's the kitchen, small but efficient. That's a combination washer/dryer, and in the bathroom I have a shower set over a deep Japanese-style tub." I pointed out all the built-in shelves and cupboards, the storage features of nearly every piece of furniture, the dining table and desk that folded away into the wall, and the set of chairs that stacked together to make an end table for the foldout love seat.

"But this is my favorite part." I put my hand on the tight, circular staircase that led to the loft bedroom above. Shelves spiraled upward beneath the steps, chock-full of books on horticulture, aromatherapy, and perfumery. "I get to climb a bookshelf to go to bed every night."

"Magical," Larken breathed, reaching for a book.

But when I saw which one had caught her eye, it was all I could do not to snatch the volume out of her hand. It was my gamma's garden journal, a handwritten and hand-drawn record of her many decades of wisdom, both botanical and life-earned. To the best of my knowledge, no hands but hers and mine had ever touched the tattered cover.

Colby looked at his watch. "We'd better get back. You might have a customer waiting, Ellie."

I breathed a sigh of relief as Larken returned the book to its home without opening it. "You're right," I said. "But I feel like I barely got a chance to see you."

"I'm going to show Larken around town this afternoon," he said. "How about we meet for dinner tonight?"

"I'd love that. At the hotel? I haven't been to the Empire Room in ages."

"Sounds good," Larken said, and Colby nodded.

We made arrangements to meet at seven.

I WENT out to the Wrangler and retrieved the bags of mulch and the rosemary topiary. After placing them around the corner by the hose faucet, I reopened the shop and headed into the office. I'd just finished making dinner reservations when the jingle of the door reached my ears, and I hurried back out with a customer greeting on my tongue.

But the newcomer wasn't a customer. Astrid Moneypenny strode inside with even more energy than usual.

"Ellie! Was that Colby I saw driving down Corona Street?"

I couldn't hide my grin. "Yup. Surprise visit." Then my mouth opened as I took in the stretchy baby sling wrapped around her torso. Inside was tucked a tiny sleeping . . . pig?

She reached the counter and pressed both palms down on it. She wore a sports skirt, trail runners, and, under the baby sling, a purple LIFE IS GOOD T-shirt was covered with pet hair. Her red hair, usually braided or at least somewhat tamed with product, rose in frizzy waves around her shoulders, and her willow green eyes sparked with interest.

"How long will he be here? Who was that with him? Is he camping nearby? When did he show up?"

A laugh escaped my throat. "Wow. Lots of questions." I ticked off my fingers. "I don't know, his girlfriend Larken, they're staying at the Hotel California, and just now." I pointed at her charge. "What's that?"

"'That' is Precious, and she's a teacup pig." She grimaced. "Supposedly. It's hard to tell. Remember when potbellied pigs were so popular, and then everyone found out they grew to be around three hundred pounds or so? Well, these are supposed to stay much smaller than that."

"She looks downright tiny."

"She looks like a baby. Which she is. Even if the guy who sold her to Mrs. Paulson—you know, the owner of the Juke Diner?—even if Precious turns out to be as advertised, she's going to end up around fifty pounds, minimum."

My nose wrinkled. "Oh, Lord."

"Anyway, she's boarding for the very first time at Dr. Ericcson's, and it turns out the poor little thing suffers from separation anxiety."

"So Astrid to the rescue," I said.

She gave me a *well, duh* look.

My best friend was a self-proclaimed petrepreneur. She worked part-time for the local veterinarian as a vet tech and also had her own business pet sitting and dog walking. She'd take care of any animal, but specialized in difficult pets and those with medical conditions that required special care.

"How long do you need to keep her with you?" I asked doubtfully.

"Another day should do it. Really, pigs are very independent. She's not nearly as disoriented as she was right after Mrs. Paulson dropped her off."

Precious opened one eye and sleepily regarded me before snuffling, sighing, and going back to sleep.

Inspiration striking, I said, "Hey, can you leave her alone long enough to go to dinner at the Empire Room with us tonight? I made reservations for seven o'clock."

Astrid shook her head ruefully. "Sorry. No can do. I have a date."

"The concert promoter?"

"Nah. I'm done with him. Too full of himself. I met this guy at the post office yesterday. He was sending post-cards back home."

"A tourist, then," I said flatly.

"Yup." She frowned. "It's just drinks and dinner at the Sapphire for some fun. It's not like I'm starting a long-distance relationship with the guy." Her hand went to her mouth. "Sorry, Ellie. I didn't mean . . ." She trailed off.

I waved it away. "Don't be silly. I'll see you tomorrow morning, then."

But after she left, I spent the rest of the afternoon try-ing not to think about Ritter Nelson, off in Alaska and up to his eyebrows in the work he was so passionate about. Trying not to think about him, and certainly trying not to miss his kind eyes and crooked smile, his easy manner and full-throated laugh.

Not to mention how great he looked in a pair of tight jeans.

DASH followed me out to the Enchanted Garden that evening and looked on as I locked the front door of my house. Growing up in Poppyville, I hadn't worried

about locking anything, but ever since finding Josie Overland dead on the boardwalk in front of the shop a few
months before, I'd tried to be more careful about security.
The corgi settled down beneath the retaining wall. I
glanced at my watch and hurried up the path toward the
front gate. I'd be cutting it close to make our dinner reservation on time.

I lucked into a parking spot on the street in front of the
hotel with a few minutes to spare, which saved me from
having to go around to the parking lot behind. As I got
out, I realized my Jeep was two cars down from a black
Escalade. Quickstepping to the front, I saw the California
license plate had a five and a six in the number. It had to
be the same one that had nearly run me down earlier that
day. I took out my phone and snapped a picture. I'd check
in later with my friend Lupe Garcia, one of the two detectives on the Poppyville police force, to find out whether it
would be worthwhile to make a report.

The Hotel California was one of the exceptions to
downtown's Western theme. Ironically, the five-story Victorian building happened to be one of the actual surviving
structures from Poppyville's inception in 1847, when
hordes of hopeful miners had streamed into the foothills
of the Sierra Nevada range in search of gold. A group of
enterprising souls had seen the opportunity to support the
rush of dreamers with supplies, food, drink, lodging, and
entertainment—some innocent, and some harking back
to the world's oldest profession.

Pauline "Poppy" Thierry had practiced the latter. She'd
been a madam with surprisingly high moral standards, and
a woman with a keen eye to efficient business practices. She'd

certainly been as powerful as any of the founding fathers. Indeed, one of them, my great-great-great-grandfather, Zebulon Hammond, had proposed they change the name of the town from Springtown to Poppyville.

Dodging a family of five, I climbed the stairs to the wide covered veranda of the hotel. To my right, two couples lounged in Adirondack chairs, wineglasses in hand. On the other side, three women played Scrabble at a glass-topped table, while their husbands recounted the afternoon's golf round over lowballs of amber liquid. A large man in a cream-colored suit and Panama hat held one of the tall double doors open for me, and I murmured my thanks as I hurried inside.

Straight ahead, a wide carpeted staircase led to the second-floor rooms. It was flanked on each side by carved wooden columns topped with stylized pineapples—a traditional sign of hospitality. Guests were gathered in clusters of sofas and brocade-covered wingback chairs, a gas fire burned merrily behind glass doors without adding heat to the lobby, and someone was tinkling out a tentative attempt at "Heart and Soul" on the grand piano. A miasma of expensive perfume, sunscreen, and clinging cigar smoke mixed with the enticing smells wafting from the Empire Room.

The clatter of dishes further beckoned, and my steps veered toward the sound. The hostess met me with a smile, and I told her we had a reservation. The smile ebbed as she scanned her computer screen.

"I'm very sorry, ma'am," she said. "I'm not showing an entry for your party."

"But I called this afternoon—" I began.

"Hey, sis!" Recognizing my brother's voice, I turned to see him and Larken approaching from the direction of the elevator.

"Hi!" she said, then gestured toward my floral handkerchief skirt. "Ellie, that blue perfectly matches your eyes."

"Thanks," I said. "You look lovely." And she did, in a simple green halter dress and white cardigan. Her hair was twisted up and clasped with a metal clip.

Colby's concession to the evening was a pair of clean jeans and a collared shirt. He kissed me on the cheek. "Sorry we're a little late."

I sighed. "No problem, since they don't have a record of our reservation." I turned back to the hostess, who was scanning her screen with a pained expression. "Can you get us in anyway?"

"It might be a while," she said. "It's a very busy evening."

Well, of course it was. August was always busy in Poppyville.

"How long?"

"Maybe an hour? Or a bit longer?"

A waiter passed behind her, the plate of pasta alle vongole in his hand filling the air with garlic, lemon, and the smell of the sea. My stomach growled. I never had managed to get a real lunch earlier. Instead I'd indulged in more of Astrid's lavender shortbread cookies than I should have.

"We could check out the Sapphire Supper Club," I said doubtfully, taking my phone out of my purse. "But they probably won't be able to get us in any faster."

"Or we could go the Roux," Colby said, his eyes dancing. "Say hi to ol' Harris."

I managed not to stick my tongue out at him.

"Behave yourself," Larken murmured to my brother. "I'm sure we can—"

"Ellie!" A woman's voice from inside the restaurant cut short whatever Larken was going to say.

Squinting into the dim light, I made out Cynthia Beck's perfectly coiffed blond tresses and the fact that she was waving a manicured hand.

I raised my own very unmanicured hand in reply. She pushed back from her table and strode toward me on four-inch heels. Her usual business attire had been replaced by a little black dress with plunging neckline, and her signature Chanel No. 5 hovered subtly around her like an aura.

"Is there a problem?" she asked, looking between us.

Glaring at the computer screen as if I could change it by sheer willpower, I said, "They lost our reservation."

The pained look on the hostess's face deepened. "Would you like me to call the manager?" she asked. "Perhaps . . ."

Cynthia flicked her fingers. "Nonsense. If they don't have a reservation, what's the manager going to do? Set up a kiddie table in the corner? We have two empty chairs at our table already. Find us one more, and Ellie and . . . Colby! I just realized it's you! Good Lord, honey, you look so rough and ready with that beard."

I suppressed a smile as my brother turned beet red.

Her attention returned to the hostess, who appeared relieved to have this tall woman deal with the situation.

"So, bring another chair to the table over in the corner. Colby, I want to hear everything you've been up to since turning into an itinerant adventurer. And we haven't met, have we?" This directed at Larken, who shook her head in wide-eyed silence.

"Well, come on, everyone. We'll make a party of it." She turned to go, but not before shooting a meaningful look at me.

Unfortunately, I had no idea what she was trying to tell me. With a mental shrug, I thought about making some excuse to be polite, but Cynthia was not one to extend insincere invitations. Besides, I was starved. So we followed behind her like three baby ducks.

Mmm, duck. Is that duck à l'orange on that woman's plate? I nearly swooned at the concentrated savory citrus fragrance.

A man sat with his back to the wall at the corner table. His mane of dark hair was combed straight back from his forehead to reveal a distinct widow's peak, and his eyes were so light blue that they looked nearly colorless in the filtered evening light coming in the windows. He didn't get up when we approached. Instead he distributed a glare among the four of us and ended by narrowing his eyes at Cynthia.

Colby stiffened beside me.

Uh-oh. Maybe this is a bad idea.

Cynthia completely ignored her companion's grumpy demeanor, cheerfully introducing us, asking Larken's name and shuffling chairs to make room for the extra one a waitress brought over. As we settled in, a waiter distributed menus and setups, poured water, took drink orders, and recited the evening's specials. When they'd left, Cynthia put her hand on the man's shoulder.

"And everyone, I'd like for you to meet my old friend Blake Sontag."

CHAPTER 3

I BARELY managed not to gape. No wonder Cynthia had given me that look. I should have figured out who her companion was. How could I not have?

Because you're all a-dither over Colby being here.

Cynthia continued. "Blake, Ellie's your interview subject tomorrow morning! She can confirm what I've been telling you about how Poppyville is on the rise."

He gave me a stony look. "The garden lady."

Beside me, Larken's quick intake of breath was audible. I felt myself redden, and my appetite fled. If I'd been nervous about the interview before, now I was sure to be a complete basket case tomorrow. I could sense a sour bitterness emanating from the man: old socks and vinegar and gall.

"Ellie's a perfume maker, too." Colby stepped in. "She's really good at it."

"Oh, my, yes . . . ," Cynthia started, then trailed off when she saw his lip curl.

Blake sniffed. "The article is on green living and small-footprint housing. I'm not here to promote her business." He spared Cynthia a glance. "Or yours, either, honey."

Her eyes flashed.

I could feel the tension coming off of my brother in waves.

Cynthia clicked her tongue. "Oh, for heaven's sake, Blake, stop being such a wet blanket." Her tone was casual, but when she turned to look at me, I realized from the pinched look around her eyes that she'd invited us over to help promote our business community. So far it didn't look like her efforts were going very well.

Thanks a lot, I thought.

However, over time I'd learned most unpleasant people were essentially unhappy people. Maybe there was a scent combination I could give him before my interview the next morning that would help. I took a deep breath, trying to release my nervousness so I could figure out what was bothering the journalist. But my spidey sense only picked up Cynthia's frustration and mild bewilderment from Larken.

Cynthia took a deep breath and tried again. "You remember Ritter Nelson, don't you, Blake? He and Ellie have been dating, and you'll be interested to know he's up in Alaska studying . . . what is it, Ellie?"

"Environmental impacts on the tundra," I said. Maybe if we all played nice, Blake would get tired of being a jerk.

"Yeah. Been there, done that," Blake said when I paused.

Colby stared at him. "But you wrote that piece in *National Geographic* about the loss of polar habitat—"

Blake started to say something, but the waiter came over to take our orders. I opted for the clam pasta dish I'd seen the waiter carrying when we'd arrived.

I checked my watch. That had been fifteen minutes ago. It seemed like we'd been sitting at the table making awkward conversation for much longer. I wanted nothing more than to bolt my food and hustle my brother and his girlfriend off to a quiet corner for a chance to catch up.

A movement in my peripheral vision drew my attention to a man wending his way through the tables toward us. His sun-streaked hair waved around his face like something out of Greek mythology, and as he neared I saw his grass green eyes spark with a combination of intelligence and humor. His brown T-shirt molded to his upper body, hinting at a ripple of muscles across his abdomen and accentuating his biceps. The shirt read, "I Shoot People," over a stylized picture of a camera.

When he stopped at our table, I felt myself staring.

Blake glowered up at him. "What do you want, Spence?"

The newcomer flashed a white-toothed grin at all of us. "Just checking to make sure everything's set for tomorrow."

Tomorrow? Oh, God, this must be the photographer.

"Yeah, yeah. All ready. We'll meet a little before ten in the lobby and go over together. Get in and get out." Blake didn't even bother to look at me when he said it. I felt my face grow pink.

Again.

"I thought you said you wanted to start at nine," Spence said. First name or last?

"That's what your assistant said, too—" I started to say, but Blake cut me off.

"Ten. It was always ten o'clock. God knows, with my insomnia I sleep little enough as it is."

"You should try a sleeping pill, Blake," Cynthia said. "I couldn't live without mine."

"Great idea, Cyn, but I don't take a pill for everything like you do."

Her nostrils flared, and I could see the effort it took not to retort.

He rubbed his eyes, and when he looked up, I could see how exhausted he was.

Was that why he was in such a bad mood? Maybe. But I'd suffered from insomnia after Harris and I broke up, and I was pretty sure I didn't take it out on everyone around me. Blake Sontag might be tired, but even if he were fully rested I didn't think he'd be a very nice guy. Still, it couldn't hurt to offer him my standard sleeping blend of lavender, vetiver, and chamomile essential oils when I got the chance.

Then I saw the smile had dropped from Spence's face. He was looking at me quizzically.

"Are you . . . ?"

"Ellie Allbright," I said. "I guess I'll see you tomorrow?" It came out as a question.

"I certainly hope so," Spence said, eyes dancing.

"Anything else?" Blake asked his photographer.

"Mind if I borrow your car keys?"

"What for?"

"Thought I'd check out the restaurants in town." He gestured around us. "No way am I going to get a table in here."

Blake sighed and fished in his pocket, then drew out a key fob and handed it to him.

"See you at ten tomorrow." Spence nodded to us, his gaze lingering on me for a few extra moments, and walked away.

Ignoring Cynthia's quirked eyebrow, I reached for my wineglass. Just because she was always on the prowl didn't mean I was.

Larken's glass was already empty, and her cheeks were flushed a delicate pink beneath her smooth tan. Now she piped up. "Mr. Sontag, I've read several of your articles in *Conscience*. I'm a subscriber, you know. To the online version, now that we travel so much." She smiled at Colby.

For the first time Blake looked pleased.

"Talk about a small footprint," I said. "My brother has been living in his Westfalia for, what—three years now?"

Colby nodded. "About that."

Blake made a face like he'd just caught a whiff of skunk.

All my big-sister defenses rose with a vengeance, but I kept my face neutral. The guy was a jerk, but it wasn't catching, and he'd be leaving town soon. Colby wasn't a child, and he could hold his own with an unhappy journalist.

I just hoped I could.

Beside me, Larken sighed. I looked over and was surprised to see a dreamy, faraway look in her eyes. "Someday," she said. "Someday I want to have a little plot of earth. Somewhere I can keep animals and sustainably grow our food, and we can support ourselves off the land. My grandpa left me some money years ago, and I've been saving it to buy a place of my own."

I blinked. *Really?* She was crunchier than I'd thought. *And what about Mr. Gadabout?* I looked at Colby, who appeared to be concentrating on his glass of beer.

Uh-oh.

Blake shook his head. "Sounds like something out of the sixties."

I bit my tongue.

Two tray-laden waiters arrived with our food. The layered fragrance floating up from my pasta reignited my appetite. Larken smiled down at her Greek salad with quinoa and roasted beets, and Colby made an appreciative noise when he saw his plate piled with Guinness-braised short ribs and colcannon. Cynthia dipped a bite of cedar-planked salmon into a pool of lemon-tarragon sauce with a sigh of contentment. Blake had requested that his New York strip be served "cremated," and his plate was the only one that didn't make me want to ask for a bite.

Silence descended as we ate. Thank God.

Then Larken spoke. "My dream might sound like something out of the sixties, Mr. Sontag, but so what? Corporate agriculture has taken over our food supply. It's ruining the environment, damaging the soil, killing the bees and other pollinators, and poisoning our water. If I want a little land where that doesn't happen, then what's wrong with that? It's a way to fight back, at least. To make a difference."

Colby put his hand on her arm. "Lark."

She jerked away from him. "Don't 'Lark' me. Mr. Sontag knows exactly what I mean. Don't you?" She directed a pleading look at the journalist.

He laughed. "You're out of luck, honey. You can do your hippie-dippy thing if you want, but corporate agriculture isn't going away. It's going to get bigger and bigger. I predict small family farms will be completely wiped out within the next decade."

Larken's fork clattered onto the table as she stood. "No! Not if enough people are dedicated to change! Not if we educate the public. Not if—"

Blake snorted his derision and shook his head.

Tears filled her eyes.

"Lark," Colby tried again.

She pushed her chair back. "What kind of environmentalist are you, anyway?"

Blake looked wry. "A very practical one. And one who understands that it's a losing battle."

"That's horrible!"

He shrugged.

"And you're a horrible man!" She whirled and ran out of the restaurant.

Colby jumped up and followed her without a word.

I started to push away from the table as well. Cynthia's hand shot out, her fingers curling around my wrist. "No," she hissed. Then she seemed to regain herself. "Let Colby handle it." *And don't leave me here alone with this guy,* she seemed to be saying.

Blake seemed utterly unaware that anything was wrong or that he'd managed to drive two of his dinner companions from the table. He took a bite of steak, then reached over and pushed Colby's chair back. Scooting his seat over, he smiled. "A little more room now."

I QUICKLY finished my meal. So did Cynthia. We skipped dessert and coffee, and as soon as it was decent to leave, I said good night and fled the restaurant.

In the lobby, I looked around for Colby and Larken. When I didn't see them, I went out the French doors that led to the swimming pool at the rear of the hotel. The only people I saw were a group of tweens playing Marco Polo while two couples sat watching them. Back inside, I checked the Horseshoe Bar. I wouldn't have been surprised if they'd decided more alcohol was in order after their encounter with Blake. However, if my brother and his girlfriend had gone to a bar, it wasn't the one in the hotel.

Colby and Larken didn't answer their room phone when I asked the concierge to call it. My brother didn't answer his cell, either. I put my phone back into my purse and rubbed my face with both hands. Then I took it out and texted Colby:

Call me when you get a chance—so sorry!

Movement in my peripheral vision snagged my attention, and I turned to see Cynthia and Blake standing outside the restaurant entrance. She was talking, gesturing animatedly to make her point. He shook his head, and I saw his mouth form the word "no." She frowned, and her eyes narrowed.

I'd seen that look before, and was happy it hadn't ever been directed at me.

Then she smiled and leaned in to say something into his ear. As she did so, her finger trailed along his arm. I remembered the gesture as one she'd used on Ritter just after he'd come back to Poppyville. I'd been sure she was making a play for him then, and she might have been. Ritter, bless his heart, hadn't even seemed to notice.

Now Blake's lips quirked up in a half smile, and he nodded.

Well, if anyone was going to get him on the side of the Poppyville business community, by hook or by crook, it was Cynthia Beck. I had to admire her success even though it sometimes seemed that she needed to get more of a personal life.

As for me, I was bone weary and had no more patience for Mr. Blake Sontag that evening. As I was going out to the hotel's front veranda, the other half of the double door slammed open with such force that it hit the wall behind it. I leaped out of the way, stumbling and catching myself on the back of a chair. A big man in a Panama hat shoul-dered past me without so much as a glance. It was the same guy that had so nicely held the door open for me when I'd arrived. Now he barreled toward the bar.

Sighing, I went out and descended the steps to the street, gratefully inhaling the sugared scent of Victorian tuberoses that dotted the beds in front of the veranda.

I heard the memory of my gamma's voice. *Tuberoses for dangerous desires. Ellie, can you hear what their scent is saying? And over there—the marigolds. Can you smell their message?*

Marigolds for cruelty, Gamma.

Very good, my child. And she'd ruffled my hair.

As I approached my Wrangler, I saw the big black SUV was gone, replaced by a red Volkswagen. The lights on the silver Lexus next to it flashed on with an audible beep, and I turned to see Cynthia coming down the steps.

She gave me an apologetic look and waved. I waved back and got behind the wheel. All I wanted was to go home and curl up with Dash.

HOWEVER, once I settled in, my little home felt foreign. Sterile. I'd spent so much energy getting it just right for Sontag and his photographer that it hardly felt like my own as Dash and I snuggled together on the love seat with my grandmother's garden journal. There would be dog hair on the cushions now, and the pillows would no longer be perfectly plump.

I just couldn't bring myself to worry about it after that horrible dinner. After how awful Blake Sontag had turned out to be.

Who cares what he thinks?

I opened the dirt-smudged cover of the journal, hoping for the peace it so often brought me. It sounded crazy, but I swore Gamma communicated with me through that book. *Her* book. It was full of drawings, some black and white, some that she'd created with colored pencil or watercolor. Mixed in were a hodgepodge of practical plant descriptions, Latin names, and snatches of song and verse. Throughout, she'd noted the meanings of plants in the language of flowers from Victorian times—and long before that. There was no index, no alphabetization, no order whatsoever.

And sometimes the journal, well, it *changed*. I'd had this record of hers since I was eleven years old, but in the last few months I'd looked at it nearly every day. Even so, I continued to stumble across pages with new information that I hadn't seen before, often information that I just happened to need to help someone. For example, the previous week Essa Mae McLory was feeling exhausted, and my usual pick-me-up blend of rosemary, peppermint, and eucalyptus wasn't working. That night Gamma's journal fell open to a page on the many uses of carnation. I'd remembered the meanings in the language of flowers as she'd written them in script around the four edges of the page:

Pink means I'll never forget you.
Red, my heart breaks.
White is sweet and lovely.
Yellow means disdain.

But Gamma had also noted that the scent could promote physical energy. The next day I'd distilled an absolute from a mixture of fragrant blooms in my garden. Sure enough, it had worked a charm, and Essa Mae was soon back to her usual, bouncy ninety-year-old self.

I flipped past a page heavy with fine-inked lines showing a murmuration of starlings in flight, and another that outlined the delicate veining of an oak leaf in pale shades of green. Finally, I closed my eyes and simply let the book fall open where it might.

When I opened my eyes I saw a drawing of a purple-red

bell-shaped flower, deep purple berries, and a cross section of a green berry surrounded by five leaves. I recognized it immediately.

Atropa belladonna.

Nightshade. Deadly nightshade, to be specific.

Nightshade for warning.

A chill shivered down my back, leaving goose bumps in its wake. Beside me, Dash sat up as if he'd heard a strange noise.

"Gamma?" I whispered.

A gust of wind rattled the window latch, and I jumped.

Stop being silly, Ellie.

To the side of the drawing, a paragraph stated,

Delicious and sweet at first but with heinous undertones. Once used by maidens to dilate pupils for beauty. Poison is naturally occurring atropine (see jimson weed and mandrake). May cause tunnel vision and hallucinations prior to convulsions and painful death. Nonetheless, extremely effective in homeopathic preparations. Slow to germinate. Grows 3–4 feet tall. Dried or fresh, scent is similar to the pungent fragrance of fresh tomato leaves.

Slowly, I closed the book and rose to put it back on the shelf. It was late, and the interview tomorrow morning, which I'd once anticipated with nervous eagerness, now loomed as a stressful event I simply had to get through. Best to do that on a full night's sleep.

But the image of the beautiful, bell-shaped nightshade flowers haunted every one of my dreams that night.

Warning . . . of what?

* * *

WITH a sense of vague dread, I watched dawn spread across the angled skylight above. Checking my phone revealed Colby had texted after I'd gone to bed, assuring me that he'd found Larken and everything was copacetic. I texted him back that I'd call after the interview.

Downstairs, I brewed strong coffee. Then I showered, taking my time under the hot water and rinsing my hair with the heady rosewater left over from my last essential oil distillation. The sweet scent helped tame my nervous tension about the upcoming interview. I dressed in a swirly skirt and simple blue tank top that Astrid had assured me would photograph well in case Sontag decided to include me in any of the pictures.

Or would that be up to the photographer? The one who had stopped at the table last night.

Those grass green eyes. And he'd smelled of grass as well, newly mown and sprinkled with fresh rain. I shook my head and ran gel-covered fingers through my dark curls in a feeble attempt to tame them.

My thoughts veered back to the garden journal. Was the appearance of deadly nightshade a real warning from my gamma? Or was I making more out of it than I should? I'd always been fairly practical, despite my gifts. I mean, smell is a sense, right? It was a kind of empiricism to trust what it told me. But in the last few months, I'd finally opened myself to things that could be sensed at the edge of awareness, still discernable but only with concentration and heightened attention. So yes: I was willing to believe my grandmother had directed me to the nightshade for a reason.

The warning had to be about Blake Sontag interviewing me. What else could it be?

Sontag hadn't been anything like I'd expected. Of course, I hadn't actually spoken to him before the disastrous dinner in the Empire Room; his assistant had set up the interview. But I'd assumed that anyone so devoted to reporting on the environment would be a decent guy. Was Gamma warning me that this interview might do more harm than good for my business, or even for Poppyville? Scents & Nonsense and the Enchanted Garden were my life. I'd worked so hard to re-create myself after the divorce, and now, despite a few hiccups along my journey, I was the happiest I'd ever been.

What about Ritter in Alaska?

I pushed the thought away.

Oh, and now Colby was back, too! Probably not for long, but it was so good to see him. And Larken was a gem.

A sudden thought stabbed through me. What if the nightshade wasn't a warning about Sontag at all? What if it was about *Colby*?

No. Not my little brother. Nothing can happen to him.

I made my bed in the loft, checked that everything was neat as a pin downstairs, and opened the blinds to show the view of the meadow and spiky Kestrel Peak. Still, doom dogged my steps as I led Dash out to the garden. As always, the lush greenery calmed me. And everything looked great, almost as if the plants were determined to make the best showing they could. I smiled as I passed the rosemary I'd planted the previous afternoon. It had been shaped into a perfect cone and now graced the edge of a miniature fairy tableau. Come December, I'd add tiny lights, and the wee folk could enjoy their own Christmas tree.

Oh. There. Three obviously dead blooms on the hydrangea. I retrieved the pointed little deadheaders from the basket by the water spigot. As I snipped off the spent blossoms, the latch to the gate rattled, and Astrid came in. Precious trotted beside her, this time outfitted with a harness and leash.

Dash ran up and stopped short as he realized this was the strangest dog he'd ever seen. He comically tipped his head one way, then the other, looked at me, and finally lay down and allowed the pig to come over to sniff his nose.

We laughed at their antics as Astrid handed me a plastic container of cookies. "Calendula tuiles." She brought cookies by Sense & Nonsense most mornings, but lately she'd been on a flower cookie kick, using fresh or dried blooms from the Enchanted Garden.

"These are gorgeous," I said, examining the delicate wafers formed into crunchy arcs that represented French roof tiles, or *tuiles*. "You really went all out."

"You want to impress the big-time journalist, right?"

I sighed, lacking the will to tell her about the whole dinner fiasco the night before.

"Now, don't worry about Precious here. I'll keep out of the way. Besides, Blake Sontag is bound to think she's cute as a button."

"I highly doubt that," I muttered.

Astrid looked hurt.

"Never mind," I assured her. "Precious is adorable."

* * *

TEN o'clock came and went. Then ten thirty. Astrid had opened Scents & Nonsense. I fussed in the house, in the garden, with my curly hair, which seemed determined to be more crazy than usual. Finally, I went into the shop.

"I don't think he's coming," I said to Astrid, who was dusting the soap displays. Then I explained what had happened at dinner.

When I was finished, she planted her fists on her hips, her face livid. "That's just wrong, Ellie. You need to call him up and tell him so."

"I only have his assistant's number," I said, opening the front door and stepping out to the boardwalk.

Immediately, I saw the silent flashing lights. Red and blue and red and blue, three blocks down. A crowd of people. Police cars and a fire truck parked in the middle of Corona Street. An ambulance in front of the Hotel California.

I took off toward them at a run.

CHAPTER 4

ALL I could think was that my brother might be in trouble, and I'd been dithering around my garden waiting for an interview that was never going to happen.

"Ellie! Wait!" Astrid called from behind me.

I kept running. When I got to the hotel, I tripped going up the steps, caught myself on the railing, and pushed into the crowd of people clustered in the doorway.

"What's going on?" I asked. "What happened?"

A few people looked over, but no one answered. Setting my jaw, I elbowed through the throng into the lobby. More people were gathered in clusters, speaking to one another in hushed tones. I scanned the faces, looking for my brother. There was a uniformed policewoman chatting with an elderly couple, jotting something in her notebook as they spoke. She nodded, and they moved away as she approached a lone man dressed in shorts and a polo shirt.

Outside the French doors, I saw more people milling around the pool. I caught a glimpse of Spence, the photographer, but didn't see if Blake Sontag was with him.

A squeal sounded behind me, and I whirled to see Astrid had made her way inside, too. She was carrying Precious, who looked none too pleased. The pig blinked with agitation and made a distinct snorting noise, which attracted the attention of those standing nearby. My friend ignored them and pointed toward the registration desk. I nodded, and we hurried over.

I vaguely recognized the woman who stood behind the computer terminal, but couldn't place her. Her pretty brown eyes flicked around the lobby, pausing for a moment here and there before moving on. Stony displeasure radiated from her heart-shaped face. Then her jaw came up in determination as she gathered her long dark hair into a ponytail and twisted it into a quick bun that she secured with a ballpoint pen off the counter.

"What's going on?" I asked again, eyeing her name tag. It read FELICITY DONOVAN and under that: MANAGER. Where did I know that name from?

She spared a glance at Astrid and did a double take when she saw Precious. She opened her mouth as if to comment but must have decided against it. Instead, she trained her gaze on me. "Are you a guest?"

"No. I own Scents and Nonsense here in Poppyville. My brother is staying here, though."

Her face cleared. "Right. You're Ellie Allbright."

"Um, yeah." I racked my brain, trying to remember. Was she a customer? Then I had it. Felicity Donovan had been the editor of the *Poppyville Picayune* for several years. I hadn't noticed when the name changed on the masthead, but she must not be working there now. But managing the Hotel California? I mentally shrugged. Maybe it paid better.

"Felicity knows everyone in town," Astrid said.

The manager's expression softened at my friend's words. "I do pay attention to what's going on. Hard not to after so many years of it being a job requirement." Now she pointed at the pig and raised her eyebrows. "I heard Mrs. Paulson got one of those."

Astrid smiled and looked down at Precious, who had settled into the curve of her shoulder. "Yep. She's boarding at Doc Ericcson's." Then she waved her hand to indicate the activity behind us and casually asked, "So, what's all this?"

"A man was found dead in his room this morning."

"Dead?" The panic I'd felt when I saw the ambulance rose higher in my throat. "Who?"

She shrugged.

"You must know," I pushed.

Her lips thinned.

"How did he die?" Astrid asked in a hushed tone.

"Don't know." Felicity's rueful expression betrayed her frustration with being kept out of the loop. "But the cops are making a pretty big deal about it."

My eyes searched the lobby for my brother again. "I said I'd call him after the interview," I whispered. "He never texted back."

"Hmm?" Astrid was stroking Precious, whose beady porcine eyes blinked with pleasure.

"Colby," I said.

Her head came up. "Oh, now. You don't think . . ."

"I don't know," I said.

"It's not your brother," Felicity said.

So she *did* know who had died.

"Hey, sis." Colby's voice cut through my agitation as he strode toward me from the direction of the stairs.

Relief whooshed through me, and I ran to give him a hug. "You're okay!" Still, I could feel worry coming off of him in waves.

"I'm fine." He grimaced. "But Blake Sontag's not."

I backed away, feeling the blood drain from my face in a strange combination of relief and horror. "That's who . . . ?"

He nodded. "A housekeeper found him a couple of hours ago."

Behind him the elevator doors opened. Two men guided a gurney into the lobby. It held a large, lumpy black bag. I gasped as I realized what had to be inside.

"Oh, now, come on," Felicity protested, hurrying out from behind the reception desk. "There's a service entrance you can use for that."

"Sorry, lady," one of the men said, even though I could see through the open elevator doors that there was another set of doors on the opposite side that must open into the hotel's service areas.

Helplessly, the hotel manager looked on as they wheeled Blake Sontag's encased body through the crowded lobby to the front entrance and down the wheelchair ramp to the waiting ambulance.

A part of me couldn't believe he was inside the bag, and another part was unreasonably glad that I didn't have to look at him. I still had disturbing dreams as a result of finding Josie Overland's dead body months before.

And yet another part of me felt like I'd been waiting for something like this to happen ever since then. My grandmother's voice rose in my mind, unbidden but clear as a bell. She'd been talking to my mother shortly before Mama died, a conversation I shouldn't have been able to remember at all, considering I'd been only three years old at the time.

We all help keep the balance, whatever our gifts . . . Your daughter will bring solace to others, but also right wrongs . . . and that will be triggered by violence.

She'd been talking about me. The original violence that sparked the memory had been Josie's murder. Now Blake Sontag was dead. Was this the beginning of a trend? The thought made me shudder.

Felicity, Astrid, Colby, and I stood in a row at the window as the men loaded the body bag into the back of the ambulance and folded the gurney for storage. Nearby, guests murmured, and I could feel their horror and curiosity buffeting my psyche.

Wait a minute.

"Colby, how did you know it was Blake who died?"

The hotel manager turned her head to look at him in a way that told me she hadn't shared that morsel of information.

Colby pressed his lips together and nodded toward the Horseshoe Bar on the other side of the lobby from the Empire Room, where we'd eaten the night before.

I took a few steps and peered into the low light. Detective

Max Lang was sitting in one of the booths. Tall and rugged, he held himself with an imposing rigidity that implied a military background he didn't actually have, and his gray eyes were narrowed beneath his straw-colored buzz cut.

Larken sat across from him, her face pale and eyes puffy from tears.

WHEN I was four, my mother died in an accident. Her mother, my gamma, was already living with us, and took over mothering me as my father grieved. Three years later, he met Wynn Stubbs—Winifred, really, but she disliked the name and said the diminutive "Winnie" made her sound either like a horse or a honey-loving bear—and they'd married a year after that. Ten months later Colby was born, and eighteen months after that my half sister Darcy had entered the world.

So I'd been an only child for nine years, and then suddenly I wasn't. I've heard of similar situations where the older sibling was unhappy about the change of events, but that wasn't me. Like all onlies, I was good at entertaining myself for long stretches of time, but it was often a lonely childhood. When Dad told me I'd be getting a little brother, I was beyond excited. Those long months had felt like waiting for Christmas, and when Colby was finally born it was like getting the best gift ever.

It didn't hurt that he was a pretty baby. I know, I know: All babies are pretty. Except some really aren't, are they? But Colby was an angel, and I'd fallen in love with him the moment my stepmother brought him home from the hospital.

We'd lived in a yellow two-story house with a wrap-around porch and big kitchen, a separate wooden garage set off to the side, and a narrow backyard. Gamma had moved into a small white house around the corner when my father remarried, but she'd already been gone for two years before the new family moved in down the block. I was thirteen. As soon as the moving van pulled away, they put a BEWARE OF DOG sign on their fence. Loud barking echoed from their yard every time I walked to school, but I soon learned it wasn't the dog I needed to worry about as much as the fourteen-year-old son. Within a week, he'd established himself as a bully at school, and I started going a block out of my way to avoid his house.

Of course, the boy found us, along with dog. It was a sunny Sunday afternoon. The dog was black and brown, a mix of too many breeds to identify any of them. The boy was gangly and pimply and mean. They stopped on the sidewalk in front of the yellow house with the box-wood hedge and the four-year-old boy playing with a toy dump truck on the lawn. I was sitting on the porch step, supposedly watching my little brother but really reading *The Wind in the Willows* for the third time. I didn't even see them until Colby started sobbing.

The dog was crouched like a jackal. The boy was just inside the hedge, grinning. His wrist was cocked back, ready to throw a second rock at my brother. Colby looked back at me with pleading, confused eyes brimming with tears. A red mark was beginning to form on his chubby arm where the first rock had struck.

In a nanosecond, I was off that porch step and running, my arms waving wildly. I ran straight at the intruders, each of them bigger than me. I didn't care. Wordless banshee shrieks of fury spewed out of my throat. Through the red haze, all I could think about was protecting Colby.

The dog straightened to its full height, feet planted foursquare, lips beginning to pull back from yellow teeth. The boy started to laugh, but I kept right on coming at them, skinny legs pumping, growl-screaming at the top of my lungs.

As I blew past my baby brother, the dog seemed to think better of whatever ill-laid plans its owner might have had and turned tail. It loped off toward home, looking back at me over its shoulder a couple of times. I remembered smelling the canine version of fear, and for a split second recognized that perhaps it wasn't an evil creature at all, merely unlucky when it came to owners. The boy looked surprised, then shocked, then scared. He threw the rock at me, but it went wild as he, too, turned tail and ran, leaving behind an impressive trail of swear words.

But I didn't care about that. I cared about Colby, who by then was looking up at me with wide eyes and quivering lips. Then he gulped, opened his mouth, and let out a wail nearly as loud as my yelling had been. Seconds later, Wynn slammed open the front door to see what in tarnation was going on.

Colby was more than a foot taller than me now, certainly not a little boy anymore. But I could see he was scared. This time it was for Larken, and not for himself, but I could feel the tight sharpness of his fear mixed with the same bewilderment that had been on his four-year-old face all those years ago.

And it twisted my heart in exactly the same way now.

"What's going on?" I asked. "Why is Max Lang talking to Larken?"

Colby put his arm around my shoulder. "He seems to be talking to everyone."

I frowned.

"But he's spending a long time with her. Apparently someone delivering room service down the hall saw Lark at Sontag's door last night." He glanced down at me. "It was before I managed to track her down. She told me she'd tried to make amends with Blake after their argument over dinner. She didn't want him to be angry and give you a hard time during the interview this morning."

It took a moment to process. "She went to see him." *For my sake.* "And that's piqued Detective Lang's interest."

My brother nodded, worry pinching the corners of his eyes.

Nightshade for warning.

Max turned his head and spotted me. A grim smile thinned his lips, and one eyebrow rose a fraction. He turned back to Larken, said something, and pointed to me standing in the lobby. She looked over and nodded. His smile stretched into something more like a grimace.

I winced as the alarm that had been forming in my solar plexus tightened its claws. Detective Max Lang was my ex-husband's best friend. He'd also tried to pin a murder on me, and I'd proven him wrong. He'd seen it as a public humiliation rather than true justice, and we'd managed to avoid each other since then.

"How did Blake die?" I asked slowly.

Colby shook his head. "I don't know. But I heard

Detective Lang say that, until they know for sure, they're treating his death as a homicide."

A tiny, desperate sound escaped my throat, and his gaze sharpened. He looked back at Larken sitting in the bar, her hands folded on the table in front of her. Her expression was one of stunned disbelief. His fingers tightened on my shoulder as he turned me to face him.

"Ellie, you think Detective Lang suspects her of killing that guy."

I didn't say anything. It took all my effort not to look away.

He gave me a little shake. "Don't you?"

"It's possible," I said.

Panic rose in his eyes. He'd suspected it, but I'd just confirmed his fear.

"You have to help her," he said.

"Colby . . ."

"Ellie, you have to. I know Larken. She could never hurt anyone. I know you just met her, but—"

"She didn't do it," I interrupted. "I believe you."

"So you have to help her."

"I don't know how—" I began.

"You cleared your own name a few months ago. Found the truth, and saved yourself. I . . ." He faltered. Took a deep breath. "I love her. Please help her."

He still had that look on his face, the one I remembered, and I kept seeing that pimply-faced boy with the rock in his hand. Only now he looked a lot like Detective Max Lang.

I heard myself say, "I'll try."

He smiled. It didn't quite reach his worried eyes, but it was better than nothing.

"First off, we need to know if it really was a homicide." I turned toward the stairs and found Astrid had been standing right behind us. She'd heard everything.

"I'll go with you," she said.

Colby whirled. "Oh, Astrid. Hey. Go where?"

"Up to Sontag's room, I assume," she said.

I nodded. "That's what I had in mind, but I think maybe it would be better if you stayed here." I nodded toward Precious, now fast asleep in my friend's arms.

She looked down, and her gaze softened as though the pig were an actual child. "Right. I'll stay here with Colby." She looked around the lobby. "See what I can see."

"I'll be right back," I said. Skipping the elevator, I headed for the wide stairway.

CHAPTER 5

Putting a slight swagger in my step that approximated confidence, I marched up the stairs. I didn't know what room Blake Sontag had been in, but the Hotel California had only five floors. I paused at each landing and listened. On the third floor my ears were rewarded with the murmur of voices and the squawk of a police radio. I turned toward the sound.

In front of one of the doorways, a uniformed policeman consulted with two women wearing white jumpsuits over their clothes. Deliberately not making eye contact, I walked toward them, scanning the room numbers. The door that was open to the hallway was number 344. The officer looked up as I paused at the threshold.

"May I help you?"

At the words, the woman standing on the other side of

the king-size bed inside the room looked up and met my eyes.

Thanking the gods of serendipity, I gestured vaguely toward her. "I'm looking for Detective Garcia."

The officer looked in and, at my friend's quick nod, lost interest in me.

Lupe came around the bed and toward where I stood in the doorway. "You can't—"

"I wouldn't dream of coming in," I said. "After all, I hear this is a crime scene."

She'd cut her smooth dark hair so it curved under her slightly square jaw. Wearing her usual uniform of slacks, crisp white blouse, blazer, and, today, penny loafers, she looked the professional from head to toe. And professional she was—unlike her colleague, at least in my experience.

Now she murmured, "What are you doing here?" as she brushed by me and started down the hallway.

It was obvious she wanted me to follow, but first I paused and took a good long look inside. A good long sniff, too, which I ended up regretting. The sour smell of vomit curled up from the other side of the bed, where Lupe had been standing, mixing unpleasantly with myriad commercial cleaning products that were no doubt part of the hotel's housekeeping supplies, the scents of mint and dirt-but-not-dirt—valerian?—and underlying it all the unmistakable fragrance of tomato leaves.

That last one gave me pause. My heart beat a little faster, and my breath grew shallow in my chest. The picture of nightshade in Gamma's journal had been so worrying by itself that I hadn't read all the notes around it, but I did remember the reference to the smell of tomato leaves.

Nightshade as a warning was one thing. Nightshade as a weapon was something else entirely.

Then I noticed the stain on the carpet in front of the bedside stand. The overturned cup at the edge of the dark blotch, white porcelain, matching the one over by the coffeemaker on the shelf by the flat-screen television.

And there, just peeking out from under the bed skirt: two dried purple berries and a length of stringy fiber I recognized as a root.

On the other side of the bedside table, the phone cord lay uselessly on the carpet under the wall jack.

"Ellie." Lupe's voice was harsh enough that the officer looked up again, eyes narrowed.

I shot him a smile and ambled down to where she waited.

"What are you doing here?" she asked again, impatience in her voice.

"My brother's in town. You remember me telling you about Colby?"

She nodded but still looked puzzled.

"Well, he's staying here with his girlfriend."

Her face cleared. "Ah. That's all. What room?"

"I, uh . . . I don't know."

The frown returned to her forehead. "I don't understand. Are you wandering around the hotel hoping to run into him? Just give him a call for heaven's sake."

My laugh sounded weak. "No, no. I know where he is. In the lobby. With everyone else, it seems." I gestured toward Sontag's room. "Quite the excitement, eh?"

She leaned against the wall and folded her arms over her chest. "So you had to come take a look at the death scene? Good heavens, Ellie. I wouldn't have thought you were so macabre."

I hesitated, then plunged ahead. "Max is downstairs interviewing my brother's girlfriend. I was just wondering what the situation is. Thank God I ran into you. Though I thought you and Max were each working solo now?" The two detectives on the Poppyville force were not the best of friends.

"The chief asked us to work this case together in order to close it as soon as possible." Her eyes narrowed. "So your brother's girlfriend is Larken Meadows." It wasn't a question, and I didn't like the way she said it.

Slowly, I nodded. "Why is Max so interested in her?"

Lupe looked out the window onto the croquet lawn that stretched behind the hotel, and didn't reply. That frightened me as much as anything she might have said.

"It's murder for sure, then?" I asked, even though I knew the answer.

She shrugged, still not looking at me. "Sontag was quite ill, and there was evidence of a rash—which may or may not have anything to do with his death. But his pupils were dilated, and he was on the floor, so he certainly didn't die in his sleep." She paused and took a breath. After a few moments she said, "There were also indications that he suffered from convulsions."

Now she met my eyes. "So poison is a possibility. We'll know for sure after the autopsy. Of course, it's also possible that he died of natural causes. Some kind of seizure, say."

I felt my nostrils flare, and she leaned toward me a fraction.

"What is it?" she asked.

This time I was the one who looked away.

"Ellie, I can tell you know something. Is it about Larken?"

I shook my head. "No, no. Nothing like that. It's just . . ."

"What?"

I sighed. "I think you'll find it was definitely poison. Atropine, to be specific."

"And you know this how?"

Deep breath. "It was the tea, right?"

She just looked at me.

"I suspect it had *Atropa belladonna* in it. I saw the berries, and a piece of the root near the bed."

"Wait a minute. Belladonna? As in . . . ?"

I nodded. "Deadly nightshade."

Not just for warning. For *murder.*

Her hands came up to her face, the long fingers massaging her temples. "Ellie, I trust that you know your stuff when it comes to anything botanical, but if you're right about the nightshade, Ms. Meadows is in a lot of trouble."

My eyes widened. "Why? Because some room service guy saw her outside Blake Sontag's door last night?"

"And because she's already admitted to giving him a jar of homemade herbal tea to help him sleep."

My shoulders slumped. I'd promised Colby I'd try to help Larken, and instead I'd just managed to plunge her deeper into hot water.

Nice going, Elliana.

* * *

As soon as I descended the stairs, Astrid and Colby stood, so I knew they'd been watching for me. Larken remained seated between them, her shoulders slumped in defeat.

I hurried across the expanse of carpet.

"Did you find out anything?" Astrid asked. She still held Precious, who was wide awake and taking in the sights.

"I'm afraid so," I said, and sank into a wingback. Larken turned to look at me with red-rimmed eyes.

"Uh-oh," my brother said. He went around back of her chair and put his hand on her shoulder.

"Larken, I talked to a detective who's investigating Blake Sontag's death. Not Lang, the other one. Her name is Lupe Garcia. She's a friend of mine."

Astrid sat down on the other side of Larken. We exchanged looks. Relief mixed with curiosity on my friend's face. "Are they working together again?" she asked.

"Lupe said the chief wants her to work with Max on this case," I said. After her first case with Detective Lang had involved him trying to pin Josie's murder on me, Lupe had asked not to work with him anymore. Her boss had agreed, since murder was such an anomaly in Poppyville.

Or had been. But now that it looked like there was another one, naturally the chief of police wanted it solved as soon as possible.

"What did she say?" Larken asked in a small voice.

I took her hand in mine. "I understand you took Blake some herbal tea."

"Uh-huh. For his insomnia, as a kind of peace offering."

I glanced up at Colby. His attention was fixed on his girlfriend like a laser.

"What was in it?" I asked.

She sighed. "Just herbs, like I told Lang. Valerian and agrimony, with a bit of chamomile and mint that I wild-crafted. For the flavor, you know."

I nodded. "He brewed some, and I could smell the valerian and the mint. Agrimony was a nice touch. Nothing else?"

Eyes wide, she shook her head. "Why?"

"The mint was wild?"

"And the chamomile. The valerian and agrimony I had in my herbal kit in the van."

Astrid looked intrigued.

"Okay," I said. "Is there any way that you might have picked up something else when you were gathering the mint and chamomile?" It was a long shot, but within the realm of possibility.

Larken's lips pressed together. "I'm very careful."

At the same time Colby chimed in with, "She knows what she's doing."

I took a deep breath, looked at Astrid and then back at Larken. "So there is no chance, no chance whatsoever, that deadly nightshade could have ended up in your tea."

Horror dawned slowly on her face. "No! Oh, my God. Is that how he died?"

I sat back. "It's very likely that's what killed him." And I'd gone and told Lupe that. Of course, she would have found out soon enough. At least we knew what we were dealing with now.

Larken's head was swinging back and forth. "No, I'd never, ever, in a million years, mistakenly harvest belladonna, and I'd certainly never give it to anyone else on purpose. Any real wildcrafter worth her salt knows to avoid that stuff."

Colby frowned. "It's that bad?"

"A few berries can kill a child. A couple of leaves can kill an adult," she said in a strangled voice.

"And the roots are the deadliest of all," I said, thinking of the shred of brown woody root next to Sontag's bed. If it hadn't been for the warning in Gamma's journal—along with the reference to the plant smelling like tomato leaves—I wouldn't have guessed that snippet of root was belladonna. Now I felt sure of it. My brother pushed away from the back of Larken's chair. "And you're positive you couldn't have given it to Sontag by accident?"

She glared at him.

"I just thought if it was an accident, then no one could blame . . ." He stopped and held up his hands. "Sorry. Okay. So Detective Lang thinks you intentionally poisoned Blake Sontag with that tea."

"And he knows that we had an argument over dinner," Larken said, ducking her head in embarrassment. "Apparently I was pretty loud when I told him what a horrible person I thought he was."

I put my hand on her arm and gave a little squeeze. "He said some pretty mean things, that's for sure."

She made a face. Then her expression turned speculative. "Where does belladonna grow around here?"

I shook my head. "I've never run across it. That doesn't mean anything, though. It grows wild a lot of places."

She nodded. "If the microclimate is right." She sighed. "You can even order plants online."

"Really?" I asked in surprise. "How do you know that?"

"A friend of mine has a poison garden. It's kind of a thing with some people, having a garden full of night-shade and foxglove and oleander and the like."

We all stared at her.

"Hey, it's not *my* thing," she said in a defensive tone.

"Can you tell us where you went when you left the restaurant?" I changed the subject.

Her eyes grew big. "That detective kept asking me that."

Swallowing, I managed a smile. "I bet he did. What did you tell him?"

"I just . . . walked. I went down the boardwalk toward your store and found the trail in the park. It wasn't quite dark yet. I followed it down to the river. I was upset, you know? And water calms me." She glanced at Colby, who nodded his encouragement. "Then I came back to the hotel and sat out on the veranda for a while. I don't know how long. I was trying to figure out how to fix what happened at dinner. Finally, I decided to offer Mr. Sontag something that would help him sleep, so I went out to the van to make up that tea."

"Colby, when did you track Larken down last night?"

"About eleven," he said.

I nodded. That fit with when he'd texted to let me know everything was okay.

"I gave Mr. Sontag the tea and came back down to sit by the swimming pool."

My lips pressed together in thought. "How did you know what room he was in?"

"Well, I was going to check at the desk, but then I saw that guy who came by the table last night. The one with the camera on his T-shirt? He was over there in the bar with a bunch of photography stuff all over the table, like he was checking it." She pointed. "I asked him, and he told me Mr. Sontag was in room 344. So I just went on up."

"And Blake was there."

"Uh-huh. I almost didn't knock, because I could hear him on the phone. It sounded like he was arguing with someone."

My ears perked up at that. "Did you hear what he said?"

She looked rueful. "Not really. He kept saying something about joy, though, which seemed weird."

Joy? Or was he arguing with his sister, Joyous?

"Anyway, when I did knock, he hung up and answered the door right away. Eager, almost, like he was expecting someone."

Interesting. I glanced over at Astrid and saw that she thought so, too.

"You told Detective Lang all this?" I asked.

She nodded.

"Did you go into his room?" I asked.

The muscles in Colby's jaw worked when he heard the question.

But she shook her head. "No. He asked what I wanted, and I apologized for what I said at dinner and gave him the jar—a little mason jelly jar, you know? He took it and thanked me and shut the door."

"He *thanked* you?" Colby asked.

She nodded, her eyes suddenly filling. "He was actually kind of nice. I mean, he shut the door in my face, but still."

I scrambled for another question, but drew a blank.

"So what do we do now?" Colby asked me.

Gathering my thoughts, I said, "Since we know Larken didn't kill him, we have to find out who else had motive and opportunity."

Astrid snorted. "From what you told me about the guy, that sounds like it could be a long list."

"Just tell us what to do," Colby said, ignoring Astrid's doom and gloom.

"Go for a hike," I said.

"What?" He looked confused.

"Seriously. You and Larken should go for a hike up Kestrel Peak. It will help clear your minds, and I need to regroup and form a plan."

Astrid pointed her finger at me. "So I'll drop Precious here off at the vet office, and meet you at Scents and Nonsense for a powwow."

I nodded. "Sounds good." I could use all the help I could get, and Astrid had proven before that she had my back.

HALF a block from Scents & Nonsense I saw Maria with her hand cupped against the glass of the window, peering into the shop. Astrid had had the good sense to lock the door before pursuing me to the Hotel California, but hadn't put the CLOSED sign in the window. I, of course, hadn't remembered either one.

"Sorry!" I said, hurrying down the boardwalk. "Let me get this open." Then I realized I didn't even have my key. "Dang it. Come around back, won't you?"

Looking puzzled, Maria followed me through the gate and to the patio. No one had thought to lock the sliding glass door, and I counted myself lucky some intrepid visitor hadn't wandered inside. At least I assumed they hadn't. Behind the counter, nothing looked disturbed. Quickly, I moved through the shop to unlock the front door.

"What can I do for you?" I asked over my shoulder.

"Well, first off," she said, leaning against the counter and stroking Nabby's velvety fur until a loud rumble sounded from his throat, "I wanted to know how the interview went this morning."

I looked at my watch. It was almost one o'clock. How time flew when murder accusations were being thrown around.

"It didn't." I moved to the coffee urn for a much-needed blast of caffeine. "You saw all the commotion at the Hotel California?"

She nodded and followed me. "I wondered what that was all about."

"Blake Sontag was found dead in his room," I said.

Maria stared at me, lips parted. "You're kidding."

We settled into the rockers in front of the big plate glass window overlooking the Enchanted Garden, and I filled her in on a few more details while we nibbled on the delicate, crispy tuile cookies Astrid had gone to all the trouble of making to impress Blake. But every bite reminded me of his murder, and I managed to finish only one.

The librarian, on the other hand, happily crunched through three cookies while I told her what I knew, leaving out the specific details Lupe had shared, which I knew she wouldn't want me to pass on, and Max Lang's suspicions about Larken. The rumors would fly around town about that soon enough.

When I finished, she said, "Murder? Really?"

"Suspicious death," I corrected. "Don't jump the gun."

"Right." She gave me a knowing look before falling silent for a few seconds, digesting it all along with her sugary snack. Finally, she said, "So . . . no interview after all. Do you think there's any chance the magazine would send someone else?"

"Oh, gosh. I can't imagine they would," I said. "And heaven knows I've lost my enthusiasm for the idea."

"Of course." She stood. "You know, as long as I'm here . . ."

Ah. There was another reason she'd come by my shop. "Let me guess. You need more foot scrub?" Maria loved my peppermint foot polish.

"Actually, I was hoping for something a bit more soothing. Don't get me wrong, I adore the peppermint, but lately my feet have been so achy."

I snapped my fingers and stood as well. "I know just the thing." I went behind the work surface where I concocted many of the Scents & Nonsense signature products and selected a small blue glass bottle from a drawer. Then I turned to the cupboard I'd dubbed the apothecary and removed two brown glass bottles.

"These are thyme and rosemary oils I distilled about a month ago. They're from my herb garden." Carefully, I measured six drops of each into the blue bottle, then screwed its lid on tight and handed it to her. "Add this to a cup and a half of baking soda and dissolve in a basin of water as a foot soak. It should help with pain and swelling, whether from standing too much, arthritis, or whatever else might be wrong."

She smiled. "I knew you could help. What do I owe you?"

I quoted her a price.

"That's not enough!"

I gave her a look. "For twelve drops of essential oil? I didn't even mix up the foot soak for you. Let me know if you like it, and then we'll talk."

She nodded happily and paid me. "Okay. Say, do you mind if I hang out in the Enchanted Garden for a while? I have some thinking to do."

I waved toward the back. "Of course not. That's why it's there. And if you want, there's some lavender lemonade mixed up in the fridge under the coffeepot."

"Mmm! Sounds good."

After she'd poured herself a glass and wandered outside, I cast around for something to do until Astrid got there. What was taking her so long?

The shop phone rang. "Scents and Nonsense," I answered.

A crackling greeted my ear, then a loud whoosh like wind blowing over the mouth of a bottle. "Hello? Hello? Elliana?" came a distant voice. "Is that you?"

"Ritter!" I practically shouted.

CHAPTER 6

Y ES! It's Ellie! Where are you?"

Mumble mumble, then, ". . . miles from Prudhoe Bay . . . a week so far. Fascinating . . ."

"You're cutting in and out," I shouted louder.

". . . are you?"

"I'm fine." I wasn't, obviously, but there was no way to go into any details about Sontag's murder with this kind of connection. "It's good to hear your voice!"

"Finally got the sat phone to work. Expensive, so I don't have long. Wanted to check in, though. Give Thea my love?"

"Of course," I said. "I miss you!"

". . . can't hear. Have to get off. Call you when I can, Elliana . . ." There was more, but it was garbled, and then the call went dead.

I'd happily pass on his love to his sister Thea. The

question was, had any of his feelings for me been included in the garbled static? Was it wrong of me to hope so, or was this long-distance relationship doomed to fail?

I hung up and found myself blinking through tears. Ritter had helped me through a tough time when Josie died, including helping me track down her killer. The experience had created a bond between us that only added to our affection for each other.

But how strong a bond?

With a sniffle, I set my jaw. *Strong enough on my end, and that's all I can control. If this Alaska–California romance doesn't work out, it won't be because of me.*

A voice made me jump. "Oh, Ellie. We'll find out who killed that nasty reporter." Astrid had come in when all my attention was on trying to decipher my boyfriend's words.

Boyfriend.

I shook my head and forced a swallow. "It's not that. Ritter just called."

Her head tipped to the right. "And it was a bad conversation?"

"Oh, Astrid! It was no conversation at all." The words tumbled out of me. "He's gone for five more months, and I couldn't even tell him what happened this morning. He didn't know Blake was going to interview me in the first place. I could barely tell Ritter that I missed him. And then he didn't say . . ." I trailed off.

"That he missed you?" she asked gently.

I sniffed. Nodded. Sniffed again.

She came around the counter and put her arm around me, squeezing me to her side. Astrid was five ten and I was a full foot shorter, so she put her chin on my head for a few seconds before stepping back and snagging my gaze.

When she was sure I wasn't going to look away, she said. "He was your rebound. You know that, right?"

I stared at her. "Astrid!"

"He was a *good* rebound, but that's still what he was. Got you back in the game, made you feel good about yourself after your ass of an ex-husband made you feel so bad. But Ritter Nelson is married to his work, and if that was going to change, it would have happened during the two months you were together."

Shaking my head, I pushed away from her.

"I just don't want to see you waste five months of your life waiting for him to come back again. Making up stories in your head about how it will be, or even how it was between you. Stories that aren't true but that you want to be—"

"No."

She blinked.

"You're wrong," I said. "I know you like to date lots of guys and have no intention of settling down soon—maybe ever."

"Honey—"

"But I'm just not built like that, Astrid. I know it's still hard for you to believe, but it was really difficult for me to divorce Harris, even after all he'd done." I'd begun pacing and now stopped, took a deep breath, and repeated what I'd just been thinking to myself. "I'm going to make this thing with Ritter work on my end. What he does is up to him, but don't you see?"

She frowned.

"I have to trust him," I said. "That's part of the deal. He's a good guy, and I'm not going to start worrying that will change just because he's in another state for . . ." I swallowed. "For a while."

I met her gaze.

She was grinning. "You love him," she singsonged.

After a few moments, I felt a ghost of a smile tug at my lips, too. I rolled my eyes. "Maybe. We haven't said that to each other yet, but yeah. You might be right."

"Ellie, just tell me you aren't thinking about getting married again so soon."

"What? That's not . . . jeez. Not to worry. I'm just thinking about getting through the next few months."

I was starting to feel self-conscious, so I changed the subject. Wiping a last smudge of wetness from my cheek and clearing my throat, I said, "That's all well and good, but let's talk about how to help Larken."

Astrid looked surprised, but recovered rapidly. "Okay."

"It sounds like Max Lang has made up his mind— again—and he's wrong—again," I said with a grimace. "When the autopsy is finished and the cause of death turns out to be deadly nightshade, he's going to close Blake's murder case as quickly as possible."

She nodded. "To show the chief that he's still a good investigator. After he messed up so badly when Josie was murdered, he has something to prove." She looked thoughtful. "What about Detective Garcia, though? Maybe she can stop his one-man stampede."

"Lupe tried to slow him down when he was so determined to make a case against me, that's for sure. But the evidence against Larken is pretty damning. Lupe's a professional, though, and I'm sure she'll conduct a real investigation despite having to work with Max again. And she'll listen to us if we find out anything."

Astrid sat on one of the high stools behind the counter. "So how do we do that?"

I grabbed a notebook and pen from under the register. "Well, Blake was a local boy. At least once he was. So it could be someone who knew him a long time, or someone who just met him."

"That's not very helpful," she observed.

I sighed. "No, it's not. Are you sure you want to get involved with this? I shouldn't assume. After all, you don't know Larken from Eve."

But my friend was shaking her head emphatically. "I don't need to. I know you, and you're my best friend in the whole world, and I'll do anything I can to help you. You'd do the same for your brother, and he adores that girl—who, by the way, I liked as soon as I met her this morning. So that's all there is to it."

Dang if those tears I'd just tamped down didn't threaten again. "Thanks," I managed.

"Besides," Astrid said with a wide grin. "I like this investigation stuff. It's exciting."

I rolled my eyes. So much for sentimentality. Tapping the pen against the notebook, I gazed out the window at Corona Street and mused, "So who would want to kill Blake Sontag?"

"So it *is* murder," Maria said from the patio doorway. "And you two are smack-dab in the middle of it. I should have known."

Shoot. I'd forgotten she was out there.

"Hey, Maria," Astrid said easily. "I don't suppose you have any books over at the library on crime investigation."

Our friend came in and leaned one elbow on the counter. "Of course we do. What did you have in mind?"

Astrid looked at me. I raised my eyebrows as if to say, *You asked her.*

"Um, how about one on motives?"

Maria blew a raspberry. "You don't need a book for that. Just talk to Cynthia." She looked between us. "Which you were going to do already, right?"

"Of course," I said breezily.

Astrid grinned.

Well, we would have once we'd gotten a plan together.

"And Blake's sister," Maria said.

Her, too. "Her, too," I said.

"Well, that should give you a start. Let me know if I can help in any way." She straightened. "I have to get back before story time is over. It's amazing how much damage a bunch of toddlers can do after cupcakes and a rousing rendition of *The Very Hungry Caterpillar.*"

Astrid gazed after her as she left. "Well, I guess we have marching orders. Next time we decide to make a plan, let's just call Maria to start with."

"Amen, sister."

A STRID had been late meeting me at Scents & Nonsense because Dr. Ericcson was having trouble with the computer at the vet office and needed her expertise. I'd never known anyone to get as flummoxed by technology as he did, and Astrid not only served as his veterinary assistant but also his unofficial office manager. It was late afternoon by the time Maria left, and since Astrid had told her boss she'd come back and get the system straightened out, she promised to go with me the next day to see Joyous Sontag.

In the meantime, I'd track down Cynthia to get her scoop on the murder victim. However, I couldn't really leave the shop until after six, so I decided to telephone someone else who might be able to share a nugget or two of information on the Sontags.

I had to wait until a woman and her two young daughters had tracked down every fairy scene in the Enchanted Garden. It was kind of like a treasure hunt, and usually I relished helping with hints and smiling encouragements of "hot" and "cold" and "Oh, you're getting warmer now!" But this afternoon I just wanted them to finish their lavender lemonade and go fly a kite. Or at least go next door to buy a kite.

After they'd found every one of the tiny troves and gnome doors tucked into the niches and alcoves all over the garden, played with Dash, and scritched a purring Nabby, the mother bought a set of scented markers, a bundle of scratch 'n' sniff stickers, and a stamp pad that smelled like strawberries. Because of the number of young people who came to see the Enchanted Garden, I'd started stocking more in the children's section of Sense & Nonsense. Despite my impatience that afternoon, I was glad to see it paying off.

When the door had swung shut behind them, I grabbed the phone and dialed the Florida number I knew by heart.

Wynn answered. "Sweetie! How are you?" My stepmother hadn't used the word "hello" to answer a telephone since the advent of caller ID.

"I'm good," I said, a knee-jerk answer that, in this case, completely belied the truth. "Well, actually, it's been a pretty weird day. I was wondering—"

"Weird? What do you mean 'weird'? What's wrong? What happened?"

I felt a small smile creep onto my face. My stepmother was a lot of things—go-getter, social butterfly, beach enthusiast, a former first runner-up for California Dairy Queen, and a woman who believed that with enough positive thinking and the occasional discreet visit to a medical aesthetician, she would never age—but she was also a born nurturer and as intuitive as a swami when it came to her kids.

She had *not* been happy to learn after the fact that I'd nearly been arrested for murder a few months back.

So she should be glad I was calling now, right?

"Well," I started. "Um."

"Elliana Elizabeth, I love you dearly and adore how you hedge around things, but will you please get to the point?"

"There was another murder," I said.

Silence. Then, "Are you in jail?"

I laughed. "No, of course not."

"Good," she declared emphatically, and I pictured her settling back in her chaise lounge on the lanai of their Fort Lauderdale condo. "Now, spill."

"Do you remember the Sontags?" I asked, easing into it.

"Bette and Jonah? Good Lord, yes. They used to throw the best parties."

"And their son, Blake?"

"Right. Blake and that sour little princess of theirs, Joyous. I do not know what was wrong with that child. Perhaps she was born on a Thursday."

"What?"

"You know, Thursday's child . . . never mind. Ellie, why are you asking . . . Oh my heavens. That's not who died, is it?"

"Blake Sontag, yes. A housekeeper found him in his room at the Hotel California this morning."

"Murdered?" she whispered.

"It does look that way," I fudged. "And unfortunately, Larken Meadows is a prime suspect."

"Who?"

Uh-oh.

"Um, Larken? You know—" *Oh, God. Why did you keep her such a secret, little brother?* But I was too far in now. "Colby's girlfriend?"

"Girlfriend!" Wynn shrieked. Moments later I heard ice cubes tumbling into a glass. My stepmother didn't ascribe to happy hour on a regular basis like the somewhat older crowd she and my father hung out with after he took early retirement. However, a solid nip of rye whiskey for medicinal purposes would be a requirement to process such shocking news.

"Colby's there?" she asked in a slightly calmer tone.

"Um, yeah. Showed up out of the blue yesterday."

"With a girlfriend."

"Um, yeah."

"Stop saying, 'um,' Ellie. It makes you sound dim."

I blinked. She must be really upset.

"What's she like?"

So much for the news of Blake's murder. "She's nice," I said. "Clean."

"Clean?"

"No, I don't mean she showers. Which, of course, she does. Shower. But she's, I don't know how to put it. Clear. Down-to-earth. Real, you know?" I hadn't thought of Larken in any of those terms until Wynn put my feet to the fire. "I guess I mean she's this sweet, straightforward, earthy type who says what she means and means what she says." I stopped, realizing that I was saying Larken seemed to possess no duplicity. There was no way she could have—or would have—killed Blake Sontag.

My stepmother was quiet for several seconds. Then she said, "I think I understand. You were always such an intuitive person, even as a little girl. I'm sure she's lovely, and I'm glad Colby managed to find someone even if he insists on living like a carney."

"You'll like her," I said, hoping she'd have a chance to meet Larken outside of a prison. "But back to the Sontags. Are you still in touch with Bette and Jonah?"

"You're doing it again, aren't you? Investigating a murder. Only this time it's for Colby."

"Wynn . . ."

"No, it's okay. It's good, I mean. You're a kind woman, and smart as a whip. I'm sure you'll fix this for your brother in no time."

No pressure. Still, her vote of confidence meant a lot.

She sighed. "But I'm afraid you won't be getting any

information from Blake's parents. A couple of years after they moved to Arizona, they were caught in a flood and killed."

"That's terrible!"

"It was, indeed. But that's what you get for camping in an arroyo during monsoon season, I guess. They should have known better."

Ouch. Did I mention Wynn didn't suffer fools gladly?

"Butterworth!" she shouted at full volume, and I held the phone away from my ear. Wynn was the only person on earth who called my dad by his given name. Everyone else called him Worth.

A grumbling in the background, followed by Wynn's rapid-fire tones, and a quick, "Bye, Ellie. Here's your father."

"Ellie? What's this about a murder? Is it really the Sontag kid?"

Well, he'd been older than me, so, "kid" . . . *anyway.*

"Hi, Dad. Yes, I'm afraid Wynn got it right."

"And Colby's girlfriend is in trouble. What can we do to help?" Bless my practical father.

"I called to find out whether you were still in contact with Blake's parents. Wynn told me what happened to them."

"Why did you want to talk to them?"

"Honestly? I'm just flailing around at this point. Blake hadn't lived here for a long time, but then he shows up to interview me for *Conscience Magazine*, and *boom*, he's killed."

"He was there to interview you?"

"Oh, God, Dad. Yes. But that didn't end up happening.

Please don't put Wynn back on. I promise to e-mail with all the details about the interview that never happened, okay?"

"I was just going to say that I hope Max Lang doesn't make too much of Blake being in Poppyville to interview *you*."

"Oh. I hadn't thought of that." *Merde*.

"So Joyous is the only owner of that parcel of land now."

It took me a moment to drag my thoughts back from Max Lang. "Wait. What land?"

"The land that's been in the Sontag family since, well, since before there was a town."

Everyone knew the Sontags had been in Poppyville for generations. Blake's great-great-great-grandfather was one of the city elders with my own ancestor Zebulon Hammond.

My father continued. "Owen Sontag claimed that big chunk of land south of town by the river around the time of the Rush. You know, off of River Road after you pass the trailhead to Kestrel Peak?"

"I thought that was public land," I said, trying to remember the last time I'd driven beyond the trailhead.

"Most of it is. Jonah's father deeded most of that property to the state with the stipulation that it be added to Clary State Park. But the family kept the parcel where the old cabin was built. It's about thirty acres, I think. Jonah had a couple too many Scotches one evening and went on and on about how he was going to keep that land in the family even though his kids thought he was being sentimental and wanted to sell it."

"How was he going to do that?"

"He and Bette willed it to their children in a joint trust. When either Blake or Joyous had children, it would automatically go to them, still held in trust until they were adults. If neither of them had children by the time they were both thirty-five, the trust would be dissolved and the land would go jointly to them.

"It was just a stopgap because, when they were in their twenties, both of his kids had already said they'd rather have the money than the land. Jonah's hope was that they would keep the old place in the family for many more generations. Actually, he used the word 'forever' when he told me about the whole thing. That's why he came up with the idea of the trust, just in case something happened to him and Bette." Dad sighed. "Which, unfortunately, it did. Of course, his assumption was that he'd still be around at that point, that he'd know his grandchildren—maybe even his great-grandchildren—and that he could convince them all to follow his wishes."

"Hmm," I mused. "Joyous is about a year older than me, so would have turned thirty-five recently. Blake was older than her, so the trust has already been dissolved."

"Does Blake have any children?" he asked. "Because if not, Jonah's will stipulated that if one of the siblings died, the ownership of all the land would automatically revert to the other one."

I hadn't even thought about Blake having kids. I'd assumed from what Maria had said about Cynthia considering Blake for husband number three meant he was single, but he could have been divorced. My throat tightened as I considered who might be grieving his loss.

"I don't know if he has children," I said. "Is the land worth anything?"

"Well, all land is worth something," Dad said. "But value always depends on what someone is willing to pay. A few people made a run at Jonah to develop those acres, but he always held out."

My stepmother's voice echoed down the line. "Butterworth! We're late for tango lessons!"

"Be right there," my dad called back. "Ellie, is there anything else I can tell you?"

"Not that I can think of. That information about the land is news, though. Um," I said. "Tango lessons?"

He laughed. "Wynn does keep things interesting."

I smiled. "I'm glad, Dad. I love you. Good-bye."

CHAPTER 7

I CLOSED Scents & Nonsense a few minutes before six, taking the chance that I might lose one last sale. It seemed more important to track down Cynthia Beck to find out what she could tell me about Blake Sontag. A telephone call didn't seem right for that. On one hand it seemed kind of cold, and on the other, I wanted to be able to see her face—and feel whatever I could feel on an empathic level—when we spoke.

As I was shutting the sliding door in back, I saw Dash and Nabby enjoying the shade cast by the mosaic retaining wall in the garden. That spot stayed damp and cool all day, no matter the August heat. The corgi was sprawled on his back, paws in the air and eyes squeezed shut in slumber, and Nabby had stretched out to his full length beside him. I left them to their peaceful snoozing and headed out to Corona Street and Foxy Locksies Hair Studio.

The boardwalk was packed with the dinnertime crowds, from those seeking a quick sandwich from Kneadful Things to those going to the opposite end of the street for a meal of barbecue brisket, tender rotisserie chicken, or baby back ribs from the Roux Grill. For a year after our divorce, I'd avoided going into the Roux, but now I went in regularly. It was, after all, some of the best food in town, even if I did say so myself. And not least because of my ex. He might be a passive-aggressive philanderer, but he was also a really good cook.

Thoughts of that chicken reminded me that, once again, I'd neglected to eat much during the day. Sometimes I thought if Astrid didn't supply the shop with cookies every morning, I'd starve to death.

So: Talk to Cynthia first, and stop in at the Roux for a to-go order of chicken after. With garlic and olive oil smashed potatoes, roasted green beans with bacon and almonds, and maybe, just maybe, a slice of pineapple cheesecake for later.

What could I say? It had been a rough day. The only thing that would be better than sitting down to that meal in the Enchanted Garden would be if Colby and Larken joined me.

Well, that and if whoever had killed Blake Sontag dropped by the police station and confessed.

I paused on the boardwalk, stepping out of the stream of traffic and barely avoiding a double stroller, and texted my brother with the dinner offer. They should have returned from their hike by then, though it was possible Colby had dragged Larken all the way to the top of Kestrel Peak.

The distinctive smell of "salon" hit me the second I opened the door to Foxy Locksies, a combination of perm solution, coloring chemicals, and expensive beauty products. All four chairs were occupied, but no one was behind the reception desk. One of the newer stylists looked up from where she was blow-drying the blue-streaked hair of a sixty-something woman. She held up her index finger in a *just a second* motion. Before she could turn away, I pointed toward Cynthia's office in the back of the building with raised eyebrows.

She gave a small shake of her head and turned back to her task. A minute later, she shut off the hair dryer, fluffed the woman's do with an expert gesture, and gave her a hand mirror before twirling the chair around. As her customer inspected the back of her head, she stepped over to where I stood.

"You're looking for Cynthia?"

"I am. Is she—"

"Not here, I'm afraid. She'll probably stop by little before eight when we close, though. At least she usually does."

I thanked her and went back outside. It was possible my fellow Greenstocking was at home mourning the sudden death of her former fiancé, but it was an even bet she'd be at the office she'd recently rented. Cynthia always had big moneymaking plans and had determined that it would appear more professional if potential investors could meet her in an office that wasn't in the back of a hair salon. Her latest venture had been purchasing the Stop N Go franchise from Lani Taylor, who was moving to San Diego. It was a lucrative concern, and I had no doubt Cynthia would only improve it.

While I'd been in the salon, Colby had texted back. He and Larken would happily join me for dinner in an hour or so.

Smiling to myself, I walked the three blocks off Corona to Cooperhawk Court. As I passed down the tree-lined streets, I reflected that it was just as well that Astrid hadn't been able to come with me. My friend always referred to Cynthia simply as "the mantrap." I got along with Cynthia well enough, and had been flattered when she invited me to join the Greenstockings. Over the course of our meetings, though, I'd learned she could be quite mercenary in her relentless striving for business success. On the other hand, her ideas usually benefited the whole town, so it was hard to complain. The woman was super intense, though. Too long in her presence sometimes made me a little twitchy. Thinking back, it was actually surprising how much Blake's negative personality had overshadowed her usual verve.

The office building was a converted two-story house with a wide, welcoming porch. It was painted sky blue with white trim, a combination that made me think of a man's dress shirt. Three cars were diagonally parked on the street in front, and I recognized one of them as Cynthia's silver Lexus. A low wooden fence surrounded the manicured yard, and a sign on the lawn listed Beck Enterprises, an accountant, an attorney, a massage therapist, and in the largest print, Gold Rush Realty. The Realtors took up the entire first floor, and the front window was plastered with sales flyers. As I approached the entrance, I saw a blond woman putting up another one. She waved, and I waved back.

Inside, an enclosed foyer led to the stairway to the second-floor offices. The blue-and-green-paisley-print carpet gave off the subtle aroma of recent shampooing. At the top of the stairs, I found a wide hallway with an open window at the end. The anticipatory fragrance of coals burning in someone's backyard grill wafted through the screen on the sounds of children playing.

All the doors except one were closed. Cynthia's Chanel No. 5 signaled to me that she was in her office before I reached the threshold. She looked up with a startled expression, which quickly relaxed into a smile.

"Ellie." She stood and gestured to an uncomfortable-looking Scandinavian chair. "Welcome to my new lair."

Scanning the rest of the room, I sat. The chair was more comfortable than it appeared. The other chairs, desk, and bookshelves boasted the same clean lines, all in light wood. Bright red blinds cut the glare of the oblique sunlight from the west, but were open at the top to allow light into the room even so. Her lemon yellow wrap dress fit in so well with her surroundings that I wondered whether she'd donned it with that intention.

"This is nice," I said. "Are you happy with it?"

"Absolutely!" She sat back down behind the kidney-shaped desk. "What can I do for you?"

I played it by ear. "Well, first off, I wanted to see how you're doing after the tragedy this morning."

She blinked.

Oh. Oh dear. She must know, right? A sick feeling chased away my formerly raging appetite.

"You mean Blake, of course," she said, rubbing delicately at her temples. "I still can't believe it."

My stomach unclenched, and a sigh of relief escaped my lips. "Yes. How did you hear?"

She looked wry. "I own a hair salon. More information goes through there than through the NSA."

"Oh. Right. So how are you doing?"

"Well, it's certainly sad for a man to die when he's so young and all." She looked thoughtful. "But to be honest, I hadn't seen him for years. And he wasn't like I remembered. When I heard he was coming back to town, I'd hoped . . ." She trailed off, staring into the past for a few seconds. Then she shook her head. "I mean, you saw him last night." She sighed. "Still, it's a tragic thing."

She didn't sound all that broken up about it.

"I'm glad to know you're okay. I'd heard you two were engaged at one time, and I thought perhaps you were still close."

Cynthia steepled her vermillion-tipped fingers on the desk in front of her and sighed. "Oh, gosh. That engagement. It didn't last long, believe me. Blake was not what you'd call a one-woman kind of guy." She made a face. "He used to be so much *nicer*, though. He grew so cynical over the years." She shook her head. "I wonder how he died."

I was silent.

It took her a few seconds to notice, but then she focused on my face. "I assumed it was a heart attack, or . . ." Her gaze sharpened. "Ellie? You know something."

Deep breath. "Gosh, Cynthia. I'm sorry to have to tell you this, but the police are investigating his death as a possible homicide." I swallowed. "It looks like he might have been poisoned."

She stood abruptly, crossed to the window, and opened the blinds. Stripes of light fell across the room as she stared through the slats. "Damn," she said under her breath. After a few seconds of silence, she squared her shoulders and whirled to face me. "That's the last thing we need in this town. Another murder. Are you sure?"

Carefully, I nodded. "Pretty sure."

Cynthia frowned. "Well, that rinky-dink police department better solve this fast." Then she looked thoughtful. "I wonder if they have a suspect."

I licked my lips.

"Aha!" She lifted one eyebrow. "Is that why you're here? You're helping the police again?"

"Well, I really was concerned about you," I began. *And my brother's girlfriend is the prime suspect.*

She looked rueful. "I'm sorry he's dead—both because he was, you know, a human being and even if he wasn't a great human being, I wouldn't wish him dead, but also because Poppyville's sweet-little-town image will be tarnished by two murders in one year."

Well, at least she was honest.

"So, do you . . ." I paused.

"Spit it out, Ellie. I'll help any way I can." She returned to her chair and leaned her elbows on the desk.

"Okay. Can you think of anyone who might have wanted Blake dead?"

"Pretty much anyone who spent five minutes with him," she muttered. Then she squinted at the ceiling and started nodding slowly. "I wonder . . ."

I leaned forward. "What?"

"Mm. More like 'who.' Do you know Felicity Donovan?"

"The manager at the Hotel California," I said.

Cynthia gave me a knowing look. "She is now. Before that she was the editor at the *Poppyville Picayune*."

"I know."

"A nice enough little weekly, but it doesn't pay beans, even for an editor. So she quit and went to work for the hotel. But before the *Picayune*, she worked for the *San Francisco Chronicle*." She paused and inclined her head. "Blake Sontag ruined her career."

"Really? What happened?

Cynthia sat back and crossed her legs, ready to impart gossip. I sat back, too, ready to receive.

"She and Blake dated back in high school. Nothing too serious—Blake was rarely serious about women, as I learned for myself—but they kept in touch when they went off to college. He went east to Princeton, and she went west to a university in Hawaii. Both studied journalism, but she had an uncle with connections and ended up as an investigative journalist at the *Chronicle*, while Blake free-lanced for a while after he graduated. He got tired of it, though, and wanted to work for a real paper. So Felicity got him a job in the features department at her paper."

"Did they start dating again?"

"Probably," Cynthia said. "But I don't really know. He was a real charmer then, though. But she's not upset about a broken heart. That would be the least of her worries."

"Why?"

"Because Blake stole a big story right out from under Felicity. And I mean *big*. You remember when Senator Callon was caught using federal funds earmarked for the cleanup of superfund sites to pay for his yacht?"

"Vaguely. The political scandals tend to run together, but he had to leave office, didn't he?"

She nodded. "Indeed. And Blake wrote that story."

I whistled. "Interesting. An environmentalist even back then, in a way."

"Not exactly. He earned a reputation with that story, and soon was getting other nature-oriented assignments. That's how he ended up in that niche. The superfund story made his whole career."

"So he's not a true environmental advocate. That explains why he was so cynical about Ritter's work and Larken's dream of farming," I said. "And I can see how Felicity would be upset."

"She wasn't just upset," Cynthia said, arching a brow. "She was *livid*. When I said he stole the story, I wasn't kidding. He was a features writer. *She* was the investigative reporter, and she did all the work. She cracked that story and was getting ready to write it when it showed up in the paper under his name."

"Oh, no!"

"Oh, yes. He'd stolen her notes and even taken an early draft she'd been working on, and claimed it all as his own."

"Didn't she protest?"

"Of course! Only instead of vindicating her, telling her editor the truth resulted in being assigned to work on terrible stories. At the same time, Blake's career rocketed."

"That's terrible. Sexism?" I wondered.

"Maybe. But apparently Felicity's editor had it in for her from the beginning because her uncle got her the job at the *Chronicle* in the first place. He eventually made her job so unpleasant that she left and came here to run the *Picayune*.

"So it was the editor's fault she left, really," I said.

"But if she'd been the one to write that story about Senator Callon, her career would have soared instead of Blake's."

I wrinkled my nose. "And you dated that guy?" I wanted to suck the words back in as soon as they came out.

Cynthia just laughed. "I know, right? But so did Felicity. As you well know, we all make mistakes."

Touché.

"So how do you know all of this?" I asked.

She shrugged. "Felicity used to be in the Greenstockings. Before your time, of course, and she dropped out when she left her job at the paper. I've tried to talk her into joining us again, now that she's running the hotel, but she hasn't bitten."

"Huh," I said, thinking. The manager of the hotel would have more access to the rooms than almost anyone else. Sontag had died sometime during the night—I'd have to check with Lupe and see if she knew anything more specific about the time of death.

Ugh.

I stood. "Anything else you can think of?"

Cynthia rose as well. "Not off the top of my head. I'll let you know if I come up with anything, though. You might check with his sister."

I nodded. "Astrid and I are going to visit her tomorrow. Today was too soon. Heck, tomorrow is probably too soon." I couldn't begin to imagine how I'd feel if my brother had been poisoned.

She tipped her head to one side. "She and Blake weren't close, but he was her family. And honestly, she's going to be a pain whether you wait or not, so you might as well tackle her soon." Her eyes bored into mine. "It's imperative that Blake's killer is brought to justice as soon as possible, and the story fades from the headlines."

Yes, I liked Cynthia. But Lordy, she could be obsessed when it came to anything related to tourism in Poppyville.

And, of course, I had to admit that she wasn't wrong. I just hoped Max wouldn't throw Larken under the bus to hurry along a conviction.

Downstairs, I let myself out of the building. The brightly colored flyers in Gold Rush's window caught my eye, and I paused to take a look. Housing prices seemed to have increased significantly since I'd been in the market for a place to live. The selection didn't look extensive, either. A tight market, then.

And then I saw the ad the woman had been taping up as I'd come in.

Pristine Property!

The heading screamed above a photo of verdant hills studded with wildflowers, a shallow red cliff to one side, and Kestrel Peak in the background.

Just ten minutes from downtown Poppyville, this undeveloped 30 acres on River Road is ripe with possibility! Water rights included in price!

Views of Kestrel Peak! Bordered by Clary State Park!

Build your dream home!

OR a prime spot for platting and development!

The possibilities are endless!

It was the parcel of land Dad had described to me on the phone that afternoon.

The old Sontag place.

I guess that answered the question of whether Blake had any children. The land was all Joyous' now.

At least until she sold it.

CHAPTER 8

As I made my way to the Roux Grill, I debated whether or not to call Lupe Garcia. Even with a possible suspect in Larken, surely she and Max would have looked into Blake's assets and checked in with his next of kin. So maybe she already knew about the thirty acres of land Joyous had inherited. But what about the information Cynthia had given me about Felicity Donovan's possible motive for murdering the man who had ruined her career?

By the time I passed between the big petunia planters that flanked the door of the restaurant I'd formerly owned with Harris, I'd decided to hold off on calling. Larken was in a jam, but the police would at least need an autopsy in hand before Max could go around making arrests. If I was going to take information to Lupe, I'd like to give her more than what I had so far.

The smell of the bite-size garlic rolls on every table hit my nose first, then the enticing aromas of roasting and grilling meats. Back in the kitchen, the brisket had slow-roasted overnight, the baby back ribs were fall-off-the-bone tender, and dry-aged steaks were ready to be seared to perfection. I still craved the rotisserie chicken, potatoes, green beans, and cheesecake, though. Maggie was tending bar and took my family-size to-go order between mixing drinks. At the last moment, I remembered Larken had ordered a Greek salad at the restaurant the night before, and might be a vegetarian. The Roux had a few options in that department, but they weren't exactly light fare. The macaroni and cheese was to die for, there was a vegetable version of the lasagna, and the Caesar salad with grilled romaine and house-made dressing was out of this world. I thought about texting Colby, but decided to go ahead and add the lasagna and salad to the order just in case.

Light from the window reflected off the liquor bottles, casting pools of color along the mahogany bar that ran down one side of the restaurant. Diners already filled the booths that marched down the opposite side. Tables took up the floor space between. The fireplace in the rear wall by the kitchen was unlit today, but provided a cheery atmosphere on chilly days.

I spied Harris sitting at one of tables. Head tipped forward so that his dark hair flopped over his forehead, he was deep in discussion with a man who looked vaguely familiar. The stranger wore a white shirt, pressed jeans, and fancy boots. Then I saw the incongruous Panama hat on the chair next to him, and pegged him as the guy who had first opened the door for me at the hotel the evening before, and then almost hit me with the same door as I'd been leaving.

Maggie came back from giving the kitchen my order and started mixing a dirty martini. Gin with two olives just like I liked it. When she put it in front of me, I said, "I don't remember ordering that."

"Drink it, honey. I heard what happened at the hotel this morning. Murder, your interview down the drain, and now Detective Lang thinks that lovely girl your brother brought home with him might have done the evil deed." She tsked. "As if. Why on earth would she kill Blake Sontag?"

I let that slide, obediently sipping the ice-cold gin, cloudy with sour olive juice. I sighed with pleasure. "No one makes a martini like you do, Maggie."

"It's a gift," she agreed cheerfully.

"How did you hear Larken is a suspect?"

Maggie nodded toward Harris. "His buddy dropped by." She meant Detective Lang. "Didn't seem too worried about being overheard, either. So, you know—I listened." Her eyes narrowed as she watched my ex wave his hands to make a point. "I wonder if Detective Lang likes that girl as a murder suspect because of her connection to you?"

I blanched. "No. You don't really think . . ." I rubbed my forehead with one hand and lifted the martini to my mouth with the other. It was possible that Maggie was right. Max and I hadn't gotten along very well when Harris and I were married; the divorce had only made it worse. And I knew he was still fuming over the fact he hadn't been able to throw me in jail for murdering Josie.

"Dang it," I whispered, and took another sip.

A couple came in and sat at the bar, and Maggie went to take their drink order. I slid off my stool and wended my way through the tables to where Harris and his friend sat. Their conversation trailed off as I approached. Stopping by the side of their table, I nodded to my ex-husband.

"Harris."

He leaned back and folded his arms across his chest. "Ellie."

I smiled at Panama Hat. He glanced at his companion, then smiled back. He was so tall that even though he was sitting down, we were nearly eye to eye. His were the color of ripe chestnuts and framed by thick lashes. He smelled of pipe tobacco and whiskey.

"What brings you into the Roux?" Harris asked, his voice tight. He liked it better during the year I stayed away from the restaurant. I reminded myself to come in more often.

"The food, of course." I nodded toward the bar. "And one of Maggie's most excellent martinis."

The look on his face was sour as he shot a look at Panama Hat. I realized I was making Harris more uncomfortable than usual. I wasn't entirely proud of the feeling of glee that thought sent through me. On the other hand . . .

I stuck out my hand. "Hi. I'm Ellie Allbright." The smile broadened on my face. "I'm Harris' ex-wife."

Panama Hat looked amused as he took my hand. His palm, dry and smooth, enveloped mine. "Well, hello, Ellie. I'm Vaughn." His voice was a deep baritone, smoothed by smoke and bourbon and rounded with a slight accent that hinted at a childhood spent deep in Texas.

"I think I saw you at the Hotel California last night," I said.

Harris abruptly stood. "Come on. Let's go back to my office where we can discuss our business in peace."

His friend's lips curved up, and one eyebrow twitched as he let go of my hand. "Sure thing, Harris." When he stood, he towered over me. "Nice to meet you, Ellie."

My ex hustled his friend toward the kitchen doorway and, presumably, to his office beyond.

Puzzled by Harris' secretive attitude, I returned to the bar. Within moments, the Roux's head chef, Raleigh, brought my to-go order out himself.

I paid for the food, gave Raleigh a big kiss on his wrinkled cheek before he returned to the kitchen, and turned to go. Then I paused. "Maggie, can you come to work at the shop early tomorrow? Say, eleven?"

She grinned. "Yep. You have plans?"

I nodded. "Hope so."

"Anything to do with this latest murder?"

I answered with an enigmatic smile, sketched a wave, and left with dinner.

Astrid and I had agreed to visit Joyous together the next day, but I also wanted to talk to Felicity Donovan and check in with the Realtor who had the listing for the Sontag family land. That meant unaccustomed time away from my shop, and I counted myself lucky Maggie was not only a great employee, but usually eager to work extra hours.

COLBY's Westfalia van was parked in front of Scents & Nonsense when I got back. I found him and Larken sitting in the wicker chairs out in the garden, Dash at their feet. My brother rose to help me with the food, but Larken was twisted around in her seat and barely spared me a glance. When I saw what had snagged her attention, I understood why.

"They gather around Nabby like that all the time," I said, nodding toward the dozens of iridescent azure wings clustered in the buddleia bush above the cat. "A kaleidoscope of blue butterflies. And when he takes a walk, sometimes they follow behind him. It's quite the sight."

"Wow," Larken breathed. "That's amazing. Magical."

"Enchanting?" I teased.

Colby had paused in unpacking the food to look at the butterflies. Now he rolled his eyes. "No wonder you named him Nabokov."

"Actually, I didn't name him. The Realtor said he came with the building. I don't know how long he's been here, but he's a shop cat, through and through. Never comes to the house, never ventures beyond the garden gate." I pulled up another chair. "I just figured someone named him that because he's a Russian blue shorthair."

My brother laughed. "Well, yeah. You're probably right. But you know about Nabokov's blues, right?"

Larken turned to sit forward again, but kept looking over her shoulder at the cluster of slowly waving wings. The blooms on the butterfly bush were a dark purple, and the combination really was stunning.

"Nabokov's blues?" she asked at the same time I shook my head in answer to my brother's question.

"Vladimir Nabokov was famous for his study of blue butterflies."

"Hang on. The guy who wrote *Lolita*?" I asked. "That Nabokov?"

"Yep. Same one. Everyone knows him as a writer, but the man was an accomplished amateur lepidopterist."

"Colby, you are a font of odd information," I said. "I'll go grab some plates." But I looked at the snoozing cat with new eyes as I passed by.

When I returned with plates and flatware, we dished up and dug in. It turned out that Larken wasn't a vegetarian, but tried to eat only organic meat that was locally sourced. I didn't know where Harris got his chicken anymore, so she stuck with the vegetable lasagna. She didn't refuse a big helping of the green beans laced with bacon, though.

As we dug in, we caught up on the minutiae of our lives. Colby and I kept in fairly regular touch on the phone and through e-mail, so he was largely up to speed. I filled in some information about Ritter for Larken, and told them both more about his project. I answered Larken's questions about Sense & Nonsense, then asked her about herself. She had two older sisters and her parents lived in upstate New York. She'd grown up there before going to college in Colorado and getting a degree in sustainable land management. Since then she'd worked on several farms to gain hands-on experience. One of those farms was where she'd met my brother.

Finally, we fell silent and there was nothing but birdsong and the sound of Dash's heavy breathing as he willed us to drop a bite where he sat by my left foot. I relented and gave him a chunk of chicken, which he made disappear faster than David Copperfield could.

Colby sat back, making the wicker chair creak. "This food is awesome. All of it. Thanks."

Larken murmured her agreement, snagging another green bean and biting it delicately with her front teeth.

"It's the least I could do, especially after that dinner debacle last night," I said, making a face.

She sighed and put down her fork.

"How was your hike?" I asked, trying to change the subject. Their noses were both a little sunburned, and Colby was suffering from a serious case of hat hair.

"It was great," Larken said. I could hear the forced cheer in her voice.

"It *was* great," Colby said. "We only got as far as Falcon Rock, but you were right—it was good to get some exercise after what happened this morning." He cut off a big bite of cheesecake and brought it to his lips. After he swallowed, he put down his fork, too. "Ellie, did you have a chance to find out anything more?"

I got up and gave Nabby a small bite of chicken so he wouldn't feel left out, then returned to my seat. "Well, I did get a chance to talk to Cynthia, and I called our folks to see if they knew anything about the family." I told them about Blake's parents' unfortunate demise in the Arizona arroyo. "Dad told me the Sontags had some land. It's been in the family since way back when Poppyville was just a supply station for the miners. From what he told me, Joyous must be the sole heir now, and get this—the place is already for sale."

Larken frowned. "Joyous?"

"Blake's sister," I explained. "Astrid and I are going to pay her a visit tomorrow. And Cynthia told me about

another possible suspect that I want to have a chat with."
I examined her face, trying to get a feel for her mood.
"We'll do our best to figure this out. The best thing for
you might be to go back to the hotel and make an early
night of it."

"No!"

I blinked.

"Sorry. But no. Not at the hotel. We checked out this
afternoon. I'm not spending another night in that place."

I looked at Colby.

He smiled a tight smile. "I'm with Lark on that. We're
back in the van." He stretched. "We do have to figure out
a place to park it, though. I don't suppose your Detective
Lang would like us camping out in front of your store."

"He's not my detective, believe me. But I might know
a place. Let me give Gessie King a call."

"At the stables?" He brightened.

"She lets people camp out in back of the barn sometimes." I watched Larken.

She smiled. "Sounds great to me."

I gave a quick nod and rose to make the call from inside
the store.

Gessie answered on the first ring, and after I'd explained
the situation, she quickly agreed to my suggestion. "Of
course your brother's welcome for as long as he likes.
They can park next to the wagons we use for the hayrides.
There's power there and easy access to water so we can
prep the chuck wagon." She made a noise in the back of
her throat, and I imagined her sitting with her muddy
paddock boots propped on the saddle stand next to her
desk while she ran her fingers through her short gray hair.

"I must say, I'd heard something about a death at the hotel, but I was out on a trail ride with a bunch of dudes all afternoon, and hadn't caught up with the latest. You let me know if there's anything else I can do, Ellie."

"Thanks, Gessie. You're a gem."

I had walked back outside as the conversation wound down. We said good-bye, and I sank into the chair.

"You're all set," I said. "She said you can stay by where she stores the wagons."

"Are there many horses?" Larken asked.

"Lots of them," I said. "You don't mind?"

"Why would I mind?"

"Some people don't like the smell of a stable."

But Colby's girlfriend shook her head. "I *love* the smell of horses. One day I hope to have one of my own."

Along with her little farm. She was a dreamer, but it was hard to fault her for it. After all, I'd followed my own dream of opening Scents & Nonsense.

Eventually.

However, Colby had developed a renewed interest in the butterflies hanging from the butterfly bush like so much enticing fruit. My brother had his own dreams, and they were very different from Larken's. He was all about freedom rather than roots. That didn't bode well for their relationship. The thought made me sad, because they obviously cared for each other.

Ritter's handsome face flashed on my mental movie screen, and suddenly the butterflies took flight, all at once. I was almost surprised by how silent they were even en masse. I joined Larken's head-back, mouth-open response as they spiraled up in a tornado of blue.

The butterflies disappeared toward the meadow, and Larken and Colby started cleaning up the after-dinner detritus. The phone trilled loudly in my hand, startling me so that I nearly dropped it. The setting sun had started to paint the edge of the sky flamingo pink, so I knew it had to be after seven thirty. Perhaps it was a customer who thought the shop would still be open.

"Scents and Nonsense," I answered.

"Oh. I'm sorry. I thought you'd be closed." The male voice was vaguely familiar.

"We are closed," I said, confused. "But why would you call if—"

"If I thought you wouldn't be there? Good question. It's just that this is the only number I could find for you— this *is* Elliana Allbright, isn't it?"

"Yes," I answered slowly. "Who's this?"

He laughed. "Let me start over. Elliana, my name is Tanner Spence. Most people call me Spence, though."

Sontag's photographer.

"Most people call me Ellie," I said.

Larken swung around and looked at me. Had there been something in my voice?

"Ellie it is, then." I heard him take a deep breath. "Okay, this is going to sound, well, unfeeling at best and horrible at worst."

"Go on."

"I was wondering if you'd still be willing to let *Conscience Magazine* interview you and take pictures of your tiny house. And by '*Conscience Magazine*,' I mean me."

"Er . . ."

"See? Unfeeling *and* horrible. I know, I know. But

here's my thinking—what happened to Bla— Mr. Sontag was tragic. Really terrible, you know? But I don't want the magazine to suffer as well. Or our readers. We go to print for next month's edition in just a few days, and that whole issue is focused on small-footprint homes. I'd really like to include yours—"

I cut him off. "Okay."

"Oh! Oh, good. Yes. You understand." I could hear actual relief in his voice. "I don't suppose you would be available tomorrow?"

"What time?" I asked.

"Late afternoon would be ideal. The light is better then."

Thank goodness Maggie was coming in early the next day. "Okay. Say . . . four o'clock?"

"Perfect," Tanner Spence said. "I'll see you then! Oh, and Ellie? Thank you. Have a great evening." And he was gone.

Until four o'clock tomorrow, at least.

"Who was that?" Colby asked.

"Apparently, my house is going to be featured in *Conscience* after all. That was Blake's photographer."

"The guy with the dreamy eyes?" Larken said with a grin.

Colby looked sharply at her.

She squeezed his arm. "Don't worry. I only have eyes for you, sweetie." She winked at me.

I muttered, "You two better get the van set up before it gets too dark."

They took the hint and left a few minutes later. I finished cleaning up and took our dishes and the leftovers to my kitchen. It was unlikely Spence would want to take pictures of the inside of my refrigerator, but just in case, I transferred the food into the old-fashioned Pyrex containers I preferred over plastic. Then I did the dishes, put them away, spiffed up the kitchen, took out the garbage, and did a quick pass on the rest of my home. Dash watched me quizzically from his bed by the back door. A few quick swipes with a lint roller took care of the dog hair on the love seat before I swept the bits of leaves and pine needles off the back porch.

When I was done, I leaned on the broom and gazed out at the meadow in the last of the twilight. The petite white flowers of daisy fleabane that nestled among the native grasses still held enough of the fading light that they looked like tiny sparks. If I let my focus soften, I could almost imagine they were fairies coming out for an evening of play and mischief.

Something moved in the nearby copse of trees to the north. I turned my head, expecting to see the buck mule deer who so often brought his harem out at this time of night.

But it was a doe. Not one I'd ever seen before. I knew because she was completely white from head to hoof. She walked toward me, apparently unafraid, perhaps curious. I glanced down at Dash, but he made no move to chase her. That surprised me, herding dog that he was. The doe stopped when she was only fifteen feet away, bent her head, and ate one of the snow-pale flowers.

That's why she's an albino. From eating the fairy daisies. I blinked away the fanciful thought and watched her with wide eyes, hardly daring to breathe.

Another dip of her head, another bloom plucked for dinner. She stood chewing, staring at me, for a full minute, then turned and walked slowly back to her woods.

I let out a long exhalation when the last of her alabaster tail had disappeared. "That was weird."

Dash looked up at me with big doggy grin on his face. I bent and scratched the blond ruff of fur across his shoulders, then stood again, suddenly realizing just how bone tired I was.

Inside, I grabbed Gamma's garden journal and took it to bed with me.

The picture of deadly nightshade was still there. I hadn't been sure it would be, since sometimes things seemed to disappear from the tattered, thick pages. I examined the precise drawing again and felt the warning inherent in it again.

Gamma had listed other names belladonna was known by over the years, her tight cursive writing giving the litany a kind of poetic quality.

Devil's cherries, nightshade, devil's herb, dwayberry, dwale, and ending with my favorite: *naughty man's cherries*.

And scribbled in a corner: *Known as the primary ingredient in witches' flying ointment.*

No doubt that was due to the hallucinogenic effects.

The symptoms of belladonna poisoning were listed on the opposite page.

Rash. Confusion to the point of delirium, along with dizziness and blurred vision.

Difficulty breathing, nausea, and panic.

In our one and only encounter, Blake Sontag hadn't been

at all pleasant to me or my companions, but I wouldn't wish a death like that on anyone. A wave of compassion washed through my body.

He didn't deserve to die like that. He didn't deserve to die at all. But he does deserve justice now.

CHAPTER 9

When I opened Scents & Nonsense at ten the next morning, Astrid had already come and gone. On the counter was a container of creamy white cookies flecked with orange peel and the delicate pink petals of sweet William flowers. She'd dipped half of each in chocolate ganache, and they smelled subtly of cloves. I downed one before even unlocking the door and flipping the sign to OPEN, and barely managed not to moan out loud at how good they were.

My thoughts flickered to Tanner Spence, and I hoped there would be some left for him to try when he showed up with his camera equipment at four o'clock. Why? Because I wanted to impress him with cookies I hadn't even made?

Yes. Just like I wanted to impress Blake Sontag until I actually met him. Spence seems nice, though. And I'm lucky he still wants to feature my tiny house in the magazine.

The vague image of his wild blond hair and the mixture of smart and funny I'd seen so briefly behind his eyes flared for a moment, but faded away as I checked the inventory of my essential oil supply and helped a few customers who wandered in off the street. Then I placed a bulk order for jojoba oil, and printed out a list of orders from the Scents & Nonsense online store over the last two days.

Maggie showed at eleven o'clock as promised. I set her to work labeling a gross of peppermint, tangerine, and cinnamon lip balms, asked her to box up the online orders for the UPS man, and headed out the door with Dash trotting at my heel.

Clutching two chocolate-dipped cookies in one hand and steering with the other, I guided the Wrangler to the curb in front of Astrid's little house. Someone in the neighborhood had recently mowed their grass, and the scent mingled with the smell of bread fresh from the oven. The combination created a sense of nostalgia that settled around me like a comfortable blanket.

I could already tell today was going to be much better than yesterday had been.

My friend opened her door and waved to me, then turned back to lock up. A few seconds later she climbed into the passenger seat. She wore a nubbly hemp sundress in soft brown, her red hair was plaited into a neat French braid, and a dark stone circle on a length of leather nestled below her throat.

I suddenly felt dowdy in my white capri pants, Breton-stripe shirt, and sneakers.

"Hey, Ellie." She twisted in the seat to ruffle Dash's pointed ears. "And how's my favorite corgi this morning?"

He nosed her hand to encourage more attention. Someone had found Dash, tired and hungry, at the rest stop out on the highway. Astrid had, of course, agreed to foster him until she could find a good home. That had taken until about ten minutes after she introduced us, because I'd instantly fallen in love with his sweet disposition, laughing expression, and intelligent brown eyes.

"I made him promise to be good if I let him come with us," I said.

Astrid smiled at him. "He will be. He's a clever boy. Someone trained him well." She turned back around as I jammed the rest of my second cookie into my mouth and pulled away from the curb.

I'd taken the soft top off the Wrangler a few weeks earlier, and the warm sun felt as good as the air rippling through my hair.

"You outdid yourself with the treats this morning," I said after I swallowed. "You should think about opening a cookie bakery. Give Kneadful Things a run for their money."

She shook her head. "I'm not like you. I enjoy making cookies too much to try to do it for a living. For you, helping people with scent is a calling, but if I had to make cookies every day, I'd get pretty cranky."

"You do make cookies every day," I pointed out.

"Yeah, but I don't *have* to."

I turned right onto Corona and kept my mouth shut. I'd come to depend on Astrid's daily baking habit, and didn't want to jinx it.

"Where does Joyous Sontag live?" Astrid asked.

"She has one of those big houses in Agate Park." It was an area known for older, stately homes, and while not the most exclusive neighborhood in Poppyville, it was up there.

"But that's on the other side of town," she said with a frown.

"Mm-hm. I want to take a little side trip before we go there."

She quirked an eyebrow. "Do tell."

"I found out from my dad that the Sontags' old family place is out past the trailhead for Kestrel Peak. I want to take a look at it."

"Because . . ."

My eyes cut sideways, then back to the road. "Because now that Blake is dead, Joyous is the sole heir to the property, and I saw a notice in the window of Gold Rush Realty that it's for sale."

Astrid whistled. "That was fast."

"No kidding. Of course, it could have been that Blake and his sister were always planning to sell it. The real estate office was closed, so I couldn't ask. Still, I'd like to check the place out."

My friend looked thoughtful. "I'd wondered how we could just show up on her doorstep the day after her brother was murdered and start asking questions. At least now we can pretend to be interested in buying her land."

"Yeah," I said slowly. I didn't like the idea of lying like

that, but maybe she was right. "I do want to extend my sympathies, though it's possible Joyous couldn't give a hoot that I was one of the last people to see her brother alive."

"Why do you say that?" she asked.

"Don't you wonder why Blake was staying at the Hotel California when he had a perfectly nice place to stay with his sister?"

"They didn't get along," Astrid guessed as we passed the parking lot at the trailhead.

"More than that," I said. "Larken heard him arguing with someone on the phone in his room the night he died. She said she heard the word 'joy.' I think he and his sister were on the outs."

The asphalt immediately became rougher, with wide cracks in the surface.

I steered around a pothole. "Though that might not mean anything. I don't know how well you know Joyous, but she doesn't really get along with anyone. She was very quiet in school, as I recall. A mousy girl who scowled a lot."

"I heard she has agoraphobia," she said.

"She's certainly a recluse," I said. "I hope it isn't as bad as that, though."

"I've never met her in person, but I've spoken with her on the phone a couple of times."

"Really?" I looked over at her.

She nodded. "Joyous does medical transcription. Veterinary, too, because Dr. Ericcson uses her." The open top had mussed her braid, and now she blew a stray lock of hair away from her eyes. "Thank God. Otherwise I'd have to input his notes on top of everything else I do in the office."

The road took us down a hill. As we came around a wide curve, I saw the property in question. It was hard to miss since it was completely surrounded by a twelve-foot metal fence topped with barbed wire.

No, make that *razor* wire.

What on earth?

I stopped the Jeep in the slight turnoff right in front of the gate and saw the fence was festooned with NO TRES-PASSING signs.

We got out. I told Dash to stay, and he watched as Astrid and I approached the gate and inspected the solid padlock that held it closed.

"I guess we won't be exploring very much," I said. "Wow, that's a lot of fence. It looks like it goes all the way around."

"How much land is in the parcel?"

"Thirty acres."

She frowned. "I could climb over."

"Twelve feet? In a dress, over razor wire? Are you out of your mind?" I squinted past the fence.

"It's beautiful," she said, leaning her head toward mine and peering through a diamond-shaped gap.

I remembered the real estate flyer urging the possibility of development and felt a twist beneath my solar plexus. A stand of houses here would be monstrous—and visible from the trail up to the peak.

"See the remains of the old log wall backed up to that hill?" I pointed. "That was probably the original house.

And that stand of willows over there? I bet there's a pond, or at least water close to the surface."

And water rights were included with the land. That was significant in this part of California, though Poppyville was lucky to have its own underground spring. Despite depleted aquifers elsewhere in the state, our spring still supplied the town with plenty of water.

I found myself irresistibly drawn to the area inside the fence, a visceral, physical reaction, and for a split second actually considered climbing the fence myself. My eyes scanned the expanse of grass punctuated with native goldenrod and monkey flower. There was a cluster of elderberry near the stand of willows, along with a messy tumble of wild potentilla studded with shiny yellow blooms.

Then I saw the first one, about four feet tall with dark oval leaves hanging from the branches. Then another, and another, the bell-shaped flowers and dark berries mocking me.

Deadly nightshade growing wild on the Sontag property. I'd never seen it anyplace else around Poppyville, but there it was, less than a mile from my house as the crow flew. Then I noticed one of the plants leaned crazily to one side, and even from that distance I could see the dirt beneath it had been disturbed.

To get at the roots.

I pointed at the plants and told Astrid what they were.

She looked surprised, then tipped her head to the side. "That's belladonna? I know people worry about livestock eating it, especially horses. But it's really quite pretty."

"Yeah. Enticing, even," I grumbled. "At least no one can get to it behind that fence."

Except I had a feeling that someone had done exactly that.

I'D looked up Joyous Sontag's address before leaving Scents & Nonsense. It turned out that she lived in the least ostentatious house in Agate Park, a three-story that was narrower than its neighbors on either side and set farther back from the street. The deep front yard had been xeriscaped with rocks, sand, flagstone, and planted with low-maintenance yuccas and multiple species of cacti. The house was painted two shades of brown, and as we walked closer I noticed the lighter color was beginning to peel on the trim. The curtains in all the windows were white, and all were drawn, giving the effect that the dwelling was fast asleep.

We rang the bell and waited.

And waited.

Astrid and I looked at each other, and she raised her eyebrows. "I think this line of investigation may have already been nipped in the bud."

Footsteps sounded from inside. I gave her a triumphant grin and turned back to the door. The footsteps stopped, and there was a long pause. I could feel eyes upon us. Then the door cracked open a few inches to reveal Joyous Sontag's thin, sallow face frowning out at us.

"What do you want?"

"Hi, Joyous. I'm Ellie Albright. I don't know if you remember me—"

"I know who you are," she interrupted. "I asked what you wanted."

I took a deep breath. "I knew your brother, Blake." That, at least, was true. Sort of. "I'm very sorry for your loss." I could feel Astrid looking at me sideways. It didn't help that I felt like I was repeating something from a bad television show. But I really *was* sorry for her loss, even if her brother had been a jerk.

Joyous scowled at us for a little longer, then gave a curt nod. "Thank you." She began to shut the door.

My foot shot out and wedged between the door and the frame.

Her eyes widened. "What do you think you're doing?"

"I'm sorry. I just . . . I would really like to talk to you. May we come in?"

Joyous blinked. "Why? We're not friends." There was something in her voice, something sad.

Intense loneliness suddenly stabbed through my sternum, a feeling so close to actual physical pain that I gasped.

Astrid's hand shot out and grabbed my elbow. "Ellie? Are you okay?"

I shook my head. "Just having a little spell."

Knowing how empathy sometimes affected me, she frowned, then nodded.

Joyous watched us through narrowed eyes.

Astrid must have heard something in Blake's sister's voice, too, because she took a step closer and said in a kind voice, "I'm Astrid Moneypenny. You don't really know me, but I work for Dr. Ericcson, and we've spoken on the phone. What happened yesterday was terrible. How are you holding up?"

"I'm fine," came Joyous' strangled reply. Her eyes glistened.

"Are you sure?" Astrid asked. She was using the voice she used to soothe injured animals. "Because, honey, I don't think I'd be fine."

The woman's expression hardened again. She shook her head vigorously, her mouth tight, and said, "I don't want to talk about Blake. Go away." She pushed against my foot with the door, squeezing my toes.

Ow. I yanked my foot away. "Wait! Please!"

The door closed.

"Can you tell us about the land you have for sale?" I called.

There was no sound of the latch clicking. Joyous' voice drifted through from the other side. "My land?" The door cracked open. Her face appeared in the gap again.

"Your property out on River Road," I said.

"Why do you think it's my land?" she asked.

"Please," I said. "Can we come in and talk about it?"

A pause, and then she nodded. "Okay. But you have to leave when I tell you to." She looked daggers at us. "Understand?"

Wide-eyed, we nodded in unison.

She turned and walked inside.

Astrid and I exchanged a glance, pushed the door open, and followed.

CHAPTER 10

THE first thing I noticed was the intense smell of lemons. It seemed to come from everywhere. I sucked it into my lungs like a drowning woman seeking oxygen, and the sad sense of solitude abated.

Somehow, Joyous Sontag had found her own scented comfort.

Then I noticed the rest of my surroundings. A part of me had been prepared for a hoarder's paradise, or something out of a dystopian novel. But the room we entered was bright, with white walls and lots of light coming in through the sheer curtains that covered the windows. Sparsely furnished with tan sofa and chairs and cream-colored rugs on a maple floor, the uncluttered space gave the impression of allowing you to breathe deeply.

So I did. More lemons. The hitch in my chest all but disappeared.

Joyous went over to a drop-lid desk and switched off the screen of the computer sitting there. A set of earphones sat to one side. Then she moved to sit tentatively on the edge of a sofa cushion. Her expression was nervous, and her eyes flicked from one side of the room to the other. Her thin shoulders were hunched. She seemed angry and scared and sad, all rolled up into one. My instinct was to help her, but I didn't know how.

Physically, she bore a definite family resemblance to her brother. Her black hair was longer, wavier, and drawn back into a ponytail at the nape of her neck, but an identical widow's peak graced her narrow forehead. Her eyes were the same light cyan, and her bow mouth was a smaller version of his. She wore yoga pants and a white T-shirt with ballet flats.

Astrid and I lowered ourselves into chairs across from her.

"How do you know about my land?" Joyous asked in a querulous tone.

"It's for sale, isn't it?" I asked. "I saw the flyer in the window of Gold Rush Realty."

She glared. "But how do you know it's *mine*?"

"My dad told me," I said. "He and your father were pretty good friends. Dad also told me about your parents' will."

"Oh." She looked down at her clasped hands and bit her lip.

"Has it been on the market long?" Astrid asked. Trying to find out whether Blake had been on board with the sale? *Good girl.*

Joyous looked up. "Are you interested in buying it?"

Astrid smiled. "We'd like to know more about it."

"It's thirty acres, just like the flyer said. It's nice. You could build a house there." She seemed to shiver. "Or do whatever you want."

"I understand your great-great-great-grandfather claimed that land back before the miners started flooding to the area," I said.

Her jaw set and she nodded. "Something like that." She bit off the words. "There was a lot more. My grandfather donated most of it to help form Clary State Park. Those thirty acres are all that's left."

"And it's never been developed? I'm sorry you have to sell it."

"I just want it gone. I don't care what happens to it." Her voice rose on the words. "Someone else can deal with . . . You need to go talk to the real estate agent if you want to know more."

"I was hoping—" I began.

"They can take you out there and show you the place, tell you everything about it. That's their job."

I tried again. "I was really hoping you'd be willing to show us the property yourself. You know, since it's been in your family for genera—"

"No!" She jumped to her feet. "I'll never go there again. *Never.* You can't make me." She sounded like a frightened child. "You need to leave now."

Astrid and I exchanged a bewildered glance.

"Now!"

"Okay," I said quietly. The woman seemed jumpy as

a cat. Was it just that she wasn't used to being around other people? Or had something terrible happened on that property?

Or did she take something terrible from there—like the deadly nightshade plant used to kill her brother?

I wanted to ask if she'd argued with her brother on the telephone the evening before his death, but this obviously wasn't the right time.

"Do the police have any news about Blake?" Astrid asked as Joyous marched us to the exit.

She turned and glared at my friend. "I told you I don't want to talk about my brother."

Astrid gave her a gentle smile and didn't say anything.

Joyous flared her nostrils. "He was murdered, the detective told me this morning. Poison. They have a suspect and expect to make an arrest soon." Her lips pinched together. "I hope whoever killed him goes to jail for the rest of their lives."

She yanked the door open with a pointed look at me. "Gold Rush Realty."

I nodded and we went outside. She slammed the door behind us.

Astrid and I walked to the Wrangler in silence. Once we'd fastened our seat belts and were on our way, she turned to me. "I expected her to be strange, but I don't understand her at all. She seemed upset about her brother, angry that he'd been murdered, but didn't want to talk about him. At the same time, the mention of her family land actually got us inside her house, yet she practically turned into a basket case when she started talking about it."

I shook my head. "I don't get it, either. I feel bad for her, that's for sure. Unless it turns out that she killed Blake and plans to let Larken pay the price."

She grimaced. "Yeah, that bit about the police having an official suspect so soon was a bit of a bombshell."

Flipping on my turn signal, I sighed. "I bet Max rushed the autopsy. I need to check with Lupe and see if I was right about the belladonna." I pulled up in front of her house.

"Well, let me know what happens," Astrid said, giving Dash one last pat and getting out of the vehicle. "I'll be around, but right now I'm due to give an asthmatic cat her inhaler."

"How's Precious the pig doing?"

She grinned. "Back with Mrs. Paulson. Don't be surprised to see her walking down Corona Street."

"It's getting so I'm not surprised at much that goes on in this town. Thanks for going with me to see Joyous," I said.

"No problem! Call me later."

I promised I would and pulled away from the curb.

I T turned out that I didn't have to track down Detective Garcia after all. I'd just parked in front of the Hotel California when my cell started buzzing, and her name lit up on the screen.

"Hey, there," I said. "I was just about to call you."

"Really." Her tone was flat.

My stomach sank. "Yeah, really. Is something wrong?"

"You tell me."

I felt my forehead crease. "What are you talking about?"

"Were you by any chance planning to tell me that your brother and Larken Meadows skipped town?"

"What? No, they didn't."

"They checked out of the hotel shortly after Detective Lang interviewed Meadows."

I backed out of the space I'd just pulled into and turned toward the north end of town. "I know that, Lupe. I had dinner with them last night. Larken didn't want to stay in the hotel after what happened there, so they're staying in Colby's Westfalia."

"Oh," she said. "I guess I can understand that. She isn't answering her phone, though. Max about popped a vein when he discovered they were gone."

Grimacing, I said, "That's the last thing Larken needs." I reached the end of Corona, turned into the stable parking lot, and stopped next to Thea Nelson's mint green step-side pickup.

"Where are they camped?" Lupe sounded a lot friendlier than when she'd first called.

"At Gessie King's," I practically crowed as I spied the Westfalia snugged up by the chuck wagon. I hadn't realized how worried I'd been than Colby might have really taken off.

Though, honestly, a part of me would have cheered him on and lied through my teeth to the police.

"Okay, thanks. I'll let Max know."

"Lupe?" I turned off the engine. Dash had jumped forward to the passenger seat, ready to get out and romp with Gessie's Bernese mountain dog. "I heard you're about to make an arrest. Is that . . ." I took a deep breath. "Is that why you wanted to know where Larken is?"

"I needed to know anyway, especially if she skipped town. But yes, you were right about the belladonna poisoning, and Max is champing at the bit to close this case." She paused. "Ellie, there are a few loose ends that don't make sense, but it's not looking good for her."

A few loose ends. I grabbed on to the phrase like a lifeline.

"Have you looked into Joyous Sontag as a suspect? Larken said she told Max that Blake was arguing with someone on the phone when she went to his room. It sounds like it might have been his sister, don't you think?"

"Maybe. Maybe not. Ms. Meadows said she didn't actually hear any of the conversation, but we're checking phone records."

"Well Blake said 'joy' a few times. That's in Max's notes, I bet. And listen, Joyous owns a piece of land—well, she and Blake both apparently owned it until his death, from what my dad told me. Blake didn't have any kids, did he?"

Lupe sighed. "No kids. No wife. Girlfriend moved to DC and dumped him a while back. Doesn't even sound like the guy had a dog."

I paused. "That's sad."

"Can I answer any other questions, Ellie? Perhaps you'd like to know his bank balance or where he got his hair cut. Whether he was a boxers or briefs kind of guy."

"Sarcasm is the lowest form of humor, my friend. Just sayin'. Back to the Sontag land—I went to check it out this morning. There are several deadly nightshade plants growing wild."

"You were there?"

"Yep. Astrid and I drove out."

She sighed. "And you went to see Joyous." It wasn't a question, and she didn't sound happy.

"Er, yeah."

"Ellie, you have to leave this to me."

"You just said it wasn't looking good for Larken."

Silence.

"She didn't kill anyone, Lupe. That field with all the deadly nightshade? It's fenced, with a locked gate. Larken couldn't have gotten in there, but Joyous could have. Or anyone the Realtor took out there, I suppose." My palms were sweating. "I know you have to do your job, but I'm not going to let Max railroad her like he tried to do to me. I'm not going to let you do it, either."

"Careful, Ellie."

But my back was up. "I mean it. I know we're friends, and I know you're a good cop. But Larken isn't going down for this."

"'Going down'?" She snorted. "You sound pretty tough there, girlfriend."

I found myself blushing, even though she couldn't see me. "Sorry. I'm just worried."

Larken came around the corner of the hay barn with Gessie. Each was leading a horse. Thea Nelson followed, pulling her work gloves off as she walked.

"Are you interested in another possible suspect?" I asked.

A pause, then, "Let's have it."

"Felicity Donovan had a problem with Blake from years

ago. He stole a big story from her when they both worked at the *San Francisco Chronicle* that made his career and tanked hers. Now she's managing the Hotel California. She would have had plenty of access to him."

"I'll look into it," Lupe said. "Listen, I have to go. I'll be in touch, though. Okay?"

"All right. Thanks," I said, and rang off.

Inhaling the warm afternoon air redolent of horse musk and alfalfa, I opened the door. Dash jumped to the ground and took off to find the Bernese, Toby. I got out and went to meet Gessie. Her iron gray curls were jammed under a stained straw cowboy hat, and her riding breeches were tucked into soft leather calf boots. Larken wore jeans and a T-shirt that read AMERICA NEEDS FARMERS.

Gessie grinned at me. "Ellie! This girl is a godsend. My stall mucker didn't show today, and this one jumped right in and helped me out. The horses love her, too."

Larken ducked her head. "Seemed like the least I could do for letting us stay here."

"Nonsense," Gessie said. "I'm paying you. Don't argue."

Looking pleased, my brother's girlfriend reached up and scrubbed at the white star between the eyes of her chestnut charge with her fingertips. The mare blinked with pleasure.

"Hey, Ellie," Thea said, joining us. She was rangy and slow moving, an old friend from high school and Ritter's little sister. She also happened to be a gifted horticulturist who had helped me design and plant the Enchanted Garden.

Talk about a godsend.

Today she wore a pair of overalls over a tank top that advertised her nursery, Terra Green, and a red ball cap.

"You hear from my brother lately?" she asked.

"Yesterday. He sends his love," I said.

"Good. Now if he'd just send me the fifty bucks he owes me." Thea was smiling, though.

Whenever someone mentioned Ritter, I was swamped with missing him. Today was one of the times his absence felt more like a muddy puddle than a wave of longing. Other times it felt like a sharp ache behind my sternum.

"What are you doing out here?" I asked Thea. "You don't ride, do you?"

"Nah. Gessie here is hosting a hunter jumper show next week and wanted one of the jumps planted with real flowers." She whistled and winked at our friend. "Fancy."

The horse trainer shrugged. "The equestrian club is celebrating fifty years. I want it to be nice."

"Where's Colby?" I didn't mention my conversation with Detective Garcia to Larken. I didn't want to worry her, not yet, and I still hadn't talked to Felicity Donovan.

"He went down to the courthouse," Larken said.

I raised my eyebrows.

"Said something about seeing if there was anything special about the Sontag land."

Thea dragged me out to the hunter course to show me the artful combination of junipers and annuals she'd come up with to approximate a natural barrier for the horses to jump over. It did look great, and I murmured my admiration before explaining I had to get going. I could practically feel the time swirling away, and my task list wasn't getting any shorter.

After saying good-bye to everyone, I called to Dash. Five minutes later we were heading back downtown.

I dropped by Scents & Nonsense to check in with Maggie. The lip balms were labeled, the online orders boxed and lined by the door for pickup later that afternoon, and she'd managed to sell a dozen sandalwood centerpiece candles to a wedding planner.

"Nice job," I said. "Those sandalwood candles were pricier than I liked, and I was about to put them on fire sale to get rid of them."

She nodded happily. "I know. But they'll be great for a wedding reception, so I figured it was a win-win. What else would you like for me to do?"

Glancing toward the coffee area, I said, "Well, it turns out the photographer who was going to be here yesterday morning is coming this afternoon at four instead. I don't know if he'll even come into the shop, but do you think you could tidy up around the back door there?"

"Why didn't you tell me?" she exclaimed. "Of course. I'll have that whole patio spick-and-span in no time." She hurried over and grabbed a broom out of the cupboard.

Laughing, I thanked her. "And I'm going to leave Dash here." He'd already trundled out to join Nabby under the retaining wall in the Enchanted Garden.

I looked at my watch. It was already two o'clock. If I hurried, I'd have enough time for two more stops.

THE lobby of the Hotel California was considerably less crowded that it had been the last two times I'd been in it. A white-haired couple played cards at the far end, and a bored-looking man stared down at his phone, obviously waiting for someone. The piano bench was empty, the fire was turned off, and the sound of a vacuum echoed from a first-floor hallway. Through a pair of French doors, I spied the corner of the outdoor swimming pool, the surface smooth and quiet. The smell of wood polish mingled with that of dust and a whiff of chlorine. The Empire Room wasn't open yet, but the Horseshoe Bar had a few patrons perched on stools in front of a baseball game on the big-screen television. I turned toward the reception desk.

A slight young man in a blue blazer stood behind the counter, his eyes glued to the computer screen in front of him. As I approached, he looked up and quickly hit a few keys.

"Can I help you?"

"Hi. Is the manager around?"

"Let me check." He turned and walked through a doorway in the back wall. A minute later he returned with the Felicity behind him.

She looked surprised when she saw who had asked for her. "Hi, Ellie. Is something wrong?"

Plenty, I thought, but said, "I just wanted to talk to you about something." I looked pointedly at the open doorway.

Lifting one eyebrow, she gestured me around the reception counter. I followed her into a messy office that also functioned partially as storage, if the stacks of cartons against the wall were any indication. I maneuvered around a pile of brochures and sank onto the guest chair. She closed the door and came to half sit on the front of a cluttered desk.

"What can I do for you?"

I'd thought about how to question her about Blake, and

hadn't come up with anything in the least bit clever. So I tried easing in to start.

"Is everything settling down after the excitement yesterday morning?"

She frowned. "On one hand, there's good turnover here, so many of the guests who've checked in have no idea there was a murder upstairs. On the other, I can only hope people aren't too awful when it comes to rating us online. It's amazing how those reviews affect our business."

I made a sympathetic noise.

Silence descended between us. I smiled.

Felicity smiled back.

Then I realized I'd never win that game with a seasoned journalist. They were trained to let the other person fill the quiet.

"You knew Blake Sontag," I said.

"I did. Lots of people did."

"Did you like him?"

She cocked her head to the side. "I have a feeling you already know the answer to that."

I donned a speculative expression. "I did hear a few things."

Her lips turned up in a smile that didn't reach her eyes. "And from whom did you hear these 'things'?"

"Er, a mutual friend . . . ?"

"I highly doubt that." Her eyes narrowed. "I really would like to know who's been spreading my business around town. It was Cynthia, wasn't it? Not many other people know, and I thought she'd keep it to herself."

I sidestepped. "You mean the business about how Blake

stole your federal superfund story when you two worked in San Francisco?" I steeled myself for her reaction.

Slowly, she folded her arms over her chest. "Yes. That's what I mean."

"You must have really hated him for that."

"I certainly did." A faintly amused look had come into her eyes.

Confused, I said, "Maybe even enough to kill him."

The amusement turned to laughter in her gaze. "Oh, yes. I may have hated him enough to kill him. I never really thought about it in those terms, but it's certainly possible that I hated that son of a bitch that much."

I blinked.

She shook her head and went behind her desk. Sat down. "But as it happens, I didn't do it."

"Oh." I groped for something to say.

"As I told Detective Garcia when she came by about twenty minutes ago, I was at home with my family when Blake Sontag checked in, and all that night until the police called me the next morning."

Wow. Lupe followed up immediately after I told her about Felicity. I owed the detective an apology.

Felicity sat back with an air of satisfaction. "At home with my two children, my husband, his parents, and his sister, who is visiting from out of town. I didn't even know Blake was in Poppyville until I found out he was dead."

I felt my shoulders slump.

She saw it, too, because something in her eyes flared. "Why do you care, anyway?"

I stood, feeling defeated. "It's not that I wanted you to be a murderer."

"That's a relief." The words dripped sarcasm.

"It's just that the police suspect my brother's girlfriend, and I know she didn't do it."

Felicity stood and snagged my gaze. "Okay. I get that. But I didn't kill him, either." She gestured toward the door, and, as I turned to let myself out, she added, "I'm not sorry he's dead, though."

CHAPTER 11

No one seemed to be sorry Blake Sontag was dead, except, perhaps, his sister. It had been hard to tell with Joyous. It made me wonder what his life away from Poppyville had been like. He'd been based out of Sacramento, but from what Lupe had told me, his personal life had been pretty dreary. Not even a dog to his name. Still, he'd had a girlfriend at some point, and he probably would have had another in the future. Maybe even a wife and kids. Maybe that would have cheered him up. It was sad that he'd never have those things now. I could only hope he'd had a best friend to tell his troubles to. Or more likely, to complain to.

And maybe a cat. Or a fish.

I'd had a fish for a short time. Astrid had tasked me with fostering Josie Overland's blue betta after Josie was killed. Unfortunately, he'd gone to fishy heaven and now lived under the Jupiter's beard in the Enchanted Garden.

Shaking myself out of my reverie, I came around the side of the reception desk and thanked the young man there. The flash of sunlight reflecting off water in my peripheral vision drew my attention to the pool at the side of the hotel. From this angle most of it was visible through the French doors.

Most of the pool, and my ex-husband sitting in a chaise lounge next to it. His pale legs stuck out of a pair of cargo shorts, and he wore wraparound sunglasses that made him look like a bug.

What the heck is he doing lounging by the side of the pool at the Hotel California in the middle of the day? I'd hardly known him to take a single day off from the Roux in the years since it had opened. During waking hours, if Harris wasn't at the restaurant, he was either running errands or . . .

On a date.

Unable to help myself, I oh-so-casually strolled over and leaned against the wall next to the doors. Then I carefully peeked around the edge.

Harris' "date" wore a Panama hat, white chinos, and a pale blue shirt open to show the considerable pelt on his chest.

His friend Vaughn with no last name. They were deep in conversation, and didn't see me spying on them.

I pushed away from the wall and went over to the bar. As I hitched myself up on a stool, Mark Kittery came over to take my drink order. He was a trainer at the Boomtown Gym. His shaved head and trademark eyebrow ring were distinctive. I'd last seen him behind the register at the hardware store, and I wondered whether he'd changed his second job or taken on a third.

"Hey, Ellie. How's it going?" His eyes flicked toward the French doors that I'd been spying through. He'd obviously seen my antics.

"Fine and dandy. How's the personal training business?" I asked, trying to deflect his attention.

He grinned. "Great! You need to come into the gym. That time you tried it out you really kicked butt on the weight machines."

I managed not to visibly shudder and pasted a smile on my face. "I'll think about it." I loathed gyms and had only ventured into the Boomtown to meet a possible murder suspect. Give me a garden workout any day.

"Heard from Ritter?" He and Mark were old friends from high school.

"Yesterday. He's enjoying his work."

"Always has," he said with a nod. "Can I get you something to drink?"

I asked for a club soda. "So, I was wondering . . ."

Mark finished filling the glass and added a twist of lemon. He pushed it across to me, leaned his elbows on the counter and grinned. "What were you wondering?"

"There's a guy out by the pool."

"Yes . . . ?" He was teasing me.

"Not Harris," I said. "The guy with the Panama hat. His first name is Vaughn."

Mark nodded that he knew who I meant.

"I keep seeing him around town. Do you know who he is?"

The bartender shook his head. "I don't know his last name. He's staying here, at least I think he is, but he always pays with cash." He rolled his eyes. "He and another guest got into it the other night, and I had to step in and break it up."

I blinked "There was a fight in here?" The Horseshoe Bar didn't exactly attract the same clientele as, say, Willie's Pool Hall.

He shook his head. "Nah. Just an argument. But it was pretty bad, and I was honestly afraid it might come to blows." He grinned. "Luckily, they listened to reason and both left."

Eyeing Mark's rippling muscles, I could see why.

"Well, I hope it doesn't happen again," I said, laying a bill on the bar for my drink.

"Oh, it won't. The man who was arguing with that guy out by the pool is the one who died."

I froze. "Panama hat was arguing with Blake Sontag?"

Mark nodded.

"When was this?" I asked, barely able to breathe.

He thought. "Well, I guess it was the night before the guy died."

"Night before last? What time?"

"I came on shift at nine, so about ten, I guess. Maybe a little earlier."

After we'd had dinner with Blake but before Larken had taken him the tea.

"Did you hear what they were arguing about?"

"Not really. It started out pretty quiet, over there in the corner. Intense, though. The guy with the hat seemed to want something, and the Sontag dude kept shaking his head. Before they stood up and it looked like Sontag was going to pop the guy in the mouth, I heard him say something like, 'I don't care what she told you. I'll never sell.'"

Oh, wow. It must have been about the parcel of land.

"Have the police talked to you about this?"

His eyes widened, and he shook his head.

"Well, don't be surprised if they do," I said, and left him gazing after me.

IT was almost three. I had just enough time to run by Gold Rush Realty before meeting Tanner Spence back at my house. But when I saw the housekeeping cart going into the elevator, I couldn't help myself.

"Excuse me?"

The dark-haired woman pushing it looked over her shoulder as I came across the lobby. She nodded with a smile, and held the elevator for me. I got on with her.

"Hi," I said brightly.

She looked at me in surprise. "Hello."

"Do you happen to clean the rooms on the third floor?" *Specifically room 344.*

She touched her cheek with her fingertips and stared at me. "No, ma'am." I detected a Romanian accent. "Rhonda cleans that floor."

"Is she working today?"

A tentative nod.

I pushed the button for the third floor. "Thank you!"

"You are most welcome, ma'am."

At three I got off, smiling back at her, and turned toward the cleaning cart in the hallway. Light spilled from the open room next to it.

"Hi!" I chirped from the doorway. "Rhonda?"

The housekeeper looked up from where she was making the bed, and I instantly recognized her. Thin as a rail and with big dark eyes, she'd been a waitress at the Roux for several years. Like Maggie, she must be moonlighting. I knew Harris had cut hours at the restaurant, but it concerned me that so many of his—formerly our—employees needed second jobs to make ends meet. Was I going to find Raleigh, the head chef, pumping gas next?

She straightened, suspicion flooding her face. But when she saw it was me, her doubt transformed into a smile. "Ellie!"

"Hi," I said again with effort. I was a natural introvert, and all this questioning people was starting to wear on me. Maybe that's why I showed all the delicacy of a bulldozer when I continued with, "Are you the one who found the body in room 344?"

However, I could tell right away I hadn't offended her by the way she said, "Golly, yeah. That detective told me not to talk about it, though."

Oh, but how she wanted to talk about it. Really, *really* wanted to. Her eyes shone with it. This was the biggest thing that was going to happen to Rhonda all year.

Small-town gossip had its disadvantages for sure, but sometimes it was a downright boon.

I came into the room and started to sit on the bed, then thought better of it. No need to make her shift any longer.

Reaching for the other side of the sheet, I pulled it toward the headboard at the same time I said, "You know, I had dinner with him the night before he died."

Her eyes grew as round as saucers. "You did?"

"Yep." I nodded toward the bed.

She dutifully grabbed her side of the sheet, and together we smoothed and tucked, then reached for the blanket.

"It must have been pretty awful, stumbling into . . ." I lowered my voice. "A dead body on the floor like that." I felt bad egging her on, especially since I'd found a dead body, too, and not long ago.

Rhonda, however, seemed far less traumatized than I had been. "It was. Oh, gosh, yes," she said. "When I told my mother, she about fainted."

"I bet," I said. "What time was it?"

We pulled the coverlet up and began arranging the sham-covered pillows on top.

"It was a little after eight in the morning, I think."

"Had he checked out?" I asked.

"Oh, no. I was cleaning the room next door, and I noticed his door was open a little ways. Not much, but as if it hadn't quite latched. So I kind of watched it while I finished cleaning the other room, you know? Because sometimes people leave their doors like that when they're going back and forth to their cars, taking out luggage, stuff like that. But no one came or went the whole time I was there, so when I was ready to move to the next room on my list, I figured the door had been left open by accident." She slid a pillow into a fresh case and fluffed it. Her face was animated as she continued her tale.

"So I could either leave it, and someone might just walk

in and take their stuff, or I could close it. The guests can always get a key from the front desk if they need to, right?"

"Uh-huh," I said.

It was all the encouragement she needed. "Well, when I reached for the door, I noticed there was this sort of, well, *smell* coming from the room. It just seemed like maybe something was wrong. So I pushed the door open."

"And there was definitely something wrong."

"Oh, gosh. I about screamed. I didn't, though. I looked around to make sure there wasn't some madman standing in the corner, and then called down to the front desk on my radio." She looked thoughtful as she gathered the dirty linens from the chair and carried them out to the bin under the cart. "And you know, I thought of you."

Right behind her in the hallway, I stopped cold in my tracks. "What? Why would you think of me?"

"Because of the little jelly jar with dried stuff in it on the dresser with all the other bottles." She smiled at me, excitement still in her eyes. "You know, because of your garden and your herbs and all."

I stared at her. "There were other bottles?"

Her head bobbed happily. "Pills. Not the prescription kind. The kind like my mom takes. Saint-John's-wort and turmeric and gingko something. For the memory. Vitamins galore. I bet that guy was as much of a hypochondriac as Mama is."

*B*OTTLES *of supplements.* Was that one of the loose ends in the case that Lupe had mentioned?

I dialed her number, but my call went to voice mail.

"Detective Garcia, I wanted to let you know that Blake Sontag got into an argument with some guy staying at the Hotel California the night he was killed. In the Horseshoe Bar, about ten or a little earlier. The bartender, Mark Kittery, had to step in before it came to blows." I paused a few seconds. "The man's first name is Vaughn, but I don't know his last name. I've seen him twice with Harris, though, so you might ask him. Or Max could. You're welcome."

I clicked the phone off, tossed it onto the Wrangler's passenger seat, and stepped on the accelerator. I probably should have thanked her for following up with Felicity so quickly, but it was her job, after all.

I backed off the gas. No need to go over the speed limit. It was quarter after three, and I had a choice: go back home and get gussied up in case Tanner Spence wanted to take my picture, or go by Gold Rush Realty and see what I could find out about the Sontag place.

After a few seconds' hesitation, I turned toward Cooper-hawk Court.

Dr. Ericcson's office was across from the turn onto Cooperhawk, and Astrid was coming out as I drove by. I honked, and she yelled something.

I slowed and waited for her to hurry across the street. "Hey!" she greeted me. "What have you been up to?"

I briefly filled her in on what I'd learned that afternoon. "Listen, I only have a few minutes before meeting the photographer from *Conscience* for the tiny house photo shoot." I'd told her about the new interview that morning after we'd gone to see Joyous. "I wanted to get some more details about the Sontags' land first."

Her eyes lit up. "I'll come with you."

* * *

THE door to Gold Rush Realty was open to the foyer, and we paused on the threshold to assess our options. A young woman hunched over a keyboard behind the circular reception counter by the entrance. Four high-tech desks with matching white computers were arranged around the edge of the room, facing the center. Only two were occupied. A hall led to private offices and a glass-walled conference room at the back of the building. Whisper blue walls and recessed lighting lent a calm, oceanic atmosphere emphasized by the large tropical fish tank. Fake air freshener tried to cover the leftover odor of a Chinese lunch.

The receptionist looked up from her computer with a wide, welcoming smile. "Can I help you?"

I gestured toward the front window. "Can you tell us anything about the parcel of land advertised on that flyer?"

She stood. "Which one?"

We went over to the window, and I pointed to the ad for the Sontag place.

"That would be Polly's listing." She turned toward one of the occupied desks, calling the agent's name.

"Thanks." Astrid and I walked toward the woman who rose to greet us, while the receptionist returned to her post.

Polly's expertly streaked, ash blond hair curled smoothly below the shoulders of her dark blue suit, and her smile was blindingly white. We introduced ourselves and settled into the two matching guest chairs. She looked between us eagerly, and I explained which property I was interested in.

"Oh, my, yes." She bobbed her head several times. "We've had a great deal of interest in that land. Are you thinking of developing it, or are you looking for a country place of your own?"

"It said something on the flyer about platting it," I said. "I'm not sure what that means."

"Subdividing it. You have to go through a process with the Board of County Commissioners to do that, apply for rezoning, and pay for a variety of assessments and permits."

"Sounds like a hassle and a half," Astrid said.

I nodded my agreement.

Polly smiled and shrugged. "But once that's all taken care of, you could build a whole neighborhood out there. With half-acre lots, you could put forty homes in and still have space for a clubhouse and pool. Wait—you do know where the plot is, don't you?"

I nodded, biting my tongue to keep from commenting on the travesty of cramming forty homes onto that pristine land. Astrid was right about it being a lot of trouble to go to, but someone might be willing to deal with all the red tape in order to reap the eventual profits—which would be considerable.

"Well, then you know the view of Kestrel Peak would add value to a development, too." Polly sounded delighted. She probably figured some nice commissions would come her way once the houses were built and on the market.

"You said there are others interested?" Astrid asked.

She nodded pertly. "Yes, indeed."

"But you just put the flyer up yesterday evening," I said. "I saw you."

Her head tipped to the side, and she leaned toward. "Ah, but that was because it went back on the market. You see, it was for sale for a few weeks, and then last week, one of the owners changed their minds and canceled the listing, but now it's for sale again."

Owners. Plural.

"Was it Joyous' brother who didn't want to sell?" I asked. "Blake?"

She looked uncomfortable. "You know who the land . . . Well, you don't need to worry. No one will be changing their minds about selling now."

"No kidding," Astrid muttered.

Polly looked horrified. "Oh, I didn't mean . . . no, only that . . . I'm sorry, but I've been asked not to talk about the owners."

"Owner," I corrected.

The agent blushed, but nodded. "Yes."

I leaned forward. "We talked to Joyous about it this morning, actually. I was hoping she'd take me out there and show me around—or at least give me the key to the gate. That's some fence! There's no evidence of it on the flyer."

Polly sighed. "Yes, well. Photoshop, you know. She told me she didn't want anyone camping there."

Or eating deadly nightshade?

Polly continued. "I told her it would be better to let people explore if they wanted to, but she's adamant."

Astrid sat back in her chair and casually asked, "So, who else is interested?"

Polly smiled enigmatically.

"You won't tell us?" I asked.

"I'm afraid we don't share that kind of information."

Jeez. You're a real estate agent, not a priest. I pushed a little more. "Are we talking about people who live in Poppyville, or outside interests?"

She shook her head. "Sorry."

"Will you at least tell me who's looked at the place? You don't have to tell me whether they want to buy it or not."

Astrid gave me a puzzled look.

Polly's jaw set and she stood. "I'm sorry. I really can't tell you who else has made inquiries."

"Would it be possible to get the key to the lock on the gate, so I can at least walk the property?"

She brightened. "Oh, Ms. Allbright, I'll be more than happy to take you out there myself. When would you like to go?"

Stifling a sigh, I said, "The sooner, the better. You know, since there are so many other potential buyers." I couldn't quite keep the sarcasm out of my voice.

The real estate agent ignored it. "How about this evening, then?" She reached for the cell phone on her desk and brought up the planner.

"It would have to be after six," I said. Surely Tanner Spence would be finished taking photos by then? I looked at my watch and saw it was already quarter to four.

"Ohmagosh. I have to go." Jumping to my feet, I started backing toward the door. "Sorry. I'm late for an appointment."

Astrid's lips parted in surprise. Then realization dawned, and she hurried to follow.

"Okay. Let's say six thirty tonight, then," Polly said, rising quickly and pacing us like a tigress. "Do you want me to pick you up?"

I shook my head. "Can I meet you here and follow you out there? I'd like to have my own vehicle."

"Sure. I'll see you then." She looked skeptical, though, and I realized she suspected I wouldn't show up.

"I'll be here," I assured her over my shoulder and high-tailed it out to the front walk.

"Ellie!" Astrid called, hurrying to catch up.

I stopped halfway to my car and whirled to face my friend.

She stopped and eyed me. "You okay?"

I hesitated, then shook my head. The nervousness I'd carried around waiting for Blake Sontag's arrival in town suddenly returned with a vengeance. Now I babbled, "What was I thinking, agreeing to this interview with Tanner Spence? I've neglected the Enchanted Garden for a whole day, and really, my house isn't all that interesting. I mean, why would anyone want to read about it? Plus, Blake Sontag is *dead*. Oh! And what about my hair?" My hands flew to my head.

My friend snorted and pulled my hands down. "Stop it. You haven't tended your plants for a *whole day*? I'm sure it all looks fantastic, as usual. And your house is charming and adorable." She arranged a curl on my temple. "And so are you. Now take a few deep breaths in the car, make like Wonder Woman, and go rock that interview."

I nodded, feeling a little better. "Right. Yes. Okay."

We hugged, and I gratefully breathed in the scents that clung to her hair: cinnamon, wet dog, antiseptic, and love.

"And thank you," I said, pulling away and heading for the Wrangler.

"Pshaw," she said. "Good luck!"

CHAPTER 12

I WENT through the garden gate and was heading to my house to change my clothes when I heard Maggie's laugh echo through the sliding glass patio door. It was high-pitched, almost a giggle, and not something I associated with the solidly built grandmother. Veering toward the sound, I stepped inside.

Tanner Spence stood across from my assistant, his right hip leaning against the counter. His hair was pulled back into a rough ponytail, and he wore surf shorts, a blue T-shirt, and flip-flops. Quintessential California guy. His forearm was casually draped over Nabby's red plush bed as he petted the rumbling feline. Maggie's expression was a lot like the cat's—intent and practically squinting with pleasure. A collection of bags and hard-sided cases were piled at the photographer's feet.

"And then the truck was swallowed whole, pulled down

into that sinkhole like it was quicksand or something. Maggie, you should have seen it." His eyes danced as he related the story.

"My word," she said with an awed shake of her head. "You've certainly had an interesting life." She looked up. "Oh! Ellie's here! Mr. Spence got here a little early and was telling me tales about his job with the *Washington Post*. War zones and everything. He's even photographed the president!"

"My former job," Spence gently corrected and turned to regard me. "I haven't worked for the *Post* for years." He stopped and searched my eyes. "Is this still a good time? I know I didn't give you much notice."

I nodded and realized I hadn't said a word yet. I took a few more steps toward them and gestured vaguely outside. "Sure. I was going to change my clothes, though. Or does it matter? I know you're here for the house, not me. So maybe it doesn't matter what I wear, or don't wear . . ." I trailed off as I felt the color rise in my cheeks. "I mean—"

"You look terrific," he cut in. "Those stripes on your shirt will photograph well, and I'll certainly include you in some of the photos." He was smiling, all his attention on me now. It was both disconcerting and gratifying. "I like to see how things pan out in a piece like this, you know? Organically. So maybe you could show me around your place first, and I can ask you some questions for the article. Then we'll capture some of that late afternoon light for the exterior shots."

"Sounds good," I said, feeling slightly less nervous. Spence seemed nice as pie. If Blake Sontag had actually interviewed me, I would have been a complete mess.

The photographer bent to pick up his camera case and a black bag. The bag made me think of the body bag they'd wheeled Blake out in, and a wave of exhaustion suddenly washed over me. I had to figure out who the real killer was before the authorities arrested Larken. And this man had worked closely with the victim.

Maybe he'll be able to help. On the other hand, any-one who had to work with the not-so-delightful Blake Sontag might count as a suspect. I sure wouldn't have wanted to deal with him for any length of time.

"Can I help you carry anything?" I asked.

Maggie moved around to the front of the counter. "I can help, too."

Spence laughed. "Thank you, ladies, but I've got it. When you've done this as long as I have, you learn to bring only what you can handle on your own."

Maggie looked disappointed as he followed me outside.

"Thanks for taking care of everything today," I called back to her.

"Elliana," Spence said. "I'm—"

"Remember, call me Ellie," I said a little too quickly. Even back in high school, Ritter had always insisted on calling me Elliana. Now he was the only one who did.

"Right. Ellie. And my friends call me Spence." He trained a dazzling smile on me, and I felt a little dizzy.

I managed a deep breath that I hoped didn't look too obvious. "Spence it is, then."

Dash trotted out from his bed under the shady pergola and stopped at my feet. Spence looked down at the corgi and grinned. "Hey, there. Who's this?"

"That's Dash," I said. "He and Nabokov—that's the cat you were petting—keep an eye on things around here."

The dog examined Spence for a long moment, then let out a quiet *woof* and sat back on his haunches.

The photographer smiled. "I'm going to take that as approval."

Me, too.

"Maggie was telling me a little about your shop. That's an interesting business." Spence walked over and stopped at the edge of the patio by the birdbath. He scanned the garden beds with an assessing eye as he spoke. "I've heard about aromatherapy, of course, but custom perfume? How does that work?"

I looked over. His eyes were fixed on me, full of sincere interest.

"Well," I started slowly. How to condense what I did into a few sentences? "All my perfumes are made from essential oils. Some I have to buy—things like sandalwood or frankincense I can't make myself. But for the really special blends, I distill the essences from the plants and flowers I grow here." I indicated the overflowing, verdant beds around us. "I use an old-fashioned copper alembic, and distill the oil from different plants at the same time, rather than mixing individual oils like most perfumers do."

"Alembic?" he asked.

"Think of it as a still, like you'd use to make moonshine. Only much smaller, or at least mine is. Only three liters. But the principle is the same. I'll show it to you, if you want."

Nodding, he looked around, very slowly. I could almost feel him figuring out compositions. I looked around at the area myself, trying to see it with the eyes of an artist rather than a horticulturist.

"This is really stunning," he said. "Impressive in its scope and variety, but there's also a feeling of, I don't know . . ." He thought for a moment, then snagged my gaze. "Peace and calm, I guess."

A quiet joy bloomed in my chest. "I feel the same way."

A current of warm air brushed through the oak tree by the corner of my little house, and the susurration of leaves rubbing together mingled with the light tinkling of a glass wind chime hanging from the shepherd's hook near the center of the garden. Several flowers from the apricot bougainvillea broke loose from their stems, rose in a cloud, and swirled among the leaves of the tree before suddenly falling to the ground.

Spence watched them, and then I saw his eyes widen. He squatted and put his camera case on the stone path, then twisted to scan the area around him.

"Do you have many of these?" He gestured to the fairy tableau near where the papery bougainvillea blossoms had landed.

"Over a dozen," I said. "The number changes, depending on the season and what I have available to work with."

He stood, a big grin on his face. "That's perfect!"

Puzzlement creased my brow.

He laughed. "You mean it's not on purpose?"

"Um . . ."

"The tiny house surrounded by tiny gardens! It's thematic genius! I'm going to use it as the backbone of the piece. I can share all the details about the house and how you came to choose such a small footprint, but the garden will make it different from any of the other tiny houses we're featuring in the magazine." He cocked his head to the side. "You're kind of tiny, too."

"Hey!"

He looked chagrined. "Oh, God. I'm sorry. I only meant that you're petite. I certainly didn't mean it as an insult." His eyes searched mine. "Only that your house, your gardens, and you have such a natural appeal that readers will want to know all about you."

Beryl. His eyes look like uncut beryl.

"You haven't even . . . even seen the house," I managed to stammer out.

He nodded. "Well, show me, then."

I led him inside and showed him all the features I'd shown Colby and Larken. Had it been only two days ago? He oohed and aahed over the round Japanese tub—just over forty-five inches in diameter but deep enough that I could sit in water up to my chin—which was a recent addition.

"I make a lot of scented bath products," I explained. "I need to be able to test them out. Plus, you know: baths."

"This is a good solution for a tiny house. Tell me about this staircase. I've never seen anything like it."

He continued asking me questions, all the time taking notes. Where had I found the barn wood for the front door? Where did the cedar shingles come from? How had I pared down my belongings to fit in such a small place?

"Divorce is great motivator," I said wryly, and he laughed. "It's also a very good way to end up with fewer possessions. I cheated, though."

Something passed behind his eyes, and I realized how it sounded. "No! Not like *that*. I meant that I didn't get rid of absolutely everything. See, Scents and Nonsense has a large storage room with enough space for me to keep my seasonal clothes, extra bedding, and a few boxes of, well, whatever."

The questions kept coming, and I answered them as cogently as I could. The man I'd hired to renovate the garden shed—"This was a garden shed? That's another fantastic angle for the article!"—was well known for his innovative solutions for storage and small-space living. It turned out that Spence had already interviewed him.

"Wait," I said. "You interviewed him? Not Blake?" Finally, an opening to talk about his boss that didn't seem too obvious.

"No. *Not* Blake."

I blinked at the sarcasm that dripped from the words.

Spence scowled and went outside. There, he began unpacking equipment. Grabbing a light meter, he carried it to different places around the garden, holding it at different angles and making notes.

What was that all about?

I sighed, and ducked back into the bathroom to take a long-overdue look in the mirror before he started taking pictures. *Conscience* didn't have a huge circulation, but it was a national periodical and especially popular in the West. I knew Astrid had been trying to make me feel better about my hair, but I didn't want to look like a ragamuffin.

At least the humidity was low, so my dark curls weren't too frizzed. The last few days showed around my eyes, though, so I dabbed a bit of concealer beneath them, added a touch of brown eyeliner to bring out the blue, and finished with a couple strokes of mascara. I was pleased to see my recent hours in the garden had added a natural blush of color to my cheeks.

Leave it at that. Otherwise it looks like you're trying.

I found Spence waiting on the front step.

"Sorry I snapped at you," he said.

"I must have hit a hot button."

His head inclined. "You did, I'm afraid. See, the idea of showcasing tiny houses and small-footprint living was my baby. I was setting it up with the editor, and had even conducted a few interviews—like with the guy who designed your house." He paused, anger clouding his handsome face. He glanced at me as if wondering whether to go on, then seemed to decide.

"Then Sontag horned in on the idea. The editor loves the cachet of having the 'great Blake Sontag' associated with *Conscience*, and Sontag knew how to play it. He told the editor he wanted control over the whole project." He met my eyes again, his lips twisted ruefully. "And that meant yours truly was out of the picture—except for the actual pictures, you know?"

"Ouch." Blake had apparently made a habit of stealing other people's story ideas. I wondered how many times he'd done it over the course of his career.

Suddenly Spence shrugged and laughed. "It's not really a big deal. Stupid professional infighting. Happens all the time in this business." Then he sobered. "Though I guess I'm more upset than I realized. Normally I'd never share this with someone I just met."

I started to wave it away.

His eyes probed mine. "I don't know. There's just something about you . . ."

I blinked.

Red-faced, Spence looked away. "Sorry. Forget I said anything." He stooped to retrieve his camera. When he straightened, he was all business. "Let's get some photos while the light's good. Would you mind standing there at the edge of the porch? Good. Chin a little higher. Right like that."

He directed me to stand this way and that, confidently in charge as he staged me in a series of photos. Maggie came out to watch from the back of the shop. She shot me a thumbs-up when he had me lean against the cedar shingles next to the overflowing window boxes, and clasped her hands over her head like a triumphant boxer when he had me point down at the gnome door at the base of the gnarled apple tree. She did all of it behind his back, and her antics relaxed me and made me laugh.

"Yes!" Spence exclaimed. "Like that. You're a natural."

Only because I have the equivalent of a dancing puppet over your shoulder. But I kept quiet and kept smiling.

Then he moved on to take several photos of the Enchanted Garden and the exterior of my tiny house, sans me. The whole time my mind was whirling.

Could Spence have killed Blake Sontag? As in Felicity Donovan's case, Blake had charmed an editor to the detriment of one of his coworkers. Spence had tried to make light of it, but he was obviously furious about Blake taking over his tiny house project.

Furious enough to commit murder, though? Poisoning wasn't exactly a crime of passion. It took planning—and in this case, a very particular knowledge. He had motive, and since he was staying in the same hotel as Blake, plenty of opportunity, too. After all, the journalist would have admitted the photographer into his room, right?

Finally, Spence finished, and we went out to the covered porch that ran the entire seventeen-foot length of my home. Taking a deep breath, he scanned the expansive meadow that reached toward the foothills and smiled. Then he turned to me and asked, "What about that, what was it? Alember?"

"Alembic," I said, smiling back. "I'll get it."

CHAPTER 13

I CLIMBED the circular stairs to the loft. Spence had taken a few pictures up there, but seemed so ill at ease in my bedroom that it was almost funny. Now I opened the special cabinet under the window and removed the elaborate copper distiller Gamma had left me along with her garden journal. Carefully cupping my hands around the spherical water pot at the bottom, I carried it downstairs. The late-day light angled through the windows, reflecting off the bright, reddish metal that had been so carefully polished over the years, first by my grandmother, then my mother, then me.

Spence waited for me on the back porch and hurried to open the screen door when I started to push it with my foot.

"Wow. That looks like something from the Middle Ages," he said, eyeing the elaborate contraption. "Can you show me how you use it?"

"Really? It's not very exciting to watch." For most people, at least. I found the process of transforming the energy of plant matter into its essence to be as powerful as any alchemy.

"Are you kidding? What you've told me so far is fascinating, and I want to see how that thing works." He pointed at the alembic.

I smiled and glanced at my watch. I'd have to hurry. It was five thirty, and I was due to meet Polly in an hour to go see the Sontag property. But I hadn't wanted to interrupt his photo session with more questions, so this might be the perfect chance to find out if Tanner Spence knew anything about plants.

"Okay, one quick demonstration coming up," I said. "Would you mind grabbing the camp stove from that cubby over there?" I gestured with my chin.

"Of course," he said, and turned to retrieve the one-burner stove. He followed me to the circular, graveled area at the back of the Enchanted Garden and set it down where I indicated.

"Give me just a sec," I said, carefully leveling the burner and placing the alembic in the center.

However, camera in hand, Spence followed me as I got my cutting basket and shears from behind the shop and went out to the garden.

"I'm going to distill one of my favorite combinations," I said. "Lavender and basil. Do you know what kind of lavender this is?" I asked, pointing at the mound of English lavender that was admittedly past its flowering prime.

He shook his head. "There's more than one?"

"Yep. They smell very similar, however. This is *La-*

vandula angustifolia." I bent and began snipping off the drying blooms. They weren't as fresh as they'd been a month before, but the buds still contained plenty of essential oil for my purpose.

"People think of lavender as being such a sweet fragrance when actually, it's quite astringent. Basil, which is thought of as a savory herb, has a sweet, licorice-like scent. Together they perform a perfect balancing act."

He obediently smelled the lavender flowers and basil leaves that I crushed together between my fingertips. "And that's the basil?"

I stared at him. "You're kidding, right?"

He looked apologetic. "I'm not much of a cook."

Or a horticulturist, I thought. Was he playing up his ignorance about plants to throw me off, or did he really not know anything about them?

"Mm," he said, sniffing the combination again. "It's nice. Not too girly. And . . . mellow?" He seemed oblivious to my scrutiny.

Relaxing a little, I nodded. "Each is considered relaxing in traditional aromatherapy. In floriography, basil means good wishes and lavender usually represents devotion or virtue. There are a lot of interpretations, of course."

He snapped a couple of pictures as a puzzled frown furrowed his brow. "Floriography?"

"The language of flowers. It's a kind of code that developed in the nineteenth century."

"Okay." He drew the word out.

I laughed. "Follow me."

My basket full of *Lavandula angustifolia* flowers and the leaves of *Ocimum basilicum*, I returned to the area

I'd set up for distillation. Spence settled on one of the large rocks that encircled the space as I lit the stove and disassembled the copper pot. Gamma had used a grate over an open fire, but I only went to the trouble of building a fire for special distillations.

I placed some of the flowers and leaves in the bottom, round pot. "This part is called the retort," I explained as I worked.

More basil. I stuffed in another handful, inhaled again to make sure the ratio was right, then filled the rest of the retort with bottled spring water. Then I added still more plant material to the dome-shaped vessel that served as the retort's lid.

"This part is called the onion," I said. "It acts as the condenser for the steam. And this is the bird's beak."

"Bird's beak," he muttered, peering at it. "It really looks like one."

I filled the onion with more cool water as the water in the retort began to boil. "The steam from the retort is full of plant oils. It travels through this coil of copper pipe inside the onion. The essential oil separates and then comes out of the bird's beak. The hydrosol—that's a fancy name for super-fragrant floral water—will stay in the pot."

"Hydrosol," he said, and I saw he'd taken out his tablet and was making notes. He rested the device on his knee. "Can you make perfume from that?"

I shook my head. "Not really. It's organic, so it can go bad. Some add rosemary oleoresin to extend the shelf life, but I usually just use a splash of vodka because it doesn't interfere with the scent. You can use hydrosols for lots of things, but lately I've been using them to rinse my hair."

Spence's eyes lit up. "Is that why you smell like roses?"

I shrugged, feeling my face turn pink.

The water had come to a boil, and the coiled condenser began to quietly hiss.

"I love the smell of roses," he said quietly.

I looked over, but he didn't meet my eye.

"There." He pointed.

The first drop of combined lavender and basil essential oil began to emerge from the bird's beak. I hurried to capture it in a tiny blue bottle. Four drops later, I turned off the flame.

Spence looked surprised. "Is that all you get?"

"Not usually. But this is just a demonstration, right? So you could see the process."

"Oh. Right." He stood.

I rose, too, and held the bottle out to him.

He breathed in the potent aroma, and a smile tugged at the corners of his lips. "For me?"

"If you want it."

He tucked it into his pocket. "Thanks. And thanks for showing me all this. And for consenting to the interview and photograph session. I thought it might be awkward after what happened yesterday, but you've been a real gem."

"It's an honor to be featured as part of *Conscience*'s tiny house issue."

It was true. And I'd had a good time sharing a small piece of my passion for scent with this interesting man.

So much so that I'd forgotten for a little while that he was a possible murder suspect.

As he packed away the last of his photography equipment, I made one more effort to draw him out about Blake.

Leaning casually against the porch support, I asked, "Did you know Blake was born here in Poppyville? That his family has lived here for generations?"

Spence's lip curled for a moment. He looked up from where he was packing away a camera filter. "Oh, yeah. He told me. In fact, that was one of the things he said to the editor in order to get him to hand the tiny house issue over to him. If we hadn't decided to come to Poppyville, I might still have control over the project."

"You do have control over the project," I pointed out, watching him.

"Yeah, now, but . . ." He trailed off. "That's not how I wanted it to happen."

"Of course not," I said, letting him off the hook. "Can I ask you something about Blake?"

One eyebrow rose sardonically. "You mean like you already have been?"

I ignored that. "Did he say anything about his family's land outside of town?"

Spence snorted. "Say anything? He insisted we go see it."

My breath caught, but I kept my tone even. "Did you go inside the fence?"

He zipped shut the compartment on the side of the bag, stood, and slung the strap over his shoulder. "Yep. The old cabin looked pretty cool. I can see why he would have wanted to keep the place in the family. Apparently there was an issue with his sister over that."

Aha!

The photographer sighed. "Listen, Blake Sontag was unpleasant and difficult to work with, but he was also a good reporter, and I'm sure his family is grieving his loss. I'm not sorry to have this tiny house project back, but I am sorry he's dead."

I walked Spence to the gate that led to the boardwalk out front. As we passed by one of the herb gardens, he paused and put down the bag so he could pick a leafy sprig and bring it to his nose.

"What's this?" he asked.

"Savory," I said. "It's great to flavor roasted meats."

His gaze snagged mine for a long moment, and I found myself unwilling to break eye contact. "Does it have a meaning in the language of flowers?"

My chin bobbed in a small nod.

He smiled and waited.

Does he already know?

"It symbolizes interest."

Spence quirked an eyebrow.

I gave in. "*Spicy* interest."

His laugh was deep, open, and utterly infectious as he handed the sprig of savory to me. "Would you have dinner with me tonight? We don't have to go to the Empire Room. In fact, I'd insist that we go somewhere else."

My mouth was suddenly so dry that I couldn't quite speak. Finally, I managed, "I'm sorry. I can't."

His face fell. "Oh. Okay. Maybe tomorrow?" He sounded almost tentative now.

"Uh . . ."

"Oh!" He smacked his forehead with his palm. "I'm

an idiot. You have a boyfriend, don't you? Of course you would." He tried to grin.

"Well, yes," I said. "It's kind of complicated."

"Right. Yes. Complicated. Got it."

A feeling of betrayal washed through me, a sharp-edged and bitter thing flavored with embarrassment that I recognized from when I'd stumbled upon Harris and Wanda Simmons in the walk-in freezer at the Roux. But this was different. This feeling wasn't actually mine. I was picking it up from Spence.

He thought I was lying about having a boyfriend.

"I do," I insisted. "His name is Ritter."

"Sure. No problem." He turned and fled through the gate to the street.

A knot of guilt formed in my stomach. I'd almost said yes to the dinner invitation. Not because I was interested in him romantically—though heaven knew he was easy on the eyes—but because I'd really enjoyed the last two hours hanging out with him, and with Ritter gone I'd been spending a lot of time at home. However, I could tell Spence's interest in me went beyond the friendship I had in mind.

I sighed and looked down at Dash, who was still looking at the gate. "Why does life have to be so complicated?"

Woof!

I QUICKLY tidied up the distillation area and returned the copper alembic to its cupboard in my bedroom. After changing into jeans, tank top, and trail runners, I took my cell out to my back porch and called Astrid. Oblique shadows were beginning to fall across the meadow.

"You want to come with me to check out the Sontag property?" I asked when she answered. "Spence just left."

"*Spence*, huh," Astrid teased. "How did that go?"

"It was fun," I said.

"Just fun? Come on, Ellie."

"I'll tell you about it on the way out to the Sontag place."

"Sorry, El. No can do. Not tonight anyway." Something in her voice.

Something I recognized. "The guy from the post office?" I guessed.

"Mm-hm. Todd. We're going miniature golfing tonight."

"You hate miniature golfing."

"Do not."

I rolled my eyes, but didn't have time to argue. "Then I'll see you in the morning. And Astrid?"

"Mm?" She sounded distracted.

"I expect a full update on your evening."

"Aye, aye, Cap'n." A male voice murmured in the background, and she laughed. "Bye."

Shaking my head, I quickly dialed Colby's cell. I had another idea.

"Hey, sis." His voice was quiet.

"Hi. Everything okay?"

"Great." He bit off the word.

I let it go. "Is Larken around?"

"Sure. Let me put her on. Lark!" he called.

"Wait—" But he'd already handed off the phone.

"Ellie?" She sounded subdued as well.

"Hey there. Are you guys up for a field trip? I'm going to look at that property I told you about last night, and I'd like you to come along."

She hesitated, then agreed.

"Great. I'll see you in a few minutes."

I left Dash with Nabby in the garden and guided my Wrangler to the stables. The van was in the same place, only now an electrical cord snaked from its side to the plug-in by Gessie's chuck wagon. The horsewoman was nowhere to be seen. Colby sat in a camp chair and waved as I approached. The pop-top ceiling of the Westfalia was raised, and the smell of onions, garlic, and ginger drifted out from the open side door.

I peeked around the side and saw Larken putting a bottle of soy sauce into the mini-fridge tucked under the sink. The floral scent of jasmine rice drifted from a pan on the fold-down table, and my stomach growled right on cue.

She looked unhappy, her lips pursed. But when she looked up and saw me, a sweet smile transformed her face.

"Hey, Ellie! You want some stir-fry? There's a bit left."

I glanced at my watch with regret. "The real estate agent is expecting me in ten minutes."

"Oh! Well, let's go, then. Colby, you're on dish duty."

"No problem," he said.

I peered at him. "You're awfully quiet."

He shrugged.

"You aren't coming with us?" I asked.

"To see a bunch of dirt? I don't think so."

I blinked. "It's not just any bunch of dirt, as you put it. It might have something to do with Blake Sontag's murder."

"I don't want to go." He scowled.

Moving to stand in front of him, I put my hands on my hips. "What's the matter with you?"

"Nothing."

"Colby—"

He abruptly stood and turned toward the house on the far side of the barn. "I'm going to take Gessie up on her offer of a shower." Without another word, he strode away.

I turned and looked at Larken, completely bewildered. "What just happened?"

She gazed after him with worried eyes. Then she took a deep breath. "We'd better get going if you want to meet that real estate agent."

"But—"

"We can talk on the way."

I gave in, and moments later we were heading to Cooperhawk Court. Larken sat in the passenger seat looking pensive. She wore the same clothes she'd had on while cleaning stalls for Gessie, and the not-unpleasant smell of horse musk emanated from the weave of her T-shirt. It was one thing for Colby to live in his van by himself, but it had to be difficult for two people in that small space, especially since there wasn't any running water. I knew he'd installed a compostable toilet, but I remembered him telling me he usually joined a gym when he moved to a new town—partly to work out, and partly to have a place to shower.

How long had Colby and Larken been together? It had been such a crazy couple of days that I hadn't asked about any details. I was about to bring it up, when Larken spoke.

"I think Detective Lang is going to arrest me," she said.

My fingers gripped the steering wheel so hard it was difficult to guide the Jeep around the corner. "Did something happen?"

"He came by Gessie's a few hours ago. Said he was just

making sure that we were really staying there and didn't have any plans to leave, but it was more than that." She sighed. "He asked me a bunch of questions about deadly nightshade—what it looks like, whether I knew the kind of places it grows, how poisonous it is." She rubbed her hands over her face and groaned. "Why did I have to open my big fat mouth? I never should have let on that I know all about belladonna."

Suppressing a frustrated sigh, I said, "Don't worry. He could have proved that you know about plants and herbs, right?"

Pressing her lips together, she nodded. "Probably."

"Then maybe it's better that you own it. But, Larken?"

"Yeah?"

"Be careful when you talk with the police, okay? In fact, maybe you should think about getting a lawyer."

She blanched. "Oh, I don't . . . Maybe." I stopped in front of the two-story that housed Gold Rush Realty and Cynthia's office and turned off the engine. Larken unfastened her seat belt, but before she could get out, I put my hand on her arm.

"What was wrong with Colby tonight? Why didn't he want to come with us? He was downright rude about it."

She bit her lip. "I'm not sure."

"Listen, I know this vacation of yours has turned out to be a real bummer." I opened my own door and put my foot on the running board. "If you want me to talk to him—"

"No, it's not that. I think he's just feeling itchy, you know? Ready to move on."

"He's only been here for three days! Doesn't he usually

stay in a place a month or more? He was in Crested Butte, Colorado, for over three months, right?"

"This isn't just anyplace, Ellie." She got out and turned to look at me. "This was home. This is where he left, not where he wants to be."

That resonated. It also kind of hurt, since I was part of "home." And honestly, though I could accept my brother's wandering tendencies, I really didn't understand them. Poppyville and the area around it was so deeply ingrained in my blood that I'd never leave. Plenty of people had suggested that I might want to after the divorce, but I'd be darned if Harris' bad behavior could run me out of town.

CHAPTER 14

P OLLY had obviously been watching for us, because
when we were halfway to the front door of Gold Rush
Realty she came out and waved. The lights inside were
already off. She quickly turned and locked the door behind her before joining us.

I greeted her and introduced Larken. "You two haven't
met, have you?"

The real estate agent shook her head and flashed her
big white teeth. "No, we haven't. It's nice that you came
along to give Ellie advice," Polly said to Larken. Then
slyly, "Or are you actually the interested party?"

I wondered how many times a day Polly used the phrase
"interested party."

Larken mumbled something incoherent.

"Sorry to make you work so late," I said.

The woman waved it away. "Honey, I work any and

all hours. Occupational hazard. Don't you worry." She pointed to a red Miata that was parked two spots down from my Jeep. "Since you already know where we're going, I'll follow you out there. Okay?"

I nodded. "Sounds good."

Larken and I returned to my vehicle and buckled up. A few blocks later, as we drove by the entrance to Raven Creek Park, I returned to our earlier discussion.

"How did you and my brother meet? Was it in Colorado?" I knew they'd met on a farm, but neither had filled me in on the details.

She leaned against the seat back and looked out at the passing landscape. "Do you believe in fate?"

"Um. I guess. Sometimes."

"We met in New Mexico, actually. I was interning at a CSA farm—you know, community supported agriculture? Anyway, he was doing some construction work for the family who lived there, and they let him park the van there. We'd seen each other around, but really got to talking at one of the monthly farm-to-table dinners, and *zing*! That was that."

I had to smile. The dreamy look she'd had on her face when she'd spoken of having her own plot of sustainable land had returned in full force as she remembered falling for my brother.

"How long ago was that?" I asked.

"Almost a year."

I did a double take. "You two have been together that long?"

She shook her head. "I was looking for a place to settle, and he was always looking for the next place to be.

So he'd stick around for three or four months and then move on."

"Wait. That sounds like it happened more than once." I guided the Jeep around a curve.

"It happened three different times," she said, grinning over at me. "That first time in Taos, but then I left, and he moved on. I ended up with a job in Texas, and lo and behold, there he was. It was a surprise to both of us. Then when it happened again, in Crested Butte, I knew we were really supposed to be together. I packed what I could in the Westfalia and came with him this last time."

Frowning, I said, "That's a crazy story, but I believe it. Sometimes life does work like that. And honestly, it sounds like you're about as itinerant as my brother."

She shook her head vigorously. "No. I'm searching. When I find what I want, I'm done."

"Hmm," I mused. "I wonder if he's searching, too."

"Of course he is," she said. I looked over at her, and she shrugged. "I just don't know what he's looking for in the end. Unfortunately, I don't think he knows, either."

We rode in silence for a couple of minutes.

Then I asked, "So you didn't live in the van with him before this trip?"

She laughed. "God, no. That's only been for a couple of weeks."

We went past the trailhead for Kestrel Peak, and I slowed to dodge a pothole. When I glanced in the rearview mirror to make sure Polly was still with us, she was talking into her cell. Her head bobbed in enthusiastic agreement.

"How's that working out?" I asked Larken. "The van thing, I mean. It's not exactly like living in an RV."

"You can say that again." There was a slight bitterness to the words. Then she sighed. "Ellie, I don't know what I'm going to do. I love that brother of yours more than I can say. And I'm pretty sure he feels the same way."

"I think you're right about that," I agreed. "I've never seen him so head over heels."

She looked pleased for a few seconds, then strain pinched the skin around her eyes. "I'm glad to hear that. I mean, I know how he feels, but coming from you . . . Still, I don't know how it's going to work out. He knows I'm looking for land." She looked miserable again. "I bet that's why he didn't want to come out here with us." A big sigh. "He's always talking about freedom this and freedom that."

My forehead squinched. "He is. But do you know exactly what he's looking for freedom from?"

Larken shrugged. "From 'the man,' from a nine-to-five job, from too many bills, from working for someone else . . ." She trailed off.

"Yeah, that sounds about right," I said slowly. "He's not irresponsible, just doesn't like to answer to anybody."

"Right," she agreed. "He's an awfully hard worker."

I felt a grin spread across my face.

"What?" Larken asked.

"Seems to me that having your own plot of land, paid for and everything, to support yourself on, is the ultimate in not having to answer to anyone else."

Her eyes widened. "I never thought about it like that."

"I wonder if Colby has," I said.

A deep inhalation, as if she was preparing to reply, but what came out was, "Son of a biscuit! What the heck is *that*?"

I'd stopped the Wrangler in the pullout in front of the locked gate. She was staring at the acres of chain link surrounding the Sontag land.

"Did I mention the place is fenced off?" I asked.

We got out as Polly steered around a rut in the road and parked the low-slung Miata. Larken was still gaping.

"Okay, that sounds good, Mr. Newton. We'll meet tomorrow morning," Polly said into her phone. "Excellent! I'm sure we can work something out. Bye!" She tossed the device into the passenger seat and turned back to us with a set of keys dangling from her finger. They jingled when she held them up and shook them.

"Ready for a little hike?" she asked.

I bounced slightly on the toes of my trail runners and glanced down at Larken's sturdy work boots. Then I saw Polly's high-heeled suede pumps.

"We are, but what about you?" I asked.

The real estate agent waved vaguely. "Oh, I'm not tromping around in there."

Was I mistaken, or was she suddenly less interested in selling me anything? Perhaps I hadn't been an interested *enough* party?

"Polly?" I said.

She paused, eyebrows raised in question.

"Do you know why Joyous Sontag fenced this place off like this?" I gestured toward the gate. "I mean, razor wire? And that padlock and chain look serious."

"Not my concern, I'm afraid."

"No toxic waste in there, right?" I was teasing but she looked alarmed.

"Of course not!"

Shaking her head at our apparent paranoia, she strode over to the gate, inserted a key in the padlock, and gave a twist. With an efficient wrench of her wrist, she opened the lock and let the chain fall away. The gate slowly swung open as if pushed by an unseen hand.

"You go on in and explore, and I'll wait here. Don't be too long, though. It'll be dark in half an hour, and I don't want to have to send in the troops to get you." She flashed a bright smile before turning back to her car. Within seconds she'd retrieved her smartphone. "Let me know if you have any questions," she called absently, already tapping on the screen.

Larken and I exchanged a wry look and went through the gate.

And stopped cold.

"Oh," she whispered. "Oh, my."

Oh, my, indeed.

A strange quiet had instantly descended, as if we'd walked through an air lock rather than a plain metal gate. But there wasn't total silence, not at all. The liquid calls of meadowlarks echoed back from the shallow red cliff, and a pair of red-winged blackbirds trilled back and forth to each other from our right and left. A ruby-throated hummingbird buzzed by, followed by another. The first one veered back and hovered a foot in front of us for a few long seconds, as if inspecting our right to be there. Then it flitted away toward the remains of the log cabin, paused and looked back, then flew on.

Larken let out a shaky giggle. "It almost looks like he wants us to follow him."

"Come on," I said, and took a few steps.

Larken didn't budge. I gently put my hand on her shoulder, and we began to walk.

A chorus of cricket song erupted around us, so loud the air throbbed with the hypnotic rhythm. I could feel more than hear Larken's gasp of surprise and delight. Colors pulsed in my peripheral vision, the slightest bit brighter than usual. I quickly turned my head to try to catch the difference, but when I looked directly at a bright mariposa lily or golden aster, they appeared perfectly normal.

Still, there was an energy here, strange and unexpected. *And yet familiar.*

With a start, I realized this place felt similar to the Enchanted Garden. It was as if the spirits of the flora and fauna were particularly alive and active.

Perhaps even aware.

I looked sideways at Larken. Her eyes traveled over the expanse of grassland and lingered on the old homestead, the cliff face, and a myriad of botanical offerings. There were woolly milkweed, paprika-colored yarrow, and orange pincushion flowers. Some of the wild onions were blooming purple, even this late in the summer. A swath of the white, oddly spiderlike blooms of soap lilies led like a path toward a stand of willows. The willows reached gentle, waving branches toward the remnants of the log home where past generations of Sontags had lived— and probably died.

Among it all, the stands of *Atropa belladonna* boasted purple-maroon flowers and berries ripe for the picking.

Larken's gaze lit on the nearest deadly nightshade plant, and she pulled me toward it.

"See?" she said as we stopped beside it. "There's no way someone would pick that by accident. Certainly no one who knows what they're doing."

"Maybe they didn't know," I said.

She shook her head vigorously. "That doesn't make sense, either. Whoever it was made a tea. You don't just throw things willy-nilly into a medicinal tea. You look for specific plants. And there's really nothing else that looks like this." She pointed to the nightshade.

"Maybe it wasn't supposed to be medicinal. Just a plain old herbal tea."

She gave me a look. "More devil's advocate?"

I smiled and shrugged. I was certain the nightshade that had been used to kill Blake Sontag came from here.

"From what I understand, nightshade doesn't exactly taste great. It's said to be extremely bitter." She looked speculative. "Though Euell Gibbons supposedly made a pie with the berries and lived to tell the tale."

I shuddered. I'd heard of the naturalist and godfather of wild food foraging, and seemed to remember he touted some healthy cereal on television. "No doubt he's an idol for a wildcrafter like you, but please promise me that you'd never try that."

Her head tipped back as she laughed. "I wouldn't dream of it!"

Then I saw the nightshade plant I'd spied through the fence before. It was still leaning to one side. I walked over to take a look. It looked like several stems had been roughly torn off, and it was obvious the area around the base had been dug up. A few roots still lay exposed against the dark soil.

"You're right about it being intentional," I said quietly, then turned. "Come on. Let's check out the ruins."

We continued on to what was left of the cabin. One wall was still mostly standing, though several logs had rolled off the very top and now lay haphazardly to one side. The mud chinking between the logs was stained dark, and much of it had cracked off.

"Careful," I said. "This doesn't look very stable."

"Oh, Ellie. Look!" Larken called from the other side.

I peered around the corner to find her kneeling on a ring of stones set before a crumbling chimney. Grass had overtaken the rest of the interior, but the stone hearth still looked like it must have when Blake's ancestors had kneeled on it to tend the fire.

"Look," she said again, and pointed to the iron bar set into the interior of the fireplace. "They cooked here," she breathed. Then she sat back on her heels. "Oh, golly. I love this place. It's absolutely perfect." She stood and ran back out.

I followed at a slower pace. Her need to put down roots was palpable, and from the look on her face, this soil would be a solid place for her to plant them.

"We could build a small house right over there, a little nearer to the cliff. It's still close to the well, but would be shaded from the sun part of the day."

My gaze followed hers to the old wellhead set into the ground. "Will you look at that. I wonder if that's why Joyous fenced this place off. It would be awful if someone were to fall in there."

Larken rolled her eyes. "Why wouldn't she just fence off the area around it?"

"Good point," I agreed.

She turned to face me, hands on her hips. "Ellie, I want to buy this land."

My jaw slackened. "But . . . really?"

"Yes. I've looked for the right place for so long, and now I've found it." She gave me a pleading look. "I don't think I can live in that van for more than a month at a time. I thought I could, for a while at least. I thought I could do anything for Colby. But it's hard." Her eyes brightened with moisture. "Maybe I'm just weak."

I ran my hand over the rough wood of the half wall. "Nah. I get it. I do. You've seen how small my place is, but it would be really hard to share it with someone full-time."

Not that I need to worry about that happening . . .

Pushing the thought away, I stepped back and turned in a circle to survey the area. Now that we were inside the gate, I could see where the chain link ran along the perimeter in the distance. The parcel was slightly wider than long, maybe five acres by six. There was room for a barn, animals, and a large flat field that practically begged to be planted with crops. I could almost see chickens pecking in the grass nearby.

Suddenly, I turned and faced Larken again. "You said you want to buy it. Is that a real possibility, though? I mean, how would you pull it off?"

She grinned. "I have the money my grandpa left me. It's not a ton, not like a big trust fund or anything, but I haven't touched it. Not a cent, even for school. I've always known what I wanted to use it for."

She ran over and gave me a big hug.

"Don't count on that freedom argument working," I warned. "My darling brother can be stubborn as all get-out."

"Don't I know it! Can't hurt to try, though. Right?" Her smile was so contagious I couldn't help but echo it.

Was I setting her up for disappointment? Still, a part of me was hoping against hope she'd be able to talk my brother into staying in Poppyville. The idea of this vibrant land being used as a small local farm rather than a big nasty housing development made me almost as giddy.

So maybe I was setting myself up for disappointment, too.

Know what? I didn't care. It was worth a shot.

The sun was nearly set over the rolling hills west of Poppyville. A quick look over revealed Polly sitting on the hood of her car, her bent elbow indicating she was still on the phone. Or again.

"If you're serious, we should look around more," I said.

Larken nodded, and we took off at a fast walk around the perimeter. The razor wire at the top of the fence lent a sour note to our progress, and we agreed that would be the first thing to come down.

Fingers of flamingo pink and raspberry were spreading across the sky. We turned and headed back toward the cabin.

Interested party, indeed.

At least we hadn't been just wasting Polly's time with this junket. I could barely keep the grin off my face even as we passed another stand of deadly nightshade.

It might be for warning, but today it seems like good luck.

"I'm going to check over there to see whether it would

be a good place for a solar array," Larken said when we reached the tumbled logs of the cabin.

"Don't take too long. I'll be over by the willows. They look so lush that there might be a small stream or maybe an artesian spring. That would make the well even sweeter."

Her eyes lit up. "Oh, that would be awesome!"

She went right and I went left. I'd pushed into the circle of seven weeping willows on the other side of the cabin when the fog came.

CHAPTER 15

THE pliant boughs of the willows bent gracefully to the ground, their delicate green leaves looking like they'd been airbrushed on. The ring of trees formed a kind of arboreal room. It was cool inside, dappled with shadow but welcoming, and I wondered if they'd been planted like that intentionally. Since weeping willows weren't native to California, I suspected some farseeing Sontag had planned this magical place.

The wellhead Larken had spied was between the willows and the cabin, so there was plenty of natural water nearby for them to drink. I breathed in the clean liquid scent of it. When I looked up, the sky appeared vibrantly rosy through the umbrellas of drooping branches.

Grinning to myself, I spread my arms wide and spun in place like a little girl.

But I wasn't a little girl, and it didn't take long to for me to get dizzy. I slowed, came to a rest, and plopped down on a tuft of low-growing grama grass.

Silly. I'm as much of a kid as Colby is.

With a start, I realized I was shivering. The temperature had dropped ten degrees over the course of only a few minutes, so quickly it hadn't registered at first. Disconcerted, I staggered to my feet and hugged myself for warmth. I turned in the direction Larken had gone—and stopped.

A heavy white mist slithered through the bunch grass and wildflowers, crawling across the ground toward where I stood. Stunned, I watched it fill the floor of the willow grove, swirling around my ankles and then my knees.

Tule fog?

The phenomenon wasn't uncommon in the valley. Not at all—except it only happened after it rained, and Poppyville hadn't seen a drop of precipitation for over three weeks.

Furthermore, we never saw tule fog in August. November, maybe. The winter months, certainly. But August?

Never.

It was known for its density and for being the leading reason for weather-related car accidents from fall to spring. And now it was up to my hips.

"Larken!" I called. "Come back to the cabin!"

She didn't respond.

By then, the mist was up to my chest, and I could barely see the remains of the cabin through the drooping branches of the willows. Overhead, the pink clouds of the sunset mocked me. Ducking my head, I took a deep breath of the humid air and hesitantly began to plod in the direction of the old homestead.

The smell hit me like a cartoon anvil. *Bubble gum.*

I stopped in my tracks, one hand on the trunk of the outermost willow. The tree was swaying. Then I realized *I* was swaying, hyperventilating as I dragged more of the sweet scent into my lungs.

No. No, that can't be. Not this time of year.

Squinting into the bushes at the edge of the willow grove, I made out the source of the fragrance. The simple white blossoms of a mock orange studded a round bush that was a foot taller than me. From it emanated not the aroma of oranges as one might expect from the name, but the intense childhood smell of Bazooka gum. There were several kinds of *Philadelphus*, all fragrant in different ways, but this one happened to be my favorite.

However, mock oranges bloomed in June. Now, in late August, the flowers should be long gone. Long, *long* gone, and with them, their candy scent.

And tule fog is unheard of this time of year, a voice whispered in the back of my mind.

It was as if this place somehow existed outside of time.

I huffed and shook away the thought. That was impossible. I might have an over-the-top sense of smell, and sure, I sometimes felt what others were feeling. But the Sontag homestead as some Brigadoon-like place?

Nah.

Distracted by my whirling thoughts, I didn't realize how far the fog had risen until I was completely engulfed.

The blanket of sweet, enticing bubble gum smell intensified. It was mixed with hints of chlorophyll and sap and bright clear water soaking into rich loam.

"Larken!" I yelled, stumbling toward the cabin again.

My foot caught on a root, and I went sprawling. My knee, still sore from hitting the bumper of the Wrangler two days before, hit the ground first.

Ouch.

The native grasses helped cushion my fall, but when I scrambled to my feet, a sharp blade of needle grass sliced across my finger. Swearing under my breath, I squinted into the blinding gray mist. The soft pink sky above had disappeared. The air around me grew heavy and dim.

A movement in the corner of my eye made me turn. "Larken! Over here."

The fog shifted. I waved my hand, and said again, "Over here!"

A figure approached. Short and sturdy.

No, wait a second. It was tall and willowy.

Languid.

With a panicked pang, I realized it wasn't Larken at all. It wasn't a *figure* at all.

It was just the fog. A trick of the light, or lack of light. That wasn't a torso, and those weren't arms, simply tendrils of water vapor curling and swirling in the breeze.

Except there isn't a breath of wind. And water vapor from where? The logical part of my brain clamored for answers. *There's been no rain. This fog can't . . . well, it just can't be.*

But it was.

And that's not *a face.*

But it sure looked like one. Then it disappeared into the undulating gray haze.

A quiet hissing began to rise around me. The fog whirled and eddied, flowing like a live thing, whispering wordlessly, reaching for me.

I should have been terrified. I knew that, but I wasn't. Along with the verdant scents, a subtle joy rose in the air, wrapping itself around me. I felt happy and calm in the friendly fog.

Sssss . . . ussssss . . .

The sound grew clearer, yet remained a bare hint of a whisper.

Oooo . . . ussss . . .

And then I made out an actual word.

Joyoussssss.

"No," I said, my voice soft as thistledown. "I'm not Joyous."

The fog swirled faster.

Feeling like a complete fool, I nonetheless continued. "Not Joyous. Ellie." I swallowed. "Elliana."

Elliana . . .

I'd heard my name on the wind before. I'd discounted it then, too. I shivered as cool humidity stroked my cheek, and I closed my eyes for a long moment.

When I opened them again, the sky glowed pink overhead, and the fog was nearly gone. As I watched, what remained of it seemed to drain straight into the ground.

"Ellie! Where have you been?" Larken came around the corner of the crumbling chimney.

I'd come closer to the cabin than I'd known.

"Whew!" I said. "That fog was something, wasn't it?"

Her head tipped to the side. "I thought I saw some mist along the ground. It didn't last very long."

"Mist! You couldn't even see—" Seeing her forehead wrinkled in puzzlement, I stopped, confused. "You didn't see that crazy tule fog?"

Looking at me like I was a candidate for a straitjacket, she slowly shook her head. "Tule?" she asked in a gentle voice. Didn't want to upset the insane lady.

Utterly gobsmacked, I stared at her. Finally, I managed to mutter, "Uh, never mind."

Had I imagined the whole thing? I didn't think so. The memory of the fog against my skin, the whispers, the smell of bubble gum . . .

Wait. The mock orange.

I turned and ran back toward the stand of willows.

"Ellie! It's getting dark. And it looks like Polly is getting a little antsy," Larken said as she followed on my heels.

I skidded to a stop in front of the bush. It was still blooming. Inhaling deeply, I turned to her and said, "See? I'm not losing my mind."

"Okay." She drew the word out, obviously skeptical.

"The mock orange! It's really here," I exclaimed. "And it *is* blooming!"

One side of her mouth pulled back as she turned her attention to the bush. "Sure is." Her eyes cut toward me, then back. "Say, isn't it kind of late for them to bloom?"

"Yes! That's my point!"

She gave me another long look, then opted for a hopeful smile. "Smells good, though, doesn't it?"

"Well, yeah, but . . ." I gave up.

"Girls!" Polly's voice drifted from where she stood just inside the gate. "Come on. Time to go."

Feeling like a ten-year-old being called inside after dinner, I trudged along behind my brother's girlfriend, mind awhirl. When we reached the gate, I stopped and gazed back at the stand of willows.

A small white doe stepped out from inside the circle of trees. *My doe.* We looked at each other for several seconds before she turned her tail toward me and went back into their shadows.

"Did you see . . . ?" I started to ask, but Larken and Polly were looking the other way, deep in discussion beside the real estate agent's car.

T HE blue hour of twilight had come and gone by the time Larken and I got back to the stables. She hadn't said much in the car, but I was pretty sure that was because she was formulating what to say to my brother about wanting to buy the Sontag land.

Colby was waiting in one of the camp chairs by the van. Gessie sat in another. Warm light spilled from the interior of the Westfalia and from the flames of two lanterns he'd set outside.

My friend rose when we approached from the parking lot. "There you are! When I heard where you'd gone, I thought about taking Sutter out and meeting you there." Sutter was her sturdy quarter horse gelding. "I've wanted to get inside that fence ever since Joyous put it up."

I climbed up on the back of the hayride wagon and perched on the edge. "It's been like that for a while, then?" I hadn't thought to ask Polly how long it had been fenced.

"At least a couple of years," she said, and gestured Larken toward the camp chair she'd been sitting in. "I've got to get going, hon. You sit here." She moved to stand by one of the lamps. Her gray hair caught the yellow light. It gave the impression of a nimbus around her head.

"But you've been on that land before it was fenced, right?" I asked. "On your trail rides?"

She nodded. "I have some standard rides I take clients on, but sometimes people want to explore a little more. I'm fine with that. Most of my rides are out in Clary State Park, anyway." She gave a kind of facial shrug. "Hard not to wander across to that edge of the Sontag place every once in a while. We never did any harm, though."

"So that's not why Joyous put up the fence?"

"To keep me out?" Gessie blew a raspberry. "Nah."

I looked at her curiously. "So why do you want to get in if you've already been there?"

She grinned. "Gotta wonder why she did it, is all. I mean, what big secret's on that land? Might be gold in them thar hills."

Colby laughed, but it sounded a little strained.

Larken had taken a seat in the open side doorway of the van, but hadn't spoken. I looked between them and opened my mouth to speak. Then I closed it again. The best thing I could do right then was butt out.

"I don't think there's any gold," Colby said. "At least

there wasn't any record of any kind of mine or claim at the courthouse."

I snapped my fingers. "That's right. You went over there today. Did you find out anything useful?"

He looked rueful. "Not useful. Interesting, though. They have some really old records there. A few go back a century and a half. They belong in a museum, not some file cabinet in the basement."

Gessie and I exchanged a meaningful look.

My brother caught it. "What?"

"For the last six months we've have been trying to get the owners of the Hotel California to reopen the museum that used to be beneath the lobby," Gessie said. "They live out of state and don't seem to think the history of our little town here is very important." She winked at me. "I think we might be wearing them down, though."

"And by 'we' she means Cynthia," I said, then explained. "Our women's business group is totally behind the idea, but that museum is definitely Cynthia's baby. There is some fascinating stuff there. It's all packed away right now, though."

"Well, if you manage to reopen it, you should see if you can get at least a few of those old documents from the county clerk." He leaned forward. "Do you know that Miss Poppy was the original owner of that parcel of the Sontag land? All the rest of it, that big section that the family donated to augment Clary State Park, was homesteaded later. But those thirty acres belonged to her."

Gessie whistled. "No kidding."

He pointed at her. "Not only that, but she *gave* the land to Blake's great-great-grandfather."

I frowned. "Why would she do that?"

He shrugged. "No idea."

"So it wasn't the original homestead like we thought."
Sliding down off the wagon, I said, "It would be a travesty
if they cut up the property that used to belong to our town's
namesake into half-acre lots and built a bunch of cracker-
box houses on it." I shuddered. "Ugh."

Larken was nodding, a thoughtful look on her face. I'd
liked the idea of her buying that land before, but now I
wanted to get out the pom-poms and cheer her on.

"The water rights are a big deal, too," Colby said. "Especially with the drought. I'd have to do more research,
but in chatting with the clerk it sounds like the owner
might be able to tap into the aquifer under that parcel and
sell the water to another county. It would take some doing
to get approved, but it's possible."

I gaped. "Oh no. That's even worse than putting houses
there!"

Gessie kicked at one of the wagon wheels. When she
looked up, her eyes were bitter. "Who's to say someone
couldn't buy the place and do both?"

Dash met me at the gate to the Enchanted Garden.
Night-blooming nicotiana sweetened the air around
us as I followed him down the path. Nabby watched us
from his red velvet bed in the window of Scents & Nonsense, the faint light from the display cases behind him
blurring the outline of his soft gray fur.

Sinking down to the moss beneath the stained-glass
birdbath, I scritched behind the corgi's foxy ears. He

panted hot breath, his eyes half-closed in bliss. They
squeezed shut when I dug my fingers into the lighter-
colored ruff along his shoulders. The fairy saddle, so they
said, where the wee ones sat upon their corgi steeds. Finally, he rolled onto his back, and I folded my arms behind
my head and reclined beside him to gaze up at the sky.

Clear as could be, with no hint of fog or the rain that
should have preceded it. The stars that glittered across
the black sea of night made me think of the fairy daisies
scattered across the meadow behind my house.

And the white doe.

Had it been the same one? Could there possibly be
more than one?

Joyoussss.

Had that been my imagination? I didn't think so, but
the episode in the willows was so otherworldly, I could
have been caught up in the moment.

But I didn't think I had. The vibrant energy of that
place, the impression there was something going on right
in front of me that was contained in the same space but
somehow in another aspect of reality that I didn't have
full access to, was *familiar* because I so often felt it in
this very garden.

"The fog called her name," I said out loud. "Or if not
the fog, something did. I swear it really happened, Dash."

He snuffled and adjusted his head on the moss. The
hoo . . . hoo . . . hoo of a great horned owl echoed from
the direction of the river. The oak leaves sighed. A colony
of bats fluttered overhead. The hollow gourd bird feeder
knocked against its post three times.

Thock.

Thock.

Thock.

From very far away I thought I heard a high-pitched giggle.

Clouds scudded across the sky, winking out the stars as if blowing out candle flames.

I sat up, and looked at my dog. A gentle snore escaped his slightly open mouth, and his paws twitched as he ran through his dreams.

Larken hadn't seen the fog in the willows, not like I had. A woman, a wildcrafter, who was so in touch with nature, she hadn't thought the late-blooming mock orange was more than an anomaly. She hadn't seen what was in the fog, or heard the voiceless naming of Blake's sister.

But I had. Whether I wanted to deny it or not, I really had.

My bet was that Joyous had heard the voices, too. And who knew what else she'd witnessed there. Because whatever they were, they weren't my . . . spirits? I just happened to be constitutionally tuned in to them. Still, I recognized they weren't looking for me.

They were looking for her.

Recently or perhaps a long time ago, she had sensed them. It had scared the bejesus out of her. Now the land was fenced off like a military base, and she was doing everything she could to pawn the land off on someone else. She wanted to be rid of it so badly she'd probably be willing give it away if she had to.

Would she also be willing to murder her own brother

if he was against selling it? Because according to Tanner Spence and Polly the real estate agent, Blake had wanted to keep that land in the family.

I sighed and pushed myself to my feet. Dash peered up at me though one slitted eyelid but decided whatever I was doing didn't require his assistance at the moment. I left him under the birdbath and went to unlock the sliding door to the shop.

Inside, I retrieved a bottle of hyacinth oil to put into my home diffuser that night. I had a feeling I was going to need a little extra nudge into sleep. As I passed the phone, I saw two voice mails had been left after Maggie closed at six o'clock. I pushed the button and listened. The first one was a sales pitch for a new kind of credit card processing service. Usually that kind of thing came in e-mail. I deleted it and waited for the second message. The sound of wind over the mouth of a bottle wasn't as loud as last time, but it told me who'd called before I heard his voice.

"Hey, Elliana. It's Ritter. Tried your cell, but no answer. Took a chance you might be working late. Sat phone's working a lot better now, but still expensive as sin, so I have to be careful. Tell you what—I'll call your cell tomorrow at, let's see, eight o'clock in the morning." A voice in the background then, and the rustle of clothing. "Okay. Gotta go. Talk to you later. Bye."

I stood there for almost a minute, staring down at the bottle of oil nestled in my palm. There hadn't been any static to make me wonder what he was saying this time. Or what he wasn't saying. He'd sounded almost businesslike.

Maybe he was in a roomful of colleagues, I argued with myself. *A bunch of scientists that don't want to hear about his personal life. That he's making a six-dollar-a-minute call in the first place is something, right?*

I knew one thing, though: It had been a woman's voice that summoned him off the phone.

Pulling my cell out of my purse, I saw he had indeed called, though he hadn't left a message. I'd missed it because I was busy giving Spence a demonstration on how to use Gamma's alembic to distill essential oil.

CHAPTER 16

SHOULDERS slumped, I went back outside and locked the door. Dash came to his feet as I went by him, and his toenails clicked on the stone path behind me as we walked to my house. Inside, I fed him some kibble and then made myself a decadent grilled cheese sandwich loaded with sharp cheddar, thinly sliced pears, and a slathering of Major Grey's chutney. Dash got a bite of the crust for his dessert as I washed down the last of my hard cider. I put the kettle on to boil and went up to don my oldest, softest pair of cotton pajamas. Back downstairs, I grabbed my nature journal and the library book on botanical drawing Maria had given me, and settled onto the love seat with a cup of steaming chamomile tea.

I opened my journal-in-progress, which was still mostly blank, to a random page and began to try to sketch the tule fog that had surrounded me only hours before. After a few minutes, I sighed and put the charcoal pencil down. I so wanted my journal to be as nice as Gamma's, as rich with meaning and the passion that I felt for plants and their scents. Instead, it looked like a ten-year-old had been doodling during class.

How the heck were you supposed to draw fog, anyway? It was like drawing air. A real artist could do it, but despite my aspirations, I was no artist. Not to mention, the fog I wanted to draw held mysterious whispers, quiet delight, and the scent of bubble gum.

I flipped through the book Maria had given me. It was a nice primer on botanical accuracy in drawing and enumerated the standard practices for precise rendering with an emphasis on science. On a whim, I checked the index and found a reference to *Atropa belladonna* on page 160.

It was a beautiful picture of the plant. Grabbing my notebook again, I turned to a fresh page and tried to copy it. I managed a decent-looking drawing of a berry and one of the flowers. At least they were recognizable. Then I put my journal aside and rose to retrieve Gamma's.

Honestly, her rendering of deadly nightshade was better than the one in the library book.

After another long look at the list of how the poison affected its victim, I flipped a few pages.

And stopped.

Dash looked up from his bed by the door when I laughed out loud. Of course, Gamma had managed to draw the fog with no problem, and using only a plain lead pencil. She'd captured the energy of the swirls, the cool humidity, and there—a face that wasn't a face, like finding a pattern in a cloud or within the full moon.

Even better was the outline of a deer peeking around the right side of the page. Just an outline on the paper, leaving the doe herself perfectly white.

I shook my head in wonder, even as the shiver ran down my back. "Gamma, you are something else."

Opposite the doe, she'd inscribed a poem along the side of the page.

Of Pan we sing, the best of leaders, Pan,
That leads the Naiads and the Dryads forth,
And to their dances more than Hermes can.
Hear, O you groves, and hills resound his worth.

—BEN JONSON

Naiads and dryads. The nymphs of spring water and trees.

Of course.

AFTER downing the relaxing tea and with the hyacinth oil lazily filling the air around my bed, I thought I'd drift off in no time. But no such luck. As soon as I lay down with Dash curled by my side, thoughts of murder began to ricochet around my brain.

Well, not murder. Murderers. Possible ones, at least.

Finally, I gave up, turned on the light, and reached into my bedside table for a pen and paper. I would write down the suspects in Blake's death in order to clear my mind enough for some nice, peaceful sheep counting. Taking a deep breath, I started in.

Felicity Donovan. Hated Blake for ruining her career, had access to his room. Access to deadly nightshade?

But she had an alibi, which Lupe would have surely checked by now.

Joyous Sontag. Blake stood in the way of her selling the family land. He likely would have let her into his room. Has a key to the gate and so has access to the deadly nightshade on her own property. Larken may have heard them arguing on the telephone the night he was poisoned.

A part of me appreciated the ironic possibility that Joyous had used a poisonous plant from the very land her brother wanted to keep and she wanted to get rid of, but the idea of a sister killing her brother made me ill.

Panama Hat aka Vaughn. Argued with Blake in the Horseshoe Bar the night Blake died. It was possible he was interested in buying the Sontag property, and Blake stood in his way.

Who else?

Any number of people who Blake had crossed or cursed or betrayed that I don't know about.

Which was really just a way to put off the obvious next person on the list. I bit my lip and made myself write it anyway.

Tanner Spence. Hated Blake for taking over his pet project. And probably hated him on principle if he had to work closely with the guy. *Was staying in the same hotel. Admitted to going inside the fenced property, so would have access to the deadly nightshade.*

The guy didn't know anything about plants, though. It seemed unlikely he'd use one as a murder weapon. Or had he been playing up his ignorance? I mean, everyone knew what plain old sweet basil looked like, didn't they? Hadn't the guy ever eaten a caprese salad?

Reluctantly, I added, *May possess more horticultural knowledge than he lets on.*

I tapped the pen against my teeth, thinking. Who were the "interested parties" the real estate agent had referred to? Could any of them want to purchase the land—to develop, or God forbid, to sell the water underneath it— enough to kill Blake for taking it off the market?

Putting the pad and pen away, I turned the light out again.

Why would anyone commit murder, really? Because they wanted something. Money. Love. To protect someone else, or even to maintain the status quo. It was the same reason anyone does anything.

That thought triggered a question on another front: What did I want from my relationship with Ritter?

I fell asleep without a clear answer.

T HE sky was a brilliant red when I took my morning coffee out to the garden.

Red sky at night, sailor's delight.
Red sky at morning, sailors take warning.

Then again, there wasn't any sailing around Poppyville, so I was simply going to enjoy the beautiful view.

I grabbed my harvesting basket and clippers and headed to one of the overflowing herb beds. I'd worked like a madwoman getting the Enchanted Garden ready for Blake Sontag's arrival, but I hadn't been able to spend much time in its soothing atmosphere over the last few days. Yesterday's distillation demonstration for Spence hadn't involved the usual quiet ritual of most of my perfume making, either. So this morning I wanted to try an essential oil extraction method that I'd recently read about.

The article that had mentioned the process called it enfleurage, but it didn't sound like traditional French enfleurage at all. That method involved immersing very delicate blooms, such as jasmine, into a solid oil. Then the more stable fat absorbed the essence without the use of heat. It was an ancient practice, but tedious.

What I wanted to try was quite different, a salt extraction technique that also took time, but didn't involve the use of animal fat.

I'd decided to use a single herb for this experiment, and one that I regularly distilled by steam so that I could compare the final results. The lemon thyme plants were looking big and beautiful and would perfectly serve my purpose. Stepping carefully around a tiny stone house surrounded by a miniature mosaic patio and plantings of moss, trimmed angel vine, and rosy succulents, I snipped and clipped the herbal mounds, keeping them neat as I gradually filled my basket.

When I was finished, I went into Scents & Nonsense and dug around in my production area until I found the ancient two-quart ceramic crock I'd picked up at a thrift store. It was glazed plain dark brown and squatted on the counter like Jabba the Hutt, but as soon as I'd seen it, I'd known it would be useful.

Nabby jumped up on the counter and *mrow*ed plaintively. His next move would be full on head-butts against any part of my anatomy he could reach, and as much as I loved him, cat hair wasn't recommended as part of the preparation for any kind of essential oil extraction.

"Okay, okay," I said, abandoning the pile of lemon thyme that was already scenting the air in the shop. "Come on."

I fed him on his place mat in the office and turned on the computer as long as I was in there. A glance at the phone revealed no messages had come in overnight. Returning to my workstation, I took my cell out of my pocket and made sure the ringer was on.

It was almost seven o'clock. Ritter would be calling in another hour.

I mulled over what I was going to say to him as I stripped the leaves and tender stems off the woodier branches of the thyme. The twigs went into the trash can, where they would continue to lend their pungency to the atmosphere of the shop. The leaves I layered on the bottom of the crock. Then I sprinkled a layer of coarse salt, followed by more thyme, another layer of salt, and so on until the crock was full. Carefully covering it with plastic cling wrap to make it airtight, I topped it with the lid and placed the crock in an unobtrusive spot on a back windowsill, where the sunlight could warm it during part of the day.

I'd leave it there for a month. The fresh herb would gradually disintegrate into a mush of organic matter, but the salt would prevent mold or bacteria from forming. Then I'd strain the liquid though muslin, and let it sit for another month to six weeks. The idea was that the essential oil would separate from the liquid, and I could skim it off. It was a lengthy process, but if it worked it would be a good way to extract oil from delicate plant material that didn't hold up well to the heat of steam distillation.

After tidying my work area, I went into the restroom to wash the strong scent of thyme off my hands. As I was drying them on a towel, a loud banging startled me. I came out and peered around the corner of a tall display of pressed-flower greeting cards, but there wasn't anyone at the front door. Colby's Westfalia was parked in front, though.

The back door slid open behind me, and he came inside. "There you are."

"Good Lord," I said. "Do you know what time it is?"

He nodded. "I know you're an early riser, and I wanted to talk to you."

I searched for the typical glint of humor in his expression, but didn't see it. "You okay?" I asked.

"Sure."

"Let me get some coffee going," I said.

My brother went outside to the garden as it brewed, and I watched him through the window. His hair stuck out from under his baseball hat, and his beard looked like it had grown half an inch in the short time since he'd been back in town. He wore his usual jeans and boots, today with an untucked chambray shirt with frayed cuffs. Standing on the edge of the patio by the birdbath, he jammed his hands into his pockets in a gesture I recognized as frustration.

But I couldn't get a better hit from him than that. For some reason I'd always had trouble picking up on the feelings of my half siblings and my dad. My stepmother's emotions, on the other hand, were obvious to anyone in her vicinity.

Dash brought my brother a tennis ball, and Colby tossed it down the path. The corgi took off at a dead run, snatched the toy out of the air on a bounce, pivoted, and was back for more within seconds. I was glad to see a grin finally break out on Colby's face.

I filled a couple of mugs and took them outside. We settled into rockers in the cool of the morning.

"Where's Larken?" I asked.

"She's at the barn, exercising some horses for Gessie. She's in heaven."

"Your girlfriend does seem to like horses. She told me about working on the CSA farms—and about how you kept meeting up by accident over the last year."

"Hmm." He took a sip of coffee.

"And knowing you as I do, I wondered whether you two mysteriously showing up in the same places three times in a row might not have been as purely serendipitous as she thinks."

He grinned mischievously.

I rolled my eyes. "You followed her!"

"Of course I followed her. In case you hadn't noticed, she's awesome." Then the smile dropped from his face.

"And now she's a murder suspect. I'm so sorry, hon. I bet you wish you hadn't come back to Poppyville at all."

He fell silent, and I felt regret twist in my solar plexus. *My regret or his?*

"Is that what you wanted to talk to me about?" I asked.

"Oh." He waved his hand. "I didn't want to talk about anything in particular. Just haven't spent any time alone with my sis yet."

That was true, but I knew he had something on his mind.

"I saw the van out front," I said. "Don't you have to pack everything up, even if you're just driving across town?"

"Yeah." He sighed and looked over at Dash, who was nosing at the lime-colored tendrils of moneywort spilling out of a pot of annuals at the edge of the patio.

"That's kind of a hassle, isn't it?"

His eyes cut to me, then back to Dash.

"Yes." .

I chose my words carefully. "Seems like there are a lot of disadvantages to living in the Westfalia."

Turning, he regarded me with scarcely concealed frustration. "Yeah, but there are a lot of advantages, too."

I smiled and nodded.

"You, too? I thought you'd be on my side, but now you're going to try to convince me to sell my van and settle down, too."

"Nah. I'm not going to try to convince you of anything. I'd never try to make you do something you don't want to do."

He settled back into his chair, slightly mollified.

"So what is it that you do want?" I asked.

"Freedom," he said instantly. It was a knee-jerk answer he'd given a hundred times. As a child he'd always chafed under routine. For a while we'd thought he had ADD, but really he simply didn't like to be stuck inside four walls all day long. College had been better for him, with its variable schedule and opportunities to explore different interests. Wynn and I had understood, but Dad still thought Colby would grow up and get a real job.

Unlikely.

I watched him through the steam rising from my mug until he met my eyes. "Seems to me that there are a lot of different kinds of freedom."

His lips pressed together, conflict written all over his face. "You know Lark wants to stay here and buy that place."

I carefully raised one shoulder and let it drop, hardly able to breathe.

Suddenly he stood, and Dash scrambled backward. Colby turned and looked down at me. "She said something about different kinds of freedom, too. The freedom of having land of my own, not having to answer to anyone, living off the grid." His eyes narrowed accusingly. "That sounds like something you'd say."

"That sounds a lot like freedom to me," I sidestepped. "But it might not be the kind you want."

He paced to the edge of the patio and looked out toward Kestrel Peak. Then spun around and came back, dropping into the rocker beside me. "Actually, it does appeal to me. But it's hard, you know? I mean, I've been so adamant about the nomadic life. And I do love it. It's just . . ." He trailed off.

"It's been three years," I said. "And there's this woman you seem to be pretty enamored with."

"Yeah."

"And you know darn well she's not going to live in that van with you forever."

He sighed. "Yeah." His palms scrubbed at his face. "Yeah," he said again. "I guess I just needed to talk it out." His hands dropped, and his gaze snagged mine. "Thanks, Ellie."

My lips turned up. "No charge."

"So what do *you* want?" he asked.

I blinked. "What? Oh. Well, I have everything I want. My dream business, this garden, my tiny house. I love my life."

"What about companionship?"

Frowning, I considered my little brother. He suddenly seemed a lot more grown-up than I'd given him credit for.

"I have lots of friends." But I knew what he was getting at. "And Ritter, of course." I looked at my watch. "He's going to be calling in about twenty minutes."

"Must be hard with him gone."

"Harder than I thought it would be," I admitted.

"Because . . . ?"

I thought about that. "He's good company. Makes me feel good. It's . . . nice."

"Nice? Jeez."

"Hey, I didn't mean—"

"Nuh-uh. I know exactly what you mean. And maybe that's all you want right now."

"Maybe," I said. *No.*

"But you can't even have that if he's not here."

I drained my mug and set it on the nearby table. "Have you been talking to Astrid?"

"No. Why?"

"Never mind."

"My point is just that you should figure out what you want and go for it. I did it when I quit the brokerage and took off in the van, and it sure looks like I'm about to do it again with Larken—whether she buys that land south of town or not." He reached over and squeezed my shoulder.

I covered his hand with my own, and smiled. "I want Ritter to finish his project and come back. It's only five more months. That's a drop of time in a lifetime."

He looked skeptical. "And then what?"

I blinked.

"Seriously. Is he going stay here after that project? Or will there be another one? And then another one? He's been doing this awhile, hasn't he?"

"I . . . I suppose there might be more," I stammered.

"And are you going to go with him? No, you are not. I know you, Ellie. You love this place. It would kill you to leave Poppyville. So does that mean you'll end up here by yourself every time Ritter goes to work?"

I stood up and checked my watch again. "I don't know. Maybe he'll find something closer. Maybe I'll go visit him. Maybe it won't work out at all. We'll figure it out when the time comes, but for now we're doing this long-distance thing as best we know how." I took a shaky breath. "Maybe it will get easier."

He rose as well. "I hope so, Ellie. You deserve every happiness, big sis." He handed me his coffee mug. "Now I need to get back to the stables and have a chat with Larken. If she's really going to make an offer on the

Sontag place, she needs to do it right away. The real estate agent told her there are other—"

"Interested parties," I chanted at the same time he said it.

But were any of them murderers?

CHAPTER 17

COLBY left, and I took my cell out to the Enchanted
Garden. I wanted the tranquil vibes of my favorite
plants around me for this call. I settled into a chair between the climbing rose and the jasmine vine that wended
around a small obelisk by the fence.

The phone rang at eight o'clock on the dot, and my
heart beat a little faster.

"Hello?"

"Elliana!" Ritter said. "Finally. It's been such a pain
getting this satellite phone to work. Turns out it works
better certain times of the day, which makes sense, I guess,
since the satellite is in orbit and all."

"Hi there," I said, amused by his rambling. It wasn't
like him at all.

Silence, then, "So how are you?"

"How long can you talk?" I asked.

A rosy finch launched off the thistle seed feeder and flew over to land on the top of the stone obelisk beside me. His bright eyes regarded me with curiosity.

Ritter made a noise in the back of his throat. "Only a few minutes, I'm afraid."

Dang it.

"We have e-mail set up on the computers now, though. I might only be able to call a couple times a week, but we can stay in more frequent touch that way. And a couple of others on the team are planning to video chat with their families once in a while, so I'm going to look into that." He paused. "This being apart blows."

I laughed at his wry tone. "It really does!"

"I miss you like sin. Actually, I miss the sinning, too."

I swore I could feel my heart swelling in my chest. "Me, too." I realized I was grinning like an idiot. "How's the project coming along?"

"I can tell you all about that in e-mail. I want to know about this new murder you've become involved with."

"You heard?"

"Thea told me."

"Thea," I said. "Oh. Right." Of course he'd called his sister.

"I have to say, I was stunned when I heard it was Blake Sontag who was killed."

"You knew him, then. I wondered," I said.

"We were actually close friends our senior year in high school. He was funny, and a heck of a ladies' man. Not a bad gig, being his wingman."

I resisted the urge to ask for details. There would be time for that later. Instead, I asked, "He was really funny?" It was hard to keep the skepticism out of my voice.

"Hilarious. Like, life-of-the-party hilarious."

"That sure doesn't sound like the guy I met," I said. "Did you stay in touch with him after school?"

"For a while, yeah. But he grew obsessed with becoming a big success, and Good Time Blake disappeared. He was all about getting ahead and making a name for himself."

"Yeah, that sounds more like him." *Even if it meant stepping over—or on—other people.*

"You know, it's too bad, because I don't think he was doing it for himself," Ritter said. "His dad was always pushing him to do better and be more. Blake revered him and craved his approval."

"Hmm. His parents both died a few years ago," I said. "A sudden, tragic accident."

Ritter whistled. "I didn't know that. That must have been devastating. Mr. Sontag was a demanding father, but they were really close."

Cynthia had mentioned how much Blake had changed. From what Ritter was telling me now, it sounded like part of that change was to please his father. However, losing his dad might have made him into the bitter curmudgeon I'd had dinner with. Bitter, but also suffering from insomnia—and possibly hypochondria according to Rhonda. I felt a flicker of real pity for the dead man.

"What about his sister, Joyous? Did you know her, too?"

"Not really," he said. "Now what's all this about your brother's girlfriend being a suspect? Thea didn't give me many details."

As quickly as possible, I filled him in. When I was done,

the only sound was static for a few seconds. Then he said, "I understand why you've jumped into investigating Blake's murder with both feet, but I can't help worrying."

"Oh, I'll be—" I began.

"Seriously," he broke in. "Promise me you'll be careful, Elliana. Remember what happened last time you took it upon yourself to track down a murderer."

That sobered me. In trying to clear my own name, I'd come close to being killed myself.

"I promise," I said quietly.

"Good. I couldn't handle it if something happened to you," Ritter said.

My throat tightened. "You be careful up there in the wilds, too, mister. I don't want to hear about any frostbite or caribou attacks, okay?"

He laughed, and soon we were murmuring a few last sweet nothings before his allotted time on the phone was up, and we had to ring off.

I sat in the garden for a while, thinking. I felt happier, but if anything, his absence felt sharper after our conversation. Ritter had been a stabilizing part of my life for months, and I missed his smile, his touch, his wry wit— heck, pretty much every single thing about him. And even before our friendship had bloomed into romance, he'd been a huge help when I was investigating Josie's murder.

I stood and brushed a bit of pollen off my sleeve. Astrid had played a big role in that case, and she was willing and able to help me prove Larken innocent now.

I might ache with missing Ritter, but I was an independent, capable woman in charge of her own life. I'd be fine.

Right?

* * *

A STRID looked up from where she was arranging oatmeal lace cookies studded with dried dandelion petals. Today she wore a loose, tie-dyed top over Thai fishing pants and Birkenstocks. Her copper hair was pulled back into a frizzy bun. I'd told her about my conversation with Ritter as soon as she'd come into Scents & Nonsense.

"So you're really going through with this long-distance thing."

I looked at the ceiling and counted to seven before saying, "I said I was before. You didn't believe me?"

She shrugged. "No. I did. I mean, you're as loyal as they come, Ellie. I guess I'm still surprised that you're in such a difficult relationship after having to put up with Harris for so long."

"The circumstances might be difficult, but the relationship isn't." I heard the defensive note in my voice.

"Right. I stand corrected," she said with a grin, and turned away to put the plate of cookies over by the coffee urn.

She set it down and looked up at me. "We all just want what's best for you, Ellie."

"I get it, and that's nice, but how would you like it if I— Say, how did your date go last night?"

"Ooh, he's hot! In fact . . ." She trailed off, and her face turned pink. "I think I'll keep the details to myself."

"I only want what's best for you," I said with a grin.

She stuck her tongue out at me.

Laughing, I looked out at her ancient Peugeot parked on Corona Street. "Who's in the back of your car?" She only drove it when she was hauling animals—or people. Otherwise Astrid made her way around town on her bike. At present, a square-headed dog was hanging his head out the window.

"That's Charlie," she said. "He's an American bulldog I'm taking care of today and tonight."

"You're boarding him at your house?" I asked.

"Yup. I don't have to go into Dr. Ericcson's today, so I thought I'd give Charlie a nice long walk in the park after I dropped off your cookies this morning."

"Any chance he'd like to hang out in the Enchanted Garden with Dash for a while?"

Her eyes lit up. "He's a good boy. I'm sure we could leave him out there. Are we going someplace?"

A glance at my watch confirmed it was nearly ten. I grimaced. "Actually, I was hoping you could watch the store for an hour or so this morning."

Her face fell.

"I want to have another chat with Joyous Sontag," I explained.

She raised an eyebrow. "Because the last one went so well?"

"Hmm. You're right about that. But I took Larken with me to see that parcel of land last night."

"That's right! How did it go?"

You mean besides the naiads and dryads and albino deer? How about the bubble gum tule fog that wasn't supposed to be there and no one else saw?

"Fine. In fact, Larken might want to make an offer on the place."

Astrid's eyes grew round. "You're kidding!"

I shook my head.

"Darn it! Does that mean she and Colby are breaking up?"

"I don't think that's going to happen. And there's nothing definite yet about Larken buying that land." I leaned my elbows onto the counter next to the register. "But, Astrid, can you imagine? She wants to have a little farm with chickens and goats and bees, and given her love of horses, probably one or two of those, too. The alternative might be a bunch of houses and a dried-up aquifer." I told her what Colby had told us the evening before.

"Ugh," she said. "I like the farm idea a lot better. So that's why you want to talk to Joyous?"

Partly. "Yes. I want to make a case for her selling it to Larken and no one else. And while I'm at it, I'm going to see if she'll tell me who else is interested in buying it. For all I know, the real estate agent was making that part up, but if there is someone who wants that land, then they might also be a suspect in Blake Sontag's murder."

"Ooh. I see what you mean." She gave a decisive nod. "Sure. I'll be happy to watch the shop. Just let me get Charlie out of the car."

While she went to retrieve her charge, I got to work mixing up a custom perfume. To a base of unscented jojoba oil, I added a few drops of frankincense, then sandalwood, and finally neroli. After taking a sniff, I adjusted it with a bit more frankincense, capped the small atomizer bottle, and tested the pump. The air filled with the intense combination of earthy, resinous scents suitable for either a man or a woman to wear.

More to the point, all three scents helped alleviate fear, and while Joyous had a reputation in town for being cranky and antisocial, her general apprehension had been nearly overwhelming when Astrid and I were in her house. It had really come to a head when she spoke of her family land. Now that I'd been there, I had an idea why the place scared her so much. The frankincense was especially effective against ongoing anxiety and fear of other people, while the sandalwood also promoted open-mindedness and acceptance of new ideas.

When I left Scents & Nonsense, Astrid was reading a magazine—she refused to take any payment those times she stepped in to help at the store, so I refused to let her do anything but answer the phone and help customers— and Dash and Charlie were lying on the cool flagstones on the shaded patio as if they'd known each other forever. Nabby glared out at the canine newcomer from where he perched on the windowsill.

All was right with the world inside Scents & Nonsense. It was nice to know, since I had a feeling my next encounter might not go so smoothly.

I was halfway to Agate Park when my cell rang. A glance at the screen told me it was my brother. I thumbed ANSWER.

"Detectives Lang and Garcia were just here," Colby said before I could even manage a hello. "They took Larken!"

"What?" I twisted the steering wheel and screeched to

a stop at the curb. A woman walking her dog across the street gave me a scowl. I ignored her. "They arrested her?"

"I don't think so." His voice was shaking. "At least they didn't say that, and there wasn't any of that Miranda rights stuff. Detective Garcia said they wanted to ask her some more questions."

Damn.

"Okay, I'll give Lupe a call," I said. "In the meantime, sit tight. This might be nothing."

"The police have suspected my girlfriend of murdering Sontag from the get-go, and now they just came and took her away," he said. "It's not *nothing.*"

I couldn't argue with that. "Okay, you're right. Call a lawyer."

"Who?"

"Is Gessie around?"

"She's giving a riding lesson."

"Go ahead and interrupt her. The only criminal lawyers I know of are over in Silver Wells, but she might know of someone closer."

"Okay. Thanks, sis."

"Did you talk to Larken about buying the Sontag land?" I asked, realizing as the words came out of my mouth that if she showed too much interest in it, Larken would be making herself look even more suspicious. So far her only possible motive to kill a man she'd just met was a rather public argument. Flimsy at best. But if the police found out she was trying to buy land that the murder victim had refused to sell . . .

What a mess.

"We were talking about it when the police showed up."

"It's going to be okay," I said with forced cheer. "I promise. I'll call you when I have news."

We hung up, and I thought about the promise I'd just made. I'd do whatever I could to keep it, but what if that wasn't good enough?

It has to be.

Lupe's phone rang three times before going to voice mail. I kept it short.

"Colby says you have Larken. Is she under arrest? We're looking for a lawyer, so hold off on questioning her, okay?" I sighed and ended the call. I knew nothing I said would stop Max Lang from asking as many questions as he wanted.

And Larken, knowing she was innocent and wanting to help, would probably try to do her best to answer them.

It was more important than ever that I find the real killer. And fast.

Joyous Sontag didn't answer my repeated knocking. I pushed the doorbell several times, as well, to no avail. Was she avoiding me? It seemed extremely unlikely that she wouldn't be home.

Leaning close to the door, I called, "Joyous? It's just Ellie. Will you please talk to me?"

Nothing.

Pressing my forehead against the door in frustration, I tried again. "Please come to the door. Polly at Gold Rush Realty took me out to see your family land, and . . ." I trailed off.

"And what?" The sharp reply came from behind me.

I whirled to find Joyous standing by the corner of the house, watching me with a critical eye. She wore khakis stained at the knee in a way that would be familiar to any gardener. A straw hat balanced jauntily on her dark hair, and she held a trowel in one gloved hand.

I stepped down and crunched across the gravel landscape to where she stood. "And I think I have an idea why you want to sell the place so badly."

"Do you want to buy it?" she asked, a glint of eagerness in her gaze.

A small shake of my head turned that eagerness to disappointment.

"Then we have nothing to discuss." She turned away and started back around the corner.

"My friend might want to buy it, though."

Joyous stopped and said over her shoulder. "Have her talk to Polly."

"She already has. But I want to talk to you about it."

She whirled back around. "What is your problem, Allbright? Why do you feel like you need to invade my privacy? Why do you want to talk to me about a real estate transaction that you aren't involved in and that an agency is handling?"

Taking a deep breath, I said, "Because the Realtor took me out to see the place last evening."

CHAPTER 18

Joyous' eyes narrowed. I felt her fear, but also an ember of hope flaring to life. Wordlessly, I reached into my purse and drew out the bottle of perfume I'd made for her. I held it out toward her.

"Smell this."

She glared at me, but it seemed more habitual than heartfelt. After a few seconds of hesitation, she set the trowel on a landscape rock, took off her gloves, and stuffed them in her back pocket. Then she reached for the bottle in my hand. Grudgingly, she pushed the atomizer down.

And blinked. Then her eyes closed, and she deeply inhaled the fragrance. I could smell it from where I stood, too, and felt the unraveling of fear that left behind curiosity and possibility.

Joyous Sontag opened her eyes and smiled.

Smiled.

Barely keeping my mouth from dropping open, I said, "That's for you."

The smile dropped away as if she'd suddenly realized it was on her face. But I'd seen it.

"Why?"

"Because it's what I do," I said.

She looked down at the bottle in her hand, then took one last whiff and screwed the cap back on. "I don't understand."

"You know I own Scents and Nonsense, right?"

She nodded. "The gift shop."

"Mm-hm. But also aromatherapy products, and I make custom perfumes." I pointed. "Like that."

She looked confused. "But I didn't ask—"

I waved it away. "It suits you, and it's a gift. Now, about your land . . ."

Her lips pursed as she considered me, but she finally relented. "You'd better come on back."

She led me around the side of the house, which was landscaped like the front with rocks and cacti. A narrow paved driveway ran along the other side, ending at an old, wooden, single-car garage that backed up to the alley. She stopped and opened a gate in the fence. We stepped through.

And I stopped still.

The backyard was completely different from the front. There still wasn't any lawn, and stone paths crisscrossed the forty-by-forty-foot area. In between them was a neat row of raised beds, each planted to overflowing with vegetables. The lettuce and spinach bed had a shade cloth protecting it, but the sun-loving plants stretched toward the sky on trellises and poles. Asian yard-long beans swung from a conical teepee, nudged by the breeze. Wide-leaved vines sprawled over the edges of their containers and crept across the pathways, studded with ripening butternut, acorn, and pumpkin squash. Root vegetables grew down into the earth while their chlorophyll-loving tops basked in the light.

Nightshades were scattered throughout, the species separate enough so as not to interfere with one another's pollination. Not deadly nightshade. Not *Atropa bella-donna*, but those in the common *Solanaceae* family that were also considered nightshades: tomatoes and peppers, eggplants and potatoes, and, in a corner by the fence, a lone tomatillo boasted its husk-covered fruit.

"This is amazing," I breathed.

Another smile threatened to creep onto Joyous' face, but she tamed it in time. "I don't trust the crap you buy in stores, so I grow my own."

I managed not to laugh. She might believe that, but she loved this garden. It was a soothing, nurtured, and nurturing space, but it didn't have the hidden throb of energy that the Enchanted Garden did.

Or that the land she was trying to sell possessed.

Without asking, I marched over and sat down at the small table outside the back door. More slowly, she settled in opposite me. There would be no offers of coffee or lemonade coming. Joyous wasn't as agitated as the previous day, but she still wasn't comfortable.

"My friend Larken might be making an offer on your land," I said. "I don't think she's had a chance to yet, but she's very interested."

I watched her closely to see if the name rang a bell. However, it didn't appear that Max Lang had revealed the name of his prime suspect in Blake's death.

"Well, she'd better hurry up, then," Joyous said.

Hard to negotiate a real estate deal when you're being held by the police for murder.

She continued. "Polly tells me there are two other people who are very interested in development."

I cringed. "Development? Really? It's a magical place, Joyous. You can't let someone just go in there and raze the land to make it into a creepy little suburb of Poppyville."

"Frankly, I don't care what they do with the place," she said through gritted teeth.

Sitting back in my chair, I regarded her with a frown. "Larken wants to have a farm there. Grow her own food like you do." I waved my hand. "Sustainable, and without damaging the land."

"Whoever is willing to take it off my hands first, wins," she said.

"What about whoever is willing to pay more?" I asked.

She shrugged.

I squinted. "Blake didn't want to sell. Polly said you had it listed, and then he came back to Poppyville and found out and took it off the market. Were you actually trying to sell it out from under him?"

"I would have given him the money," she said, picking at a sliver working its way loose from the wooden table. "Blake only cared about that place when my dad was alive. He never came back here. Then he shows up to interview you, finds out I'm selling, and throws a fit. Accused me of fraud, said he wanted it for his heirs." She snorted. "As if he'd ever settle down."

"Fraud?" I seized on the word. "My dad told me that your father arranged it so you owned it in common, right? So you would have had to forge your brother's signature if it sold."

She shrugged again.

"Joyous," I said as gently as I could manage. "Why do you want to be rid of it so badly?"

A squirrel ran across the yard. She watched it instead of looking at me.

"Why is it fenced like Fort Knox?"

Still no answer. Anxiety rose within her like a tide.

"Joyous."

She wouldn't look at me.

"When I was there last night, the tule fog came."

I waited. Seconds ticked by.

Finally, she turned her head and met my eyes. Her own were full of wonder. "You saw the fog?"

Nodding, I said carefully. "Thick, white fog. In August, and with no rain for weeks. I was in the willow grove."

Her breath caught.

"You've seen it, too," I said.

She started to shrug again, but it turned into a tentative nod.

"And the, uh, presence? The ones who live there?"

Her eyes filled and her throat worked.

I sat quietly until she got herself under control again.

"I always thought I was crazy," she whispered.

Shaking my head, I said, "Nope. Not crazy. In tune,

for sure, though." I paused, choosing my words. "It's a friendly place, you know. They're friendly. It was a strange experience, but I felt happiness and joy in the fog, too."

A tear splashed down her cheek. "My parents used to take us camping there as kids. Blake loved it." She took a shaky breath. "But he never saw the fog. They didn't, either. Only me. They laughed. They told me I wasn't right in the head, that I was seeing things." She gulped. "After a while, I came to believe it myself."

My heart ached for this woman. She was like me, able to see a little further, a little more than most people. My mother and gamma had assured me that my intuitive sense of smell and empathy was a gift. For a long time, I'd taken it for granted. But Joyous had been ridiculed and belittled, so she'd withdrawn into herself.

No wonder she avoided people and never smiled.

I plunged on. "I think the, uh, spirits? That are there in the willow grove? I think they might be naiads and dryads."

She stared at me like I was crazy now.

In for a penny . . . "See, my gamma kept a journal, and in it I found something she recorded about them. The picture she drew beside the entry—it was of the fog, the willows, and the white deer."

Joyous had been hanging on my every word, but now she interrupted. "White deer?"

"You never saw a white deer?"

She shook her head.

"Hmm. Yeah. That might just be mine, since I saw it near my house, too. Anyway, there in the trees, with the spring underneath, I think that place is protected by their presence—whatever you want to call them." I paused, wondering if I should tell her the rest. I made a decision.

"At first, I think they thought I was you. The voices in the fog called your name. Well, they were sort of voices."

She blanched. Swallowed. "Really?" she whispered.

"I heard it." I reached my hand out and touched her wrist with my fingertips. She stared at it but didn't pull away. "That's happened before, hasn't it?"

Her head jerked up. "When we were camping." Her jaw worked. "And then it all happened again a couple years ago. I thought I'd imagined it all as a child, and I went back out there to prove to myself that I was normal after all." She blinked away tears. "But they came again, and called my name, and I knew I was really and truly insane. I fenced off the whole shebang right after that."

"There was no one you could tell," I said.

"No one."

"Including Blake."

Her look was enough answer.

Standing, I put my hands on my hips. "Well, honey, you aren't crazy. Not at all. You have a gift, like I do. That thing with the perfume? Let's just say it's a knack I have. And those spirits protecting your land out there? They're good. You know that, right?"

She looked torn.

"They are. Trust me. And now you want to sell that land to a developer who is going to cut down those trees and suck out the water." I looked at the sky, then back at her. "If you allow that, you would be destroying them."

Her chin came up, and, as our eyes locked, I realized a part of her knew that. The part that was scared of what she'd experienced. The part that thought it might make her believe she wasn't nuts. We stared at each other for a long time.

"You really did see them," she said at last.

I sat back down. "And heard them."

"Why?"

I blinked. "What?"

"Why you? Why no one else?"

Now it was my turn to shrug. "I don't know. But you should come to the Enchanted Garden behind my shop. It has the same kind of vibe."

"Enchanted Garden?" she snorted.

My face reddened. "I only call it that because of the fairy tableaus I've placed throughout the place. You know, miniature gardens and furniture and winged figurines?"

"Seriously?"

"Yes, seriously. But it does have a vibe. You need to come see it. You'll know right away what I mean." I waved my hand. "Anyway, about the land. Are you positive you want to sell it?"

She hesitated. "I'm not sure now."

Sorry, Larken. And yet, I was happy to hear it.

"Will you tell me who else is interested in buying it?" I asked.

Her head tipped to the side. "Why?"

"Or just tell me whether any of the, uh, currently interested parties, as Polly likes to say, were interested before Blake came back and took the place off the market?"

Joyous frowned and asked again, "Why?"

Lord, she was stubborn. I felt time trickling away. Had

Colby found a lawyer? For all I knew Max had officially arrested Larken by now.

I unclenched my jaw and said, "Because if they wanted to buy your land, and then Blake came back to town and nixed any chance of a sale, then that could be a motive for murder."

Her lips parted in surprise. "Oh! I hadn't thought of that."

"Well, the police have, I bet. And I'm afraid you're on that list, too. The detectives don't know that you want to sell the land that's been in your family for, what, five generations because you saw things there that others can't. They'll think you want the money." I stopped myself from going further, but every antenna I had was aquiver, waiting for her reaction.

"And that I killed my brother for it?" she said, flabbergasted. "I'd never do that!"

"That plant poison they told you killed him? It's atropine. It comes from deadly nightshade—belladonna—and there was nightshade in Blake's tea. Someone gave it to him, and your land has belladonna growing wild all over it. I even found a plant that had been partially harvested. I need to know who's been inside that fence."

I saw her lips form into the beginning of another "why," but when she saw the look on my face, she thought better of it.

"There are only two that I know of," she said. "One is your ex-husband, and the other is Vaughn Newton."

My head silently exploded. *"Harris?"*

And then I saw him in my mind's eye, sitting at the

table with "Vaughn" in the Roux Grill, and then again beside the pool at the Hotel California. From what I knew of my ex's financials, he might be able to mortgage everything he owned to get the land, but there was no way he could afford to develop it.

But what if he could sell the water? Or the water rights?

I rubbed my hands over my face, then looked up. "Vaughn *Newton*?" The name tickled my memory.

Then I had it. Polly had called someone "Mr. Newton" on the phone when she'd gotten out of her Miata to unlock the gate for Larken and me.

Joyous had been watching my face. Now she nodded ruefully. "I can tell you that even if I do sell, it won't be to either of them now. I'd much rather your friend have it."

"Um, there's something you should probably hear from me first."

"What?" The word held dread.

"You know that suspect in your brother's murder that Detective Lang told you about?"

She nodded once, very slowly.

"Well, she's the suspect. My friend. Larken." I held my hand up. "She didn't do it. I know she didn't do it. She barely knew the guy, but they had a little tiff in the restaurant, and the police are under a lot of pressure to solve Blake's case, so they're using her as a scapegoat."

Joyous stared at me. "You're kidding."

"No, I'm not, but really, you have to believe me." I grimaced as I heard the words. I, for one, immediately stopped believing someone the second they said I should.

Her eyes narrowed. Then suddenly she stood up. "Okay. I believe you."

I barely stopped myself from blurting out a "why?" of my own.

"Wait here," she said, and turned toward the screen door that led into the house.

Alarm Klaxons went off in my head. What was she going to do?

"Joyous," I said, scrambling to my feet.

"On second thought, come inside. It might be too windy to show you out here." She turned and went inside.

Puzzled, I followed her through a kitchen with periwinkle walls, white cupboards, and old-school linoleum cracking in one corner. We ended up in the pale and serene living room Astrid and I had been in the day before, just as redolent of lemon. I breathed it in, my curiosity warring with impatience and my worry about Larken.

"Wait here," Joyous said, and went through a hallway and to the stairs. "I'll be right back."

I perched on the tan sofa and hoped my new friend didn't turn out to be as crazy as she'd always thought she was. And that if she was, she didn't own a gun.

A minute later, I heard her on the stairs again. She came into the room holding a shoebox. She sank down on the cushion next to me, opened it, and spread the contents out onto the coffee table.

"I'm choosing to believe you about your friend's innocence because you've convinced me what I saw out by the old homestead was real. And because you can, er, sense things, too."

"Okay," I said, drawing the word out as I tried to make out some of the writing on the pile of papers in front of me.

"I think it might be hereditary."

"What is?" I asked, confused.

"This gift you referred to." She leaned forward and selected a small bundle of folded sheets wrapped with a ribbon. "Ellie, you and I are cousins."

CHAPTER 19

✿

I GAPED. "We're *what*?"

Joyous smiled for the second time that day, maybe that year. I, on the other hand, was too dazed by her statement to do anything but stare at her with my mouth hanging open.

"Apparently we have the same great-great-great-grandfather. Zebulon Hammond."

One of the original founders of the town. Any native of Poppyville worth their salt knew their names.

She went on. "And from what I can figure out, that makes us fifth cousins."

"But . . . but . . . ," I stammered. "But Zebulon . . . my gamma said . . ." I swallowed. "He married Caroline Pickle." Gamma had thoroughly schooled me in her family history when I was a child.

"In 1850."

"Then how could he be related to you?"

The smile turned into a laugh. It was a nice laugh, really. I would have appreciated it more if I hadn't been reeling. "The usual way. He had a relationship with someone else."

Leaning forward, she handed me the packet of letters. "It's all in here. Before he married Caroline, he was, er, involved with another woman. She wouldn't marry him, though, and gave their son to a young couple, the Sontags, to raise."

Hands trembling, I untied the ribbon on the packet of what I now saw were letters, and unfolded the first sheet of paper.

Dearest Pauline,

Though we are not far apart, in truth and candor I think of you every second and must needs communicate my feelings. Your golden hair and sky blue eyes and gaily ringing laugh haunt my waking hours. Please tell me, dearest, that I may call after business hours tonight.

I await your answer.

Your admiring,
Zebulon Hammond

I stared at the spidery script. Stilted, old-fashioned, even a little goofy, but the sentiment was clear. I looked at the names again.

"Hang on," I said. "Pauline? Evening business hours?"

I looked up at Joyous. "My great-great-great-grandfather dated Poppy Thierry? The town madam?"

She nodded, her eyes dancing. "Not just dated. Miss Poppy was my great-great-great-grandmother. Here, let me show you the rest."

One by one, she laid out the letters so that they demonstrated the timeline she described: Zebulon and Pauline's love affair followed by its dissolution, the letter that informed Zebulon that Poppy had given birth to a baby boy after he'd already married Caroline Pickle, and the details of her subsequent foster arrangement with the Sontags.

"She named her son Horace," Joyous said. "That's the name of my great-great-grandfather."

I flopped back against the arm of the sofa, nearly gasping from the sudden influx of new information.

"So see how we're cousins?" she said. "Blake was your cousin, too." Her eyes clouded. "I wish I'd had a chance to tell him." A heavy sigh. "I wish I could have told him a lot of things. He didn't want to have anything to do with his weird sister, though. And he was furious that I was selling the land."

"Do you know where that land came from?" I asked with a half smile.

She looked surprised. "From the Sontags."

I shook my head. "Not those thirty acres. My brother was at the county clerk's office yesterday and found some old documents that said that particular piece of property came directly to our great-great-grandfather from Poppy herself."

Joyous' eyes grew wide. "Really?"

I nodded. "She gave it to her son."

She got up and walked over the front window. Drawing back the gauzy curtain, she gazed out at the cacti and rocks. "I guess I'll be doing some thinking about that place."

I rose and joined her at the window. "How long have you known we're related?"

"Since my parents died. Blake couldn't have cared less about the past, but they knew I was interested in history. They left me all that documentation along with a bunch of other old stuff in the attic."

"So they knew about Poppy and Zebulon?"

One shoulder lifted and dropped. "They never said anything to me about it. I bet Daddy knew, though. It was probably why he was so set on keeping that land in the family." Her eyes were wet.

"I'm sorry about what happened to them." I patted her shoulder.

A deep, shuddering breath. "Thanks."

"I'm glad you showed me the letters," I said.

She turned to look at me. "Me, too. And I'm glad you're looking into my brother's murder. We might not have been close, but he was family and I want to see justice done. If your friend didn't kill him, then someone has to find out who really did."

"Which reminds me, I have to get going."

"Of course." She walked me to the front door and smiled. "Good luck, cousin."

I nodded. "I'll take all I can get."

Outside, I walked to the Wrangler, started it up, and

pulled onto the street. Two blocks later, I pulled over and turned off the engine, mind awhirl.

I'd thought that I didn't have any family on my mother's side ever since Gamma had died. Now, I found myself liking the whole idea of having a cousin. I didn't know if I would have picked Joyous, but she was starting to grow on me.

And you can't choose your family, right?

L UPE had texted me while I'd been relearning family history with Joyous.

Will call when I get a chance.

There was no voice mail, though, so apparently she hadn't had a chance.

My watch read almost noon. Astrid was going to kill me, but I took a left, away from the shop, and pulled into Cooperhawk Court. I'd brace Harris at the restaurant after I closed Scents & Nonsense that evening, but I still didn't know exactly how Vaughn Newton fit into the picture. Maybe I could get Polly to tell me more.

My phone rang as I parked in front of Gold Rush Realty. "Colby! Did you find a lawyer?" I asked.

"Apparently, criminal lawyers are hard to come by in Poppyville."

"Yeah. That's because we don't have that much crime." *Or at least we never used to.*

The front door of the blue-and-white converted house opened, and a man emerged. His streaked hair was braided and jammed under a porkpie hat, but the rest of his clothes echoed what he'd worn yesterday afternoon while photographing my tiny house—surf shorts, T-shirt, flip-flops.

What was Tanner Spence doing in Gold Rush Realty?

"Gessie knows a guy who might be able to help," Colby went on. "But he's semiretired, and today he's in Sacramento. We're waiting for him to call us back."

"Dang. Okay, I'll try Lupe again."

We hung up, and I climbed out of the Wrangler.

Spence had come down the walkway and now stopped in front of the Jeep. He looked it up and down. "Nice ride."

My forehead wrinkled. "Most people think it's an old piece of crap."

He patted the hood. "Now, don't talk about her like that. This is a classic. What year? Ninety-eight?"

Surprised, I nodded. "You know your cars."

"This just happens to be a favorite of mine."

I gestured toward the office building. "Checking out the real estate here in Poppyville?"

He grinned and shrugged. "Maybe."

My eyebrows rose. "Why? You live in Sacramento, don't you?"

One side of his mouth turned up. "Sometimes." His eyes narrowed. "Any more questions I can answer for you?"

"I was just—"

"It's all over town, Ellie. You're trying to find out who killed Blake. I wish I'd known that before I opened my big mouth yesterday and told you all about how I hated the guy." He made a rude noise. "I didn't realize you thought I was a murderer."

"But you aren't, right?" I tipped my head to one side.

I watched to see if he reacted to what amounted to an accusation. I liked Spence; however, I couldn't be sure he was innocent, and Larken was being questioned by the police at that very moment.

When Spence did react, it was only with a look of disgust and a shake of his head.

I held up my palms in front of me. "Okay, so you hated the guy. You know you weren't alone in that."

"No wonder you wouldn't go out to dinner with me," he muttered.

I shook my head. "I told you that I'm involved with someone."

"Oh, I remember. It's 'complicated.'" He grimaced. "Too bad, because I really enjoyed hanging out with you. I'll see you around, Ellie." And he walked away.

Is this going to affect how he writes the feature on my tiny house? I wondered. Then I set my jaw. I hoped not, but it was out of my control. And what was he doing in Gold Rush, anyway? After all, now that he'd finished the article for *Conscience Magazine*, why was Spence still in Poppyville at all? Maybe he was after the Sontag land as so many others seemed to be.

When I climbed the steps to the wide porch, I saw the sales flyer for the parcel was still up in the window.

The door opened, and I almost collided with Cynthia. Today she wore a seafoam green linen suit, and her hair was in a smooth chignon.

"Ellie! How are things?" It was a rote question, but she caught herself and peered into my eyes. "Really. How are things going with the investigation into Blake's murder?"

I sighed. "Confusing, mostly. Too many suspects, but

none are quite right. The only thing I know is the one person the police suspect the most didn't do it."

"What about Felicity?" she asked. "Did you talk to her?"

"Absolutely. So did Detective Garcia. You were right about how much she loathed Blake. She didn't even bother to deny it, but she has an alibi that night from multiple people."

"And no other progress? It's been two days."

"Jeez, Cynthia. I'm doing the best I can. It all seems to revolve around some land out past the Kestrel Peak trailhead. You know, where the Sontag place is?"

She frowned. "I thought that was all a state park."

"All but thirty acres."

Hitching her Coach bag a little higher on her shoulder, she said, "Well, real estate isn't exactly my bailiwick. Max Lang said they have a suspect. Maybe you should just leave it to the police after all."

I stared at her. "Did he tell you that suspect is Larken Meadows?"

She raised her eyebrows. "No, he didn't." A speculative look settled on her patrician features. "Of course. *That's* why you're involved. It doesn't have anything to do with saving Poppyville's reputation as a sweet little tourist town."

"I want to preserve Poppyville's good name as much as anyone," I said. "But you know as well as I do that Larken had no reason to kill Blake Sontag. You were there when they met, and when they argued. I'm looking for real justice, not a quick fix."

The look she gave me made me wonder if a quick fix wouldn't suit her just fine, but then she shrugged and smiled. "Of course, Ellie. We all want justice for Blake. Now, you be sure and let me know if there's any way I can help, okay?"

I agreed, and she clicked out to her Lexus on heels that would have killed me within an hour.

Inside Gold Rush Realty, the receptionist was on the phone. From what I could hear, there was some snafu with a signing. She smiled and waved me toward a chair.

Antsy, I perched on the edge. My cell phone buzzed, and I saw Astrid had texted.

How much longer? Just wondering. Wouldn't mind taking Charlie for his walk before it gets too hot.

I put the phone back in my pocket and stood just as the receptionist finally hung up and apologized for making me wait. I went over and leaned my elbow on the counter, trying for casual.

"Say, I'm supposed to meet Vaughn Newton here." A total lie, but at least it might get the conversation going.

She frowned, and I sighed inwardly. The no-tell policy regarding potential clients would of course extend to everyone in the office. Quickly I scrambled for an excuse to find out more about Mr. Newton.

Then she said, "I'm so sorry, but you already missed him. He and Polly left together to look at the property."

The property.

I pasted a look of deep disappointment on my face.

"But you can probably catch them," she said brightly. "They left about half an hour ago."

"The place out past the Kestrel Peak trailhead, right?"

She pointed at me. "That's the one!"

"Okay, thanks!" I turned to go, then whirled back. "Say, that guy who was just in here?"

"Mr. Dreamy Eyes?" she said, and propped her chin with her hand.

"Uh, yeah. Sure. Him. What was he interested in?"

She pursed her lips while still trying to look friendly. "Oh, I don't know . . ."

I leaned forward and said in a conspiratorial voice, "He is awful cute, isn't he? His name is Tanner Spence. I was just wondering if he was meeting Polly and Vaughn, too."

She hesitated, then shook her head. "He didn't say anything about that. Looked at all kinds of listings. Land, houses, rentals. Said you can tell a lot about a town by the real estate market."

Well, that wasn't very helpful. It did make me wonder why he'd be interested in learning about the town, though.

I thanked her and quickly went out to the Wrangler. If I hurried, I might be able to "accidentally" run into Polly and Vaughn Newton.

But first I needed to run by the shop and see if Astrid was okay with holding down the fort for a little bit longer. High clouds had moved in, cutting the sunlight and lowering the temperature a bit. If they held, it would be a cooler afternoon than usual.

All the spots in front of Scents & Nonsense were full, so I pulled into a space in the lot across Corona and got out. Astrid was on the boardwalk in front of the shop with the watering can, thoroughly dousing the myriad of potted plants and window boxes that I'd neglected of late.

She looked up and saw me. Waving, she stepped past the parked cars and out into the street as I started across from the parking lot.

A roaring filled the air from the direction of Raven Creek Park. In slow motion, I twisted to see a huge black form coming toward us.

A car. SUV.

A Cadillac Escalade, in fact.

Déjà vu—right down to the freezing in place.

The gleaming chrome on the enormous boxy front flashed in the sunlight as the SUV bore down like an evil predator on its helpless prey. The engine howled. The smell of hot oil and burning metal seared the air.

Hands gripped the steering wheel at ten and two, pale and mesmerizing, looking as if they were floating behind the windshield without benefit of being attached to a body. Suddenly they wrenched the wheel, and the vehicle swung straight for me.

A frantic shrieking pierced through the roar of the engine.

Then I realized I was the one screaming. The colorful emblem set in the middle of the leering mouth of the grille was almost upon me when my muscles miraculously unlocked. I launched myself backward with all the strength I had.

It was enough to propel me away from the vehicle, but only by a hair. I felt the wind created by the rushing mountain of metal blast my face as I fell. I landed hard, crying out in pain as I bashed into the curb on my backside and bounced down to sit in the gutter.

A scorching screech of metal on metal saturated the

air. It made my teeth hurt, and I squeezed my eyes shut against it. I heard footsteps running toward me as the engine gunned, and looked up in time to see the black SUV turn the corner onto a side street.

"Ellie! Oh, my God. Are you okay?"

With an effort, I turned my head. Spence was leaning over me, horrified worry all over his face.

He ran his hand over my neck and the back of my skull, then tipped my chin up so he could look first in one eye and then the other. "Ellie? Say something."

"Something," I croaked out.

His laugh was short, but relief softened his gaze. "At least you don't seem to have a concussion. Can you move your neck?"

I slowly obliged. "I didn't hit my head."

"But you landed really hard, didn't you? I can tell by the way you're moving. Or rather, not moving. Does your back hurt?"

"It's fine. Sitting down is going to be unpleasant for a while, though." I tried a smile.

He didn't seem to notice. "Wiggle your fingers."

I wiggled.

Apparently satisfied, he sat back on his heels on the sidewalk beside me. A smooshed bakery bag with the Kneadful Things logo on it lay a few feet away.

"What happened?" he asked. "I was getting a sandwich and heard a car engine and then a scream. When I came out you were . . ." He gestured to where I still sat in the gutter. "Here." His hand was shaking.

"I was almost hit by a car," I said. "I've seen it before. In fact, it almost hit me before." I scowled. "I meant to report the driver, but with everything that's been going on the last few days, I forgot. But believe you me, that is going to be one sorry tourist when I find out who it is."

Spence looked down the street. "What a jerk. You could have been killed!"

"Uh-huh," I agreed in a quivering voice. Gingerly, I scooted up to the curb. "Ouch." My bruised behind started to throb with pain.

Raising my head, I looked across the street. A gawker knot was gathering on the boardwalk in front of Scents & Nonsense, and a few other people were gathered around a prone figure on the street.

With a start, I recognized her red hair and quirky fisherman pants.

"Astrid!" I screamed.

CHAPTER 20

I PUSHED myself painfully to my feet, ignoring Spence's protests and pointing to my friend, who lay alarmingly still on the asphalt. With a halting gait, I limped across to her and fell to my knees.

Thank heavens, her eyes were open. When she saw me leaning over her, she smiled weakly.

"You're okay," she whispered.

"I'm fine, honey." It took all my effort to kept my voice soft and calm. I scanned her all over, looking for blood or any sign of damage. It was hard to tell with her loose clothes.

"Did they hit you?" I leaned in to check out how her pupils looked, just as Spence had with me.

"Only the rearview mirror," she grunted.

Her left hand was cupped around her right shoulder. Gently, I touched it, and she yelped with pain.

"Sorry!"

"The ambulance is on the way," someone said from nearby.

"Thank you," I called out, without looking up from my friend's pinched face. "It's going to be okay," I said to her. "They'll be here soon and fix you all up."

"I don't need an ambulance! The clinic is only six blocks away. Can't someone just drive me over there?" She shifted to one side and tried to push herself up with her good hand. The movement made her gasp with pain.

"Now stop that," I said, exasperated. "They're on their way already."

"Help me sit up," she said, and tried again.

Strong male hands pushed her upright. Spence had elbowed through the growing crowd to join me beside her.

"Thanks," she rasped. Cleared her throat and winced.

"Here. You forgot this," he said, and handed me my purse. Then, with tender fingertips, Spence probed at her shoulder a couple of times. This time, she allowed it in silence.

"It's dislocated," he said. "And there might be a fracture. They'll x-ray it at the hospital."

"Clinic," she said.

"What?" he asked.

"The nearest hospital is in Silver Wells," I explained. "The ambulance will take her to the Poppyville Clinic. Don't worry—they know their stuff there."

The sound of a siren split the air, and I lurched to my feet. Spence grabbed my elbow to help steady me, and together we tried to move the gathered onlookers away from my friend.

The crowd parted to let Lupe Garcia through. As always, she looked official in dark slacks and white oxford shirt. Today's blazer was the color of oatmeal. She took in the situation with a sweeping glance and turned back to the milling people.

"Please step back, everyone. Let the paramedics through." She held up her hands with her palms out and patted the air as if pushing them away. "Come on, folks."

Everyone obeyed, murmuring as they broke away into the smaller clusters and gave us some space. The ambulance parked nearby. A uniformed man and woman got out and ran over.

I explained what had happened to them as quickly as I could. Lupe stood beside me, listening closely, her frown deepening with every word. Her eyes flicked to the onlookers, who had moved several yards away to inspect a dark blue pickup truck diagonally parked a few doors down. Its shiny side was crumpled and buckled where the SUV had sideswiped it.

When I was finished, she motioned me over by the front door of Scents & Nonsense. Lupe seemed a little surprised when Spence trailed along, but didn't say anything.

"Is there anything else?" she asked me. "Do you know what kind of car it was?"

"Cadillac Escalade. I have the license plate," I said. From the corner of my eye, I saw Spence's head jerk up.

Lupe's smile filled her whole face. "Good girl."

Pointing to an unmarked Ford Taurus that had been part of the police department for so long that it might as well have had the town logo on the side and a light bar on top, she said, "Let's go sit in my car to talk."

Spence stepped forward. "Ellie's hurt, too."

Lupe paused, her eyes traveling over me. "Are you hit?"

I gave a little laugh. "You make it sound like I was shot."

"The car didn't hit her, but she fell pretty hard," Spence said. "I don't think she has a concussion, but she should be x-rayed."

"You sound like you've had medical training, Mr. Spence," Lupe said.

He shrugged. "I've been in some dicey situations. Occupational hazard in my old job. You learn a few basics."

She considered him, then nodded. "Okay. Ellie, just tell me the license plate number and then we'll get you checked out."

"I'm fine," I protested as I reached into my purse for my cell. "I just hope my phone fared all right."

Gingerly, I removed it. "Dang it." The screen was crisscrossed with cracks, but when I pushed the ON button, Ritter's handsome face grinned up at me.

I accessed the camera function, found the picture I wanted, and handed it to Lupe.

She stared down at the screen, then up at me, then back at the screen. "You got a *picture* of it?"

"Oh!" I said. "Not just now, no. But that jerk driver almost hit me a couple days ago. Then I spied the same SUV parked in front of the Hotel California and took this picture. I was going to text it to you to see whether it would be worth reporting . . ." I trailed off. "What? Why are you looking at me like that?"

Frowning, Spence sidled up next to the detective and looked over her shoulder at the photo. His eyes widened.

"Because I know this plate number. I've been trying to find this vehicle for three days," she said.

One side of my mouth drew back. "You mean someone else reported the driver? Jeez, what a—"

"It's Blake's Escalade," Spence broke in. "That's why she's been looking for it."

My mouth closed. Opened. Closed again. I looked between them.

"He's right," Lupe said. "Mr. Spence told us he'd used the vehicle the night before Mr. Sontag was killed, but assured us he returned it to the parking lot of the Hotel California."

"Right. And I found him in the bar and returned his keys," Spence said.

"Did you stay in the bar for a while?" I asked.

Spence nodded. "Blake left, but I stayed."

"Did you hear him argue with anyone?"

Puzzled, he shook his head.

So the argument with Vaughn Newton must have happened before Spence came back to the hotel.

"But a woman asked you which room Blake was in," I said.

Another nod. "Right. You were eating dinner with her earlier when I stopped by the table. I told her Blake was in room 344."

Lupe directed a speculative look at him. "We didn't have any reason to disbelieve him about the vehicle, except we didn't find it in the parking lot the next morning in the course of our investigation."

Another of the loose ends Lupe mentioned?

Spence said, "I'd ridden here from Sacramento with Blake. When his car disappeared, I ended up renting a car for the rest of my stay here."

Suddenly, I pointed at him. "Wait. The first time that thing almost ran me down was before I'd ever met Blake Sontag. And I remember seeing the passenger in the rear-view window."

Light hair, wraparound glasses.

He ducked his head. "Guilty as charged. Not that I was driving. But I remember Blake almost hitting someone." His gaze softened for a moment. "I didn't realize it was you." Then it was gone with a shake of his chin. "He was a terrible driver."

And they were heading south out of town on River Road. "Was that when you went out to see his land?"

He nodded.

"Well, that obviously wasn't Blake behind the wheel today," I said.

"Obviously," Lupe said wryly.

"So who was it?" I asked. "Whoever took his car the night he was poisoned?"

We looked around at each other. At least I knew for sure Spence hadn't tried to run me down. The thought brought a surge of relief completely out of proportion to the situation.

"Maybe," Lupe said slowly, "just maybe, your investigating is going a little too well, Ellie."

"What do you mean?" Spence said.

She gave him a *why are you still here* look.

"She means I might be getting too close to the truth," I

said. "Because whoever was behind that wheel, a) shouldn't have the car in the first place, and b) came very close to killing me." I met Lupe's eyes and bit my lip.

His jaw slackened. "You mean it was intentional?"

"Maybe they were trying to scare you," Lupe said to me.

I nodded and shivered. "Maybe. Or maybe they just didn't get the job done."

She looked over my shoulder. "They're loading Astrid into the ambulance."

"Oh!" I turned. "I have to talk to her."

"Fine," Lupe said.

"Aren't you going to the hos— I mean clinic?" Spence asked me with a stern frown.

"I'll give her a ride," Lupe said.

Leaving them to deal with each other, I hobbled over to where Astrid was now being wheeled into the back of the ambulance on a gurney. She saw me coming and tried to raise herself up.

"Will you stop moving around?" the female paramedic admonished with a smile.

"Charlie," Astrid said. It came out *Chaahlie*.

I looked sharply at the medic.

"I gave her a little something to take the edge off the pain," she said.

"Oh, right. That's good." I patted my friend's hand. "Don't worry. Charlie's fine with Dash out in the garden for now. I'll check on them before I come see how you're doing over at the clinic. If we have to figure something else out, we will. Don't worry."

She nodded and closed her eyes. "Mmkay. Thank you, Ellie-boo."

Guilt stabbed through me. The driver of the SUV might have been aiming for me, but they'd hurt my best friend. A dark red spark of anger joined the guilt.

The paramedic climbed in with her and closed the doors. I watched them drive away toward the clinic for almost a full block before I turned back toward the store. Spence and Lupe were both watching me.

Taking a deep breath, I made my way over to them. "I'll send you that picture," I said to Lupe.

She nodded. "Good. Now, let's get you over to the doc's."

"I have to check on the dogs first, and close the shop." At this rate, I was going to be out of business. "I'll be right back."

"Can I help?" Spence asked.

I shook my head while gazing into his verdant eyes. "You've done enough. Really." Standing on tiptoe, I kissed him on the cheek.

It was possible that his cheeks turned pink, but it was hard to tell with his tan. "No problem. Um . . ."

I raised my eyebrows in question.

He looked up at Lupe, who hadn't budged and was watching us with interest. Then he grinned and shrugged before meeting my eyes again. "I'm going to call you later to check up and see how you're doing."

"Oh, you don't need to—"

"Nonsense. I'll talk to you later."

With a nod at Lupe and one last smile at me, he turned and went back across the street—probably to get another sandwich to replace the one in the smooshed bakery bag. I could still see it lying by the parking lot entrance.

I turned to go inside Scents & Nonsense, only to find Lupe watching me with amusement.

"He's cute," she said.

I pushed past her. "I'll be right back."

The dogs were looking through the sliding glass door, no doubt wondering what all the commotion was about. Once I went out and gave them some scritchin's and peanut butter treats and fresh water, they settled down on the patio again. Soon I'd changed into a pair of soft yoga pants and rejoined Lupe out front. I dialed my cell and locked the front door to the shop as it rang.

When Maggie answered, I said, "Hey there. It's Ellie."

"Good Lord, girl. Are you all right?"

That was fast.

"I'm fine. You heard about the attempted hit-and-run?"

"Nan Walton came in for lunch and told all of us." Nan was the town's 911 dispatcher. "Is Astrid okay?"

"She has a dislocated shoulder at the very least," I said. "I'm heading over to the clinic now. I don't suppose there's any chance you could come watch the shop this afternoon, is there? I know it's not your usual day . . ."

"Oh, honey. I'm on shift at the Roux now. But I could tell Harris I need to help you out—"

"No, Maggie, don't do that. You know how he is about you working for both of us. Don't make it worse. It's not a big deal—I just thought I'd try."

"You sure?"

"Absolutely. I'll check in with you later, okay?"

"Okay, hon."

Cynthia wasn't wrong that murder is bad for business. I don't think she meant it quite like this, though.

Maggie and I hung up as I stepped out to see Lupe talking with the owner of the sideswiped pickup truck. I went over and got into her car and put on my seat belt.

"You're moving like you're ninety," she said when she slid into the driver's seat a few minutes later. "Should I have insisted you ride over to the clinic with Astrid?" the detective asked in a concerned voice.

"Nah. I fell backward and landed on my behind. I'm bruised but not beaten!" I pasted on a big smile.

She rolled her eyes and started the engine.

"Is Larken still at the police station?" I asked as she pulled into the light traffic on Corona.

Her expression was grim. "She was when I left."

"Now, come on, Lupe. She sure as heck wasn't behind the wheel of that Escalade."

"We don't know for sure it was the murderer, either."

I gave her a look.

One side of her mouth turned up in a wry half smile. "You'll go pretty far to help your brother's girlfriend."

"You mean like getting my best friend hit by a truck?" I said bitterly.

She sobered. "Sorry. I shouldn't joke." Pulling out her phone, she gave it a voice command to call Max Lang and put it to her ear.

"Hey, Max? Lupe here. I think you need to let Ms. Meadows go about her business for right now."

A loud male voice spoke rapidly. I couldn't hear the words, but the volume and register increased.

"I don't think that's relevant right now," she cut in, and told him about Blake's vehicle almost running Astrid and me down in the street.

He balked.

She insisted.

Finally, she hung up and looked over at me. "He's letting her go and putting out a watch for the Caddy to all our cruisers."

"Which is, what? Three cars?" I asked.

"Two, actually. So what was that about Tanner Spence and the victim going out to see some land?"

"Remember I told you that Joyous inherited the family land when Blake died?"

"Right."

"She already had it on the market," I said. "When Blake got into town, he found out and took it right back off." I hurried on. "But now it sounds like she might have changed her mind about selling, too. Second thoughts and all."

Her lips thinned. "Which you know about because you two are such good friends all of a sudden."

"Something like that," I hedged.

She looked thoughtful. "So Joyous had a motive."

"Maybe, but less so if she's not going to sell the place now." *If that was even true. Could Joyous be playing me for a fool?* I plunged on. "But there were a couple of people who were very interested in buying that land. Once it's developed, it could be worth a lot of money. Once Blake took it off the market, one of them might have killed him because they knew Joyous wanted to sell."

"Who were these people?"

I wrinkled my nose. "Joyous told me one of them was Harris."

Lupe's eyes cut toward me. "Really."

"Yeah, but I doubt he was serious. He might have been

able to afford the undeveloped land itself, but developing it to the point where he could make a profit would cost a lot more money than he has."

"But maybe he could get the money," she said.

"Maybe," I agreed. I didn't like the idea of Harris being a murder suspect, but it wasn't the first time the thought had crossed my mind. And seeing him twice with Vaughn Newton made me wonder if my ex might have found someone from out of town to fund the project.

"Who's the other prospective buyer?" she asked.

"A guy named Vaughn Newton. He's the one Blake argued with in the Horseshoe Bar the night he died. I don't know how he fits into things, but I was at Gold Rush Realty this morning and learned he went out to look at the parcel again with one of the agents. I was about to go out there and see if I could meet him."

Lupe looked at the roof lining of the car as if invoking the patience of Job. "Just now?"

I looked at my watch. "About an hour ago. I was kind of waylaid, you know? I don't know if they'd still be there. Either way, you could check with Polly at Gold Rush about the guy. She wouldn't tell me anything, but maybe you can convince her."

"Hmm. You think?"

"There's no need for sarcasm."

Lupe turned on her blinker and slowed as we approached the small parking lot in front of the Poppyville Clinic. She pulled up in front of the door, and I got out.

"You want me to go in with you?" she called through the open passenger window.

"You have a killer to catch. I'm good."

"You're going to get those x-rays, right?" Her look was knowing.

"You bet!" Smiling, I waved and turned to go in. I had a killer to catch, too, and no time for unnecessary medical tests. My plan was to check on Astrid and then head over to the Roux Grill to ask my ex-husband about Mr. Panama Hat Newton.

CHAPTER 21

🏃

T HE clinic was small but efficient, and equipped for urgent care as well as dispensing everyday flu shots to the public. There was a small blood lab for basic testing, and a radiology room where Astrid no doubt had already been scanned and diagnosed.

The reception area was twenty by twenty-five feet, with maroon carpet, bland art on the walls, and a small play area for the kiddos in one corner. Six boxy chairs upholstered in rough peach-colored fabric lined the walls, interspersed with a couple of tables stacked with donated magazines. It smelled of antiseptic, toner ink, and Zoe Ulrich's retro Jean Naté perfume.

The receptionist bounced to her feet behind the check-in counter when I entered, a brunette woman in her forties with a pale face and sunny smile. Zoe had been a staple at the clinic for twenty-five years. To the best of my knowledge she hadn't ever worked anywhere else. Like Nan Walton, Poppyville's 911 dispatcher, she was not above breaking the rules and talking out of school. I could count on her giving me the scoop on Astrid.

She bustled out to where I stood saying, "Hi, Ellie! We're all ready for you. I hear you've had a fall. Let's get you into a room."

And then I knew why Lupe had given me that look before she drove off. She'd called ahead.

Dang it.

I wasn't getting out of those x-rays after all.

"Thanks," I muttered.

"Sure thing!" The perky receptionist led me into an exam room and told me the doctor would be right with me.

"Can you tell me how Astrid Moneypenny is doing?" I asked.

"Oh, she's going to be fine. No fracture, thank goodness—just that nasty dislocation. Doctor's already done a closed reduction. That means she popped that shoulder right back into place, no fuss, no muss, no bother. Astrid's resting comfortably now." She leaned toward me with a conspiratorial glint in her eye. "She's pretty doped up, actually. Doctor had to give her a big ol' muscle relaxant in order to do the reduction."

Poor Astrid. "Okay. Thanks."

"You hop up there on the table now. Doc will be right in."

My backside had gone from painful to numb, but now the pain was returning, a pulsing ache. Ignoring the instructions to hop up on the table, I gingerly sat in a peach-colored chair exactly like the ones in the waiting room, leaned to one side to take the worst of the pressure off, and tried to distract myself with speculation.

It looked like Spence was off the list of suspects, at least for now. But what about Joyous? I'd revealed an awful lot to her, including the possibility that she was a suspect in the murder of her brother. She'd desperately wanted to get rid of her family land, at least until I convinced her that the things she'd experienced there didn't mean she was crazy. But before that, could she really have been willing to kill her brother because he wouldn't sell?

I had a hard time believing that she'd have taken his SUV that night, though. Heck, I had a hard time imagining her leaving her house and going to the hotel. However, I couldn't be sure.

What if she really had killed Blake, and I made her nervous? We might be newfound relatives, but if Joyous did kill her brother, we weren't well enough acquainted for me to know if she'd hesitate to kill a fifth cousin to cover her tracks.

The door opened and the doctor came in. She stopped, put her hands on her hips, and tsked. "Ellie, I hear your posterior met with a hard concrete surface at a rather high velocity this afternoon."

I smiled, and found myself relaxing. "That's one way to put it."

"Shall we take a look?"

Dr. Eliza Scott was a tall African-American woman pushing fifty who wore her gray-streaked hair in a thick braid down her back. Her compassionate eyes viewed the world from behind thick black-framed glasses, and she always seemed to smell faintly of strawberries.

I did not hop onto the table, but did climb slowly. The doctor poked and prodded and moved my legs this way and that, all the time quizzing me about whether it hurt here or there or more or less.

Finally, we were done, and she proclaimed, "You have a severe hematoma, but that will heal. Nothing's broken. We'll take a few films to make sure everything is okay with your spine, though. Better safe than sorry, you know. Oh, and let me write you out a prescription for pain-killers."

She looked up at me from under her brows as she tore off a sheet from prescription pad. "You're going to want them tonight, for sure." She turned and rustled through a drawer. "Here are a couple of sample packets in case you just want to go right home."

I sighed and slid off the table. "After the x-rays can I see Astrid?"

She checked her watch. "Sure. The muscle relaxant should be wearing off in another twenty or thirty minutes. When it does, you can take her home."

"Thanks, Eliza."

She smiled and patted my shoulder. "You're very welcome."

A nurse I'd never met before came in and led me to the x-ray room. When that was finished, she said they'd contact me if there were any problems and took me to see my friend.

At least Astrid was in a real bed, in a nice room that, while small, looked more like a hotel room than a recovery room in a clinic.

She saw me come in and raised her head. Instantly, it fell back to the pillow, and she closed her eyes. "I'm a little woozy," she said.

"Don't worry. Doc Scott said you'll feel better in twenty minutes or so."

"Muscle relaxer," she slurred. "I know. God, I can't think straight."

"I'll stay with you, and then when you're ready, you can come home with me."

Her eyes widened in alarm. "Oh, no no no no, Ellie. Not *that*."

My brow knitted. "What's wrong with my place?"

"Ooooh, that staircase." She made a swirling gesture with her hand. "It's so twisty! Whew! It makes me dizzy to think about it."

I laughed. "You don't have to go upstairs. The love seat folds out. It's super comfy, and the television is right there, too."

She blinked. "Oh. Well, then that's fine." Her eyes started to drift closed, then snapped open. "Can I watch *Game of Thrones*?"

Smoothing her hair back from her face, I said, "All night long, if you want."

"Mmmkay, then."

In seconds, she was snoring.

I was itching to go see Harris and find out what he knew about Vaughn Newton, but Astrid needed me. I needed to get her settled at home first. I looked at my watch. After two. There was plenty of time.

I waited for a whole five minutes before I couldn't take

it any longer. Waving at the ebullient receptionist, I went out through the peach-and-maroon waiting room to the parking lot and called Lupe.

"They weren't out at the Sontag place," she said without benefit of greeting.

"Vaughn Newton and Polly?" I asked.

"Right. I've gone by the real estate office, and they don't have any idea when Polly will be back. I called the number the receptionist gave me, but she isn't answering."

"Polly loves her cell phone," I said. "It's strange that she'd not answer."

"I plan to keep trying," she said. "Listen, I have to go. Max wants to talk to me."

"Ugh. Sorry."

"Yeah, me, too. Later."

I called Colby next. He answered on the second ring.

"Els, I don't know what you did, but Larken is back here with me." The relief in his voice was palpable.

"I almost got run down in the street," I said.

"What?"

"You mean the news hasn't reached you guys yet? An attempted hit-and-run in front of Scents and Nonsense. There's a good chance that whoever was behind the wheel was aiming for me, and since I'm pretty sure I haven't made anyone that mad by making perfume, it must have something to do with Sontag's murder. Lupe thinks I'm getting too close to the truth."

"My God, Ellie. Are you okay? Did they hit you?"

Ruefully, I rubbed my backside. "I'm fine. Astrid has a dislocated shoulder, but the doctor fixed her up and we're heading home soon."

"If I hadn't asked you to help Larken—"

"Don't be ridiculous. I called to find out whether you reached that lawyer."

"Not yet."

"Well, keep trying. It would be nice to have someone on retainer if we need them, but Larken might be out of the woods since she was being questioned by the police when I was almost hit. Hard to ask for a better alibi than the police themselves."

I heard him take a shaky breath. "Thanks, sis. I'm glad you're okay. Do you think it would help if we left town?"

"No, Colby, I do *not* think that would help."

"Okay, okay. What do you need me to do?"

"Just sit tight," I said. "I'll call if we need anything. I'll be taking Astrid to my house to recuperate in just a few minutes."

We hung up. As I turned to go back inside, I realized we had a slight logistical problem.

A STRID was awake when I came back into her room. Not only awake, but sitting on the edge of the bed and sliding her feet into her Birkenstocks. Her arm was held immobile by a royal blue sling. She looked tired, but otherwise back to my old Astrid.

"I'm ready to go," she said.

"Me, too," I said. "Unfortunately, Lupe gave me a ride, so we don't have a car."

She sighed.

"Don't worry. I've called Spence. He'll be here any minute."

She looked surprised but didn't comment.

There were lots of people I could have called, of course. Colby would have come and picked us up, but I knew he'd have to pack up everything in the Westfalia first. Not only would that be a pain, it would probably take a while, and I wanted to get going.

Astrid signed some paperwork at the desk, and we went out to wait on the bench in front of the clinic. Spence pulled up within less than a minute. We bundled my friend into the back of his rental sedan, and I slid tentatively into the passenger seat.

"You were right about the dislocated shoulder," I said. Astrid murmured agreement from the behind us.

"And your . . . back?" Spence asked.

"All x-rayed. Doctor Scott thinks it's fine. Did you get another sandwich from Kneadful Things?"

He nodded.

"What kind?" I asked.

A snort sounded from the backseat.

His lips twitched. "Ham and Swiss on marble rye with avocado, alfalfa sprouts, mustard, and mayo."

"Wow."

Astrid giggled. "You are so weird, Ellie."

"She's still kind of drugged up," I said in a low voice.

"I see," he said, a smile still tugging at his lips.

We'd reached the end of Corona by Scents & Nonsense. A small school bus was parked in front, painted white and decorated with green trim.

"Oh, no," I groaned. "It's the church bus from Silver Wells. They usually let me know when they're going to be here." For all I knew, they had. I hadn't exactly been checking my e-mail as faithfully as usual.

"What's the problem?" Spence asked.

"I closed the shop. Darn it. They spend a ton whenever they show up."

We got out, and I heard voices coming from behind the store.

"Oh, they wouldn't." I shook my head. "They wouldn't just go into the garden if I wasn't here, if the store was closed. Would they?"

Swearing under my breath, I abandoned Astrid to Spence and trotted to the half-open gate. I pushed inside to find two dozen people milling around the Enchanted Garden. Adults pointed out the fairy gardens to children, and more than one hand clutched one of Astrid's dandelion cookies.

Wait a minute. How did these people get cookies?

"Ellie's back!"

I turned to see Maria standing on the back patio. Gessie stood beside her, and I saw Thea pass by inside the open sliding door.

The librarian hurried over. "Maggie called. Said you needed help." She blew a wisp of hair out of her eyes. "Boy, I'll say. This crowd is buying up everything. Oh, there's Astrid!" she said looking over my shoulder. "Honey, is that bulldog one of yours?"

"Sure is," Astrid called.

Tears stung my eyes. It had been a long and strange day already. I'd reconnected with my boyfriend, gained a cousin, almost been killed, eliminated at least one murder suspect in Tanner Spence, and seen my best friend lying in the street, injured. Not to mention my own bruises.

But this simple, practical gesture, and by so many of my friends, to step in and take care of my business when I couldn't—it undid me.

I let out a sob, but managed to clamp a hand over my own mouth as a couple of customers looked over.

"Come on," Spence said, and guided both Astrid and me down the path to my house. He nodded to people as we went, friendly but not inviting comment.

I fumbled out my keys and got the door open. Dash and Charlie greeted us at the door. Spence closed the door behind us, and led Astrid to a chair.

"This sofa folds down, as I recall," he said.

Her eyebrows climbed her forehead.

My laugh was shaky, but it damped down the urge to cry. "The tiny house article, remember? Spence knows all the space-saving features of this house."

"Uh-huh," she said.

He just grinned.

"Jeez, you two," I muttered.

He helped me unfold the bed. Then he took the dogs out back to let them run in the meadow for a few minutes while I got her situated. When he brought them back inside, he headed for the front door. "See you later."

"Wait!" I said.

"You need a ride someplace?"

"No, it's not that. I just wanted to say thanks. You know—again."

"You're welcome again," he said. "And I'm still going

to call." He waggled his eyebrows and went out, closing the door behind him.

"What a great guy," Astrid said from the love seat behind me. "Not to mention hot."

"Here," I said and reached toward the shelf by the television. "Let me show you how to use the remote."

CHAPTER 22

WITH her blessing, I left Astrid on my sofa with Charlie and Dash on either side to keep her company. She was drowsily watching the television when I slipped out the door.

The church bus had loaded up and trundled away, leaving me with a till full of sales, and a store in disarray. I didn't care about the mess.

"You guys are so awesome," I said. "Thank you for coming to my rescue."

"Pshaw," Gessie said. "You'd do the same for me. Heck, I think you might have found me a full-time employee, if I can get her to stay."

"Larken?" Thea asked.

Gessie nodded. "The girl doesn't know everything, but she's smart as a whip and willing to learn."

"I like her," Thea said. "Colby chose well."

"I think so, too," I said. "But she's not out of danger yet. Not until Blake Sontag's real killer is found."

"You let us know if there's anything we can do, okay?" Thea said.

"Well . . ."

"Spit it out," Gessie said.

"I hate to ask, but I think Harris might know something about this whole business."

Maria let out a low whistle. "You're kidding."

"I don't know for sure. But I'd like to go talk to him."

"And you need us to keep watching the store."

"You've already done so much," I said. "And all those sales! It'll be okay if I close—"

"Nonsense," Maria said. "We don't have any programs going on at the library until this evening. My assistant can take care of things."

Gessie nodded. "I can stay for another hour or so, but then I have a lesson."

"I have a delivery to make, but I can come back in an hour," Thea said.

My eyes grew hot again. I coughed. "Thanks. I don't think I'll be gone too long."

"You're going to the Roux?" Thea asked. When I nodded, she said, "Get yourself a burger. You don't eat enough."

"I am kind of hungry. Can I bring anyone back anything?"

They all turned me down. As I went to leave, Thea followed me. "I'll walk you out."

On the boardwalk, she stopped me. "You and Ritter okay? When I talked to him he sounded pretty down."

I smiled. "We talked this morning. Now that they have phone and Internet, I think we're going to be fine."

"Glad to hear it. You two are good together."

"I think so, too," I said. "I'll see you later."

OLDER Jeeps are not known for providing a smooth ride, and the Wrangler was no exception. For all I knew, the shocks had never been changed. I sure hadn't had it done, and now I regretted that fact with every bump in the road, every pothole and manhole cover, and every raised crosswalk on the six-block drive to the Roux Grill.

It was too late for the lunch crowd, and too early for the happy hour crowd, but there were customers all the same. A few were scattered in the outdoor seating with cool drinks and appetizers. An Australian shepherd lazed at the feet of one couple, supplied with a water bowl from the restaurant.

Rhonda was taking their order and saw me. She waved with the tips of her fingers and gave me a look as if we had a secret. In a way we did. Not everyone knew what it felt like to discover a murder victim.

The cinnamon chocolate scent of mole sauce overrode everything except the garlic that had likely become part of the actual structure of the Roux Grill. I inhaled deeply, my mouth watering. It took days for Raleigh to make a big batch of his famous mole. He did it only a few times a year, and when it was gone, it was gone.

Forget the burger. Chicken mole was in my very near future.

I sidled up to the bar and waited for Maggie to finish mixing a bloody Mary. She handed it to the customer and came down to where I stood.

"Pull up a stool, hon. Too early for a martini?"

After my day, I almost said no. "How about a ginger ale?"

"Done." She eyed me as she poured the fizzy liquid into a tall glass filled with ice. "How bad are you hurt?"

"Not as bad as Astrid." I filled her in on the details. "And I want to thank you for calling Maria. I got back to the shop this afternoon and found a bus full of people checking out the Enchanted Garden and buying things up left and right. That wouldn't have happened if not for you."

"Hey, it's in my interest for you to make money. You can afford to hire me for more hours, then." She winked.

I laughed and took a swig of ginger ale. The sticky sweet iciness of it slid down my throat like a balm. "Is Harris around?"

Her lips pressed together. "In his office."

Turning toward the back of the restaurant, I nodded. "Thanks."

"Ellie, he's not alone."

I paused.

"Detective Lang is back there, too."

Great.

It was one thing to brace Harris about Panama Hat, but I'd never get anything out of him with Max there.

"Hmm. Changed my mind," I said. "I think I'll order some of Raleigh's mole and wait a few minutes."

"Good plan," she said with a grin. "I'll put in the order."

When it arrived, I took the plate over to a table in the corner and eased myself into the seat. I soon lost myself in the complex flavors of the Roux's head chef's version of the dish—creamy and spicy, laced with garlic and pineapple, peppers, and plantain. I was wiping up the last of the sauce with a soft corn tortilla when a shadow fell across my plate.

I looked up to see Max Lang standing over me.

Sitting back, I finished my bite and swallowed. "Detective Lang."

"Miz Allbright."

"Have you tried the mole?"

"I'm not here for the food."

"That's a shame. It's some of the best in town."

"Is that why you're here? Or are you on another one of your illegal investigations?"

"Illegal?"

"You're not licensed."

There was a time when he would have intimidated me. Not now. "I'm not getting paid, and I don't need a license to ask a few questions." I stood. Even so, I came up only to his chest. I didn't care. "But you are getting paid, and you should be asking questions. There are a lot of possible suspects in Blake Sontag's murder. Suspects other than a girl who'd never even met the victim before."

His response was a stony look.

"You know I'm right."

The tiniest, teensiest nod. "You might be."

You could have knocked me over with a feather. Until, that is, he leaned down and got in my face. "But don't you ever accuse me of not doing my job again, Allbright."

It was my turn to nod. "Fair enough."

He turned and walked away without another word. I

stared after him until the door shut behind him, then looked over at Maggie. Her eyes were wide.

Grabbing my plate, I bused it back through the door to the kitchen. Raleigh was by himself, rubbing dry spices into a huge brisket.

"Ellie!"

"Raleigh, you've done it again. Love the mole."

"Already running low," he said. "Glad you got some before it's gone."

I rinsed my dish and asked over my shoulder, "Is Harris in his office?"

Raleigh nodded toward the door. It was shut, but I was pretty sure my ex could hear me. I went over and knocked.

"Yeah, come in."

I twisted the knob, walked in, and closed the door behind me.

My former office seemed more coated with dust every time I went into it. The Venetian blinds were gray by now, and the poor plant in the corner had gone to philodendron heaven. The room smelled of coffee dregs and hair gel.

Harris looked up from his desk. His dark hair curled down over his forehead, and his sneering lips gave him the slightest resemblance to Elvis Presley.

"What do you want, Ellie?"

I would have been offended if that wasn't his usual greeting. Now I just took it in stride. Taking a seat in the chair opposite him, I said, "Tell me about buying Joyous Sontag's land."

Surprise flitted across his face before he could tame it. "Not really any of your business, is it?"

"You know better than that."

"Any investments I make are my own. We don't share finances any longer." His lip curled. "You made sure of that."

Stunningly, Harris still blamed me for our divorce.

"It's my business if someone interested in that property had to kill Blake Sontag to make sure it stays on the market."

The blood drained from his face, then returned with a vengeance. "You're accusing me of murder?"

I shrugged. I didn't think Harris had it in him, but he didn't have to know that. "Someone did it, and it wasn't the suspect Max Lang jumped at before gathering all the evidence." I leaned forward. "You have some of that evidence, though. Don't you?"

Spots of outraged indignation mottled his cheeks. "Of course not."

"You know, it's also my business, though only morally, if you are putting this restaurant—and my friends' jobs—in jeopardy in order to afford that parcel of land." I was watching him carefully. Then I shook my head. "No, you love this place too much. You haven't mortgaged it."

"No."

Ah, but there was something in his eyes.

"Joyous already told me you looked at the property. So how were you thinking you'd swing it financially?"

He looked away. "It's just a possibility. God, Ellie. I'm open to opportunity, is all. Just like my partners."

"Uh-huh. Vaughn Newton?"

He threw up his hands. "Yes! Okay, yes. That's the guy. Real estate investor from Houston. Wants to develop the place."

"And the water rights? What about those?"

Harris shrugged, but he had a nasty grin on his face. "There are a lot of untapped natural resources around here."

Idiot.

"Wait, you said *partners*." Joyous mentioned that Harris and Vaughn were interested in buying. "Who else?"

"A silent partner." That grin again.

"Who is it?"

"Ellie, do you know what 'silent partner' means? In the business world it means someone who invests in a business endeavor but isn't part of the day-to-day running of it. It's someone who is, as you might expect, silent. And in this case, secret."

I found myself growing angrier with every word that came out of his mouth. "Listen, Harris. I have had a really weird day. Make that *days*. A man has been killed, your overbearing cop friend wants to arrest my little brother's girlfriend for murder, and my best friend is lying on my sofa in a lot of pain with her shoulder in a sling. The last thing I need from you is a mansplanation of what a silent partner is." I stood and leaned across the desk on my hands so that my face was nearly in his.

He pulled back.

"Now tell me: Who is your silent partner?" I demanded.

His eyes narrowed as we stared each other down. Then he smirked. "Fine. But it's on you when she finds out I told you."

I felt myself start to frown, but forced a poker face. "She who?"

"Cynthia Beck."

Well, that took the wind right out of my sails.

On the other hand, it narrowed the field of suspects. The mysterious Vaughn Newton was looking better and better.

O UTSIDE, the clouds scudded across the sky and the temperature had dropped. I looked upward, trying to judge if it was going to rain. The Wrangler had been doused plenty of times, and I had a dash cover to protect the fussy electronic bits, but I didn't relish getting soaked. I might have time to get the soft top on if I hurried home.

My phone rang as I stepped on the running board. It was Lupe. "Someone reported a black SUV careening down a street in Agate Park."

My stomach did a flip-flop around Raleigh's lovely mole sauce.

Agate Park.

"Joyous?"

"That's what I'm thinking."

I really didn't want my new relative to end up being a murderer, but it was still a possibility. Starting the engine, I said, "I'll meet you there."

"No! Ellie, wait—"

I hung up and tromped on the accelerator.

CHAPTER 23

I ENTERED the neighborhood and turned toward Joyous' house. A block away, Lupe stepped out from behind her Taurus and flagged me down. When I stopped, she climbed into the passenger side.

"Ellie, you need to go home."

I shook my head.

"I know you want to clear Larken Meadows' name, but I'm on your side. I'll handle it."

"Lupe, someone tried to kill me, and they hurt my friend. It's personal now. I'm not going home."

We locked eyes for what seemed like a long time before her head inclined an infinitesimal amount. "Let's just check out the neighborhood first, okay? I want to make sure we're not jumping the gun."

"Okay."

"Then if we find the Cadillac, I'll call for backup."

Again, I agreed. "Can you drive?"

Her forehead wrinkled. "Of course."

I pulled into a parking spot and put on the dash cover. The wind had picked up, and leaves were eddying against the curbs as the trees stretched and shifted their limbs in the moving air. When I was satisfied the dash of the Wrangler wouldn't get wet, I grabbed my purse and got out. It took me about four times as long as it should have for me to exit my vehicle.

Lupe looked on with a skeptical eye. "I think you should go home and join Astrid on the sofa."

"Funny," I said, and got into her car.

We drove around for a while. Up and down each street, peering into driveways and noting cars on the street. Unfortunately, there weren't very many of those. Agate Park was a neighborhood where people took their vehicles to the car wash every week and then parked them safe inside their garages.

"There's an alley," I said.

Lupe turned and maneuvered down the passage between backyards. We didn't see the black SUV, though. A block later, she turned down another.

"You know where we need to go," I said.

She gave me a sideways look.

I sighed. "Sorry. I'm a little cranky."

"Did Doc Scott give you any pain pills?"

"Yeah."

"Did you take any?"

"Not yet. I want to keep a clear head."

Her chin dipped. "I get it. But Ellie, do you really think I don't know where the murder victim's sister lives? I'm just covering all our bases." She grinned at me then. "Which I've done. Let's check out her place."

She turned down another alley and stopped by a back fence. "This is it. Come on."

We got out and quietly shut the doors on the Taurus. I was torn, but that didn't matter. The truth was the truth, even if Joyous was my cousin. After all, Blake had been, too.

The sky rumbled overhead as we sidled down the alley to the wooden garage. Lupe peered around the corner, then nodded back at me and edged around it.

I felt like I was on a military mission.

We reached the front of the garage and stood in the driveway looking back at it. There were no windows on the side or front of the building. Turning, I gazed up at the white curtains on the second floor of Joyous' house. I knew from experience you could look through them without anyone seeing in.

Was she watching us?

Lupe tried to lift the garage door, but it was locked.

"Come on," Lupe whispered. "I want to look in the backyard."

"It's just a vegetable garden," I said. "There's no place for a car back there." Then I looked down the side of the garage we hadn't sneaked around.

"Look." I pointed.

The side door was slightly ajar.

Lupe walked down to take a look. Relieved that we didn't have to act like something out of a *Law & Order* rerun, I followed. I was right on her heels as she pushed the door open a little farther and slipped inside.

The Escalade took up the whole space. There was barely

enough room for us to scoot around the outside of it. Max would have been too big to fit, I thought uncharitably. When we got to the right side, I saw the crumpled front panel and torn fender.

This was definitely the vehicle that had hit the pickup on Corona.

And had nearly sent Astrid and me to the next world.

Anger flared deep underneath my sternum, and I turned back toward the house even though I couldn't see it through the wooden garage wall.

"Time to call in the cavalry?" I asked Lupe.

"Yep," she said, and sidestepped out of the garage with her cell phone in hand.

I started to follow, but then I smelled it and paused. Where was it coming from?

There. The scent wafted, ever so faintly but ever so recognizably, from the open window of the Escalade.

Chanel No. 5.

After a moment's hesitation, I opened the door and climbed in. It was entirely possible I was contaminating a crime scene, but I had to be sure.

Yes. Subtle but distinct. Recent.

The one and only perfume Cynthia Beck ever wore.

I closed my eyes and tried to think. Lots of people wore that perfume. Thousands. Hundreds of thousands, if not more.

But not in Poppyville, and not in Blake Sontag's missing vehicle.

Unless she was in it the night we all had dinner together in the Empire Room!

For a moment, relief whooshed through me.

Then I remembered Cynthia coming down the steps of the Hotel California that night and unlocking her silver Lexus with her key fob. She'd driven herself to dinner that night.

And I pictured her running her finger down Blake's arm as I watched from across the lobby. The whisper in his ear that made him smile. Had she been making plans to come back later?

I felt a little sick as I thought about Cynthia's motive to kill Blake Sontag. Harris had told me less than an hour ago that she was his silent partner, and I'd been going on and on in his office about anyone interested in the Sontag property being a possible suspect.

I'd completely discounted Cynthia as a killer. But now I thought about the mercenary look she got when she talked about money, about how her whole life seemed to revolve around it. Did she even have friends that weren't in her women's marketing group?

I thought that was all state park, she'd said when I told her about the thirty acres of Sontag land.

Real estate really isn't my bailiwick, she'd said.

She'd lied.

And just that morning I'd told her I was interested in justice, not a quick fix. Perhaps she'd been counting on Max arresting his "suspect," but I was the fly in the ointment.

Had Cynthia actually tried to kill me? It was easier to believe than I liked.

"What are you doing?" Lupe hissed from the doorway.

I got out of the Cadillac. "Joyous didn't kill her brother, and she didn't try to run me down on Corona Street this afternoon."

Lupe frowned. "What are you talking about? Why else would Blake's SUV be in her garage?"

I was searching for an answer when we heard a scream from inside the house.

We took off at a run.

Lupe veered toward the front yard, but I opened the back gate Joyous had led me through. Was that just this morning? So much had happened. I passed the raised beds, where the sun shade over the greens rippled in the wind. Trying to see through the curtains, I hurried to the back door that led to the kitchen, and gave the knob a twist.

It was unlocked. Slowly, I pushed it open.

The high-pitched squeal of unoiled hinges broke the silence. Swearing under my breath, I opened the door with a silent jerk and stood on the threshold.

"What was that?" came Cynthia's voice from the living room.

"I don't know." Joyous sounded terrified.

"Let's go find out, shall we?"

Crossing quickly, I saw them both sitting in the living room. Cynthia held something shiny in her hand.

A gun.

My blood chilled.

She was coming to her feet when I stepped out of the kitchen. She startled and quickly held the gun behind her back as she sat back down.

"It's just me, Joyous," I said casually. "I think I left my scarf here this morn . . . Oh! Hi, Cynthia."

She looked utterly confused.

They were sitting side by side on Joyous' tan sofa. There was a steaming cup of tea on the low table in front of my cousin, along with a single sheet of paper and a fountain pen.

I gave a little laugh. "I swear, I'd forget my head if it wasn't screwed on." I snagged Joyous' gaze. "Have you seen it?"

"Uh."

"The scarf. It was blue, with those little yellow sparkles?" I'd never owned a scarf with any color of sparkles.

"Oh!" She looked at Cynthia, then at me. Her eyes grew bigger. "*That* scarf. No, I haven't seen it."

Over their shoulders, I saw movement through the curtains.

Lupe.

"I wonder if I left it out front," I said and walked past them to the door. "Maybe I took it off when we were looking at that yucca. I'm helping Joyous with her garden," I said to Cynthia.

"Hold it," she said.

I arranged a puzzled frown on my face and kept reaching for the door handle. "What's the matter?"

She leaped to her feet. "Stop right there, Ellie." Her lips twisted, and she raised her hand toward me. It held the gun. The small revolver should have appealed to my fondness for miniatures, but despite its pink pearl grip that was nearly eclipsed by her pink pearl–tipped fingers, I didn't care for it one little bit.

I stopped right there. "Gosh, Cynthia. What are you doing with that?"

"Who's out there?" she demanded.

"No one." I gave a half shrug.

"How stupid do you think I am? You heard Joyous

scream, didn't you?" She shook her head. "You give someone a little push and they get all hysterical."

Eyeing the gun, I shook my head. "I really don't know how stupid you are."

Cynthia sneered.

"But you must be stupid if you think you're going to get away with this."

Her lips pressed together in anger. "Why do you have to stick your nose into *everything*, Ellie? If it hadn't been for you, I'd be free and clear. Now I have to figure out what to do with you, too."

I looked at Joyous. "What do you mean, 'you, too.'"

"She brewed up some more of that tea," my cousin said in a shaky voice. "She said she was going to make me drink it."

I hadn't thought I had any more adrenaline left in my body, but it turned out I did. "Did you? Drink it, I mean?"

She shook her head, and my shoulders slumped in relief. "I haven't written my suicide note yet."

It clicked together. "Right," I said slowly. "You write a note that admits you killed your brother, then kill yourself using the same poison because you feel so guilty."

Cynthia gave a satisfied nod. "Pretty good, huh? I mean, as long as you alerted the cops to the fact that it was a plant poison that killed Blake, I might as well use that."

"They would have figured that out anyway," I said. "You said you'd be free and clear, but they'd know."

She smirked. "Actually, they wouldn't have. See, unless they have something to specifically test for in an autopsy, it's very difficult to narrow down plant poisons."

I stared at her. "You did a lot of homework, didn't you?"

"Something like that." She took a deep breath.

Moving cautiously, I sat on one of the chairs across from Joyous. Cynthia moved as if to stop me, but I was already seated by the time she'd made up her mind.

I thought I heard the tiniest squeal from the direction of the kitchen. "You killed Blake so Joyous would put their land back on the market, right?" I asked loudly, hoping to cover any noise Lupe might make as she entered the house.

"Do you know how much profit you could make from that place?" Cynthia said, looking up at the ceiling as if praying to the god of money.

"Were you really going to work with Harris?" I couldn't keep the dismay out of my voice.

She shrugged. "Commerce makes strange bedfellows."

I shuddered. "Did you make Blake drink *his* tea at gunpoint?"

I was firing every question I could think of at her.

Come on, Lupe.

"Of course not. No one is going believe I'd shoot a gun in a crowded hotel. Think, Ellie." she tapped her temple. "I was going to open one of his gingko capsules and put the belladonna in there, but your little Larken had already brought Blake a nice tea to help him sleep. So I just added the belladonna to that when I helped him brew it up. Then, when the police decided his death was suspicious, I had a built-in scapegoat." She rolled her eyes. "Until you decided to get involved."

"So after dinner you left the hotel, but then you went back. Blake was expecting a good time, and got killed instead," I said.

Joyous let out a small moan.

Cynthia ignored her. "I might have given him a good time if my partner could have convinced him to sell the land."

"Your partner," I said. "Not Harris, but Vaughn Newton. That's what they argued about in the bar that night."

Cynthia nodded. "But as persuasive as Vaughn can be, he couldn't talk Blake into selling that land. Nor would Blake develop it with me. That was what I tried first, before he even came back to Poppyville. So I had to get my old beau here, so I could talk to him in person."

"*That's* why you told him about my tiny house?" I breathed.

She gave a very unladylike snort. "Tiny house. God. Only you would want to live in a garden shed."

I bit my tongue.

She went on. "But Blake had grown remarkably attached to that family land over the years. He was quite unreasonable about it. So when Vaughn called me to let me know he hadn't been successful, I knew there was only one thing to do."

"Vaughn was in on it, too?" I asked, wondering about Harris.

"God, no. Vaughn is a good ol' boy from Houston who's willing to use a little intimidation, but that's about it."

"Unlike you," I said flatly.

"You're a woman. You know how hard it is for us to get ahead."

I stared at her.

"You won't get my land if you kill me," Joyous suddenly said.

Cynthia sank into the other chair, gun still pointed at me. "I thought about making you sign it over, but that might look too suspicious. It will come up at public auction eventually. I can wait."

"It won't," Joyous shook her head. "I already decided to take it off the market, and this afternoon I updated my will. The land will go to my next of kin."

Our captor smirked. "Nice try. I checked. You don't have any next of kin."

Joyous smiled, and I saw Cynthia stop herself from opening her mouth in surprise. "Actually, I do have a distant cousin." She nodded at me. "Ellie."

Cynthia's nostrils flared. "You have got to be *kidding* me," she yelled. She raised the gun. "Drink the tea!"

"Don't," I warned Joyous. And to Cynthia, "Frankly, I'd rather be shot than die from nightshade poisoning. Hallucinations, vomiting, convulsions—and those are just a few of the things that happen before you finally lose consciousness."

Joyous blanched at my words, but then her face turned stony, and she pushed away from the coffee table. "You did that to my brother?"

A flash of lightning lit the sky outside. Seconds later, thunder boomed overhead.

"Oh, please. I'm sure it wasn't that bad," Cynthia said.

"It was," I said. "And you unplugged the room phone from the wall so he couldn't call for help."

"Well, of course." She sounded exasperated. "I hid his cell phone in his dresser drawer, too. Now, let's face it: You're both going to drink the tea," Cynthia said, as if she hadn't heard a word I said. "The police won't be able to tell exactly what happened. In the meantime, I'll think of some way to explain it to my advantage."

"Oh, come on. We're not all that incompetent," Lupe said, stepping into the kitchen doorway. She was training a gun on Cynthia. "Put down the weapon."

I would have been terrified, but Cynthia just looked furious. She hesitated, then looked toward the front door.

"I hate to sound trite," Lupe said. "But we have the place surrounded."

Finally, the leader of the Greenstockings' shoulders slumped. Lupe stepped up and took her gun, then opened the door to let two uniformed police in. They quickly frisked Cynthia and put handcuffs on her. Lupe led Joyous into the kitchen.

As the uniformed officers were taking Cynthia out the door, I asked them to wait a minute. Standing in front of her, I considered telling her what a horrible, evil woman she was.

But condemnation would slide off her like warm butter, so I settled on, "Trying to kill me and then dumping Blake's Cadillac in his sister's garage was genius, but I still don't understand why you took Blake's vehicle the night you gave him the poison. Didn't you drive your own car back to the hotel?"

She looked down her nose at me. "Of course not. Someone might have seen my Lexus. It's rather noticeable, you know." She sniffed. "I walked."

I felt my forehead crease. "But why not walk back home then?"

She turned bright red. "I broke a heel."

I stared at her. My lips began to twitch. "You broke a heel."

"Yes. You'd know what that's like if you ever wore proper business attire."

"You stole the car of a man you killed because your heel broke and you needed a ride home." A laugh snorted out of my mouth, and it was all I could do not to tip over into hysteria.

Outside, it was raining, steady but gentle. Thunder rumbled in the distance, but the storm was already passing.

CHAPTER 24

LUPE, Astrid, and I sat in rocking chairs on the Scents & Nonsense patio and looked out at the Enchanted Garden. Dash and Charlie gnawed on rawhide chews at our feet, while Nabby stalked the perimeter of the fence in the cooler weather. Yesterday's rainstorm had knocked the heat right out of the atmosphere, and while the temperature would still climb considerably as the day went on, there was a feeling that the relentless swelter of summer was falling behind us. The plants in the garden appeared refreshed, and after the events of the last few days, I was feeling better than I had a right to.

After I'd arrived home the night before, I filled Astrid in on what had happened while she was binge watching *Game of Thrones* with Charlie. Then I finally took one of the painkillers that Dr. Scott had given me and tumbled into bed. I'd slept like a dead person for ten solid hours and woken after eleven in the morning. I'd hurried out of my house, only to find Astrid and Lupe sitting on the patio of Scents & Nonsense, nibbling on buttery anise-and-cinnamon bizcochitos, and sipping strong tea.

Maggie was keeping an eye on things inside the shop and insisted that I join them. Now I gratefully took another sip of steaming Darjeeling.

"You have to give me this recipe," Astrid said. The bright blue sling that kept her arm and shoulder immobilized reminded me of the baby sling she'd carried Precious the teacup pig around in. Had that really been only four days ago?

"It's my mother's," the detective said. She'd brought the cookies over, saying that Astrid being unable to bake gave her an excuse to cook in her tiny apartment. "She always made them for the holidays, but I figured this was a kind of celebration, too."

I shifted the soft pillow on the right side of my seat and carefully stretched my leg out. Even my falling injury was less painful today, though it would take a while to heal altogether.

"We might need something bubbly if we're celebrating bringing a murderer to justice," I said.

"A double murderer," Lupe said.

I stopped my fussing and turned. Astrid was staring at her.

Now that she'd snagged our attention, Lupe gazed out at the garden and smiled a grim smile. I was glad it wasn't directed at me. "Cynthia Beck had used deadly nightshade to kill before, when she lived in San Diego. Husband number one."

"Holy moly," Astrid breathed. "So one of her divorces wasn't a divorce at all?"

"Oh, no. She had the two divorces, too. She didn't advertise being a widow after she moved to Poppyville, I take it?"

Astrid and I shook our heads. She said, "I always called her a mantrap, but I had no idea she was a black widow."

The detective nodded. "She got away with it for years. Probably wouldn't have ever been caught if she hadn't tried it again." She looked pointedly at me. "And if you hadn't known right off the bat what killed Sontag."

"So that's why she knew plant poisons were hard to detect in an autopsy," I said. "She'd done her research a long time ago, and then she'd recognized the belladonna when she saw it on the land she wanted to buy."

"Exactly."

"But how did you find out?" Astrid asked the detective. "Her husband's death must have been a long time ago."

"Thirteen years ago," Lupe agreed. A cat-who-just-ate-the-canary look settled on her face. "She confessed."

I frowned. "You're kidding. I mean, it just doesn't seem like Cynthia to say or do anything that isn't in her own best interest."

"Ah. But I convinced her it was in her best interest. Once I found out she'd had three marriage licenses, I called the police in San Diego and found the guy who'd investigated her first husband's death. He sent me her file online, and I spent all night going over it."

I searched her face. Now that I wasn't dwelling on my own posterior and had a modicum of caffeine in my system, I could see the dark circles under her eyes. Lupe hadn't slept at all since I'd seen her last. A true professional. I couldn't imagine Max Lang losing one second of sleep, or sacrificing one beer or ball game, in order to dig deeper into crime.

Not to mention then baking up a batch of yummy cookies.

She continued. "I found enough that I thought I could build a case." She shrugged. "When I talked to Cynthia earlier this morning, I managed to convince her of that and told her the prosecutor would likely go easier on her if she came clean. It took some persuading, but eventually, she did just that."

"Nice job!" I lifted my cup.

"To getting Larken off the hook," Astrid said, holding her tea aloft.

"To good police work," I said.

Lupe grinned and her weariness seemed to drop away. She lifted her cup as well. "To justice." A wry expression crossed her face. "And to no more murders in Poppyville and never having to work with Max Lang again."

"Amen," Astrid and I intoned.

THE bell over the door to Scents & Nonsense jingled, and I looked up from where I was pricing a new shipment of scented drawer liners to see Tanner Spence silhouetted in the light from the street. It had been almost a week since Cynthia's arrest, and he'd called a couple of times to check on how I was doing.

He strode in and stopped in front of the counter. "Lookie what I have." He slid a folder across to me.

Raising my eyebrows, I opened it. Inside was a mock-up of the article on my tiny house.

"Oh, this is great," I said, flipping through the pages. "Longer than I thought it would be, too."

"Read it," he said, and went over to pour a cup of coffee and grab a chocolate chip cookie.

Astrid might not want to *have* to make cookies, but as long as she could manage recipes that only required one hand and a stand mixer, she was determined not to stop. She was back at work at Dr. Ericcson's office and still pet sitting, too.

I read through the article. It was informative, with a casual voice that was friendly and accessible, so the reader learned a lot while feeling like they were getting to know the author—and the subject, which in this case was me. It was a strange feeling.

The pictures were artful compositions that also conveyed the creativity and ingenuity of the man who had designed my tiny house. There was a mention at the end that he was interviewed elsewhere in the magazine.

After all that posing Spence had made me do, the only photo of me was a candid shot I hadn't even known he'd taken. I was leaning over the alembic, and he'd caught the steam starting to swirl from it into the air. The expression on my face was as dreamy as any I'd seen on Larken.

I didn't know whether to be flattered or dismayed.

"You like it?" he asked, and handed me a cookie.

Absently, I bit into it while flipping through the article

again. "I love it." Looking up, I said, "You aren't required to show it to me, are you?"

"God, no. But I wanted you to see it before it comes out in the magazine." He shrugged disarmingly. "I'm pretty proud of it."

"You should be."

He smiled.

I smiled.

"Is that why you're still in town?" I asked finally.

His eyebrows rose in amusement. "Not exactly."

I waited.

Spence's grin widened. "I love small towns."

I stared at him.

"I live here now," Spence said. "Just signed a lease on an apartment on the west side of town."

I blinked. "Because . . . ?"

"Like I said, I love small towns. And in the short time I've been here, Poppyville captured my interest."

I couldn't keep the skepticism out of my voice when I said, "Poppyville captured your interest."

"Uh-huh. Along with some of its inhabitants. One in particular, but she's not available. So it's not like I'm moving here for her." Then he dropped the teasing tone. "Listen, Ellie. I'm a freelancer. I work all over the place, and I live wherever I want to. For a long time, I was overseas for months at a time, but I'm done with that gig. Still, it never made sense for me to own a home."

He took a breath, watching me as he spoke. "I'm on a month-to-month lease in Sacramento, but I'm tired of the city. I like Poppyville. A lot. And I like you." He held up his hand as I began to protest. "I know you have a long-distance relationship going on, and I respect that. But we can be friends. Or not, if that somehow feels wrong to you. Either way, I'm going to stay here for a while." He seemed to struggle for the right words, then shrugged. "It just feels right here."

"Okay," I said.

"Okay, what?"

"Friends." I stuck out my hand.

He grinned and shook it.

After all, how could I argue about Poppyville feeling right to someone else, when my whole life it had been the only place I'd ever wanted to be?

I STOOD beneath the circle of willows and listened. Mead-owlarks, red-winged blackbirds, and the cawing of crows. A breeze pushed the tree branches back and forth. Far overhead, a jet plane carried passengers to a faraway place.

The air smelled of sage and dust and sun-warmed clay. No bubble gum. Nothing weird.

But the weird was there, hiding. I could feel it.

The fences were all down, the gate gone, the edges of Miss Poppy's original parcel of land left to the imagination. It all felt so much bigger as a result, even the shallow red cliff, the crumbling chimney, and half-fallen wall.

Leaving the trees behind, I joined Larken, Colby, and Joyous in the remains of the old cabin. They were discussing the particulars of the agreement they'd reached. The ruins would stay right where they were, but Joyous would bring in an expert to make sure they were structurally safe. Ditto for the wellhead.

Joyous kept looking over her shoulder at the willows as if they were going to spontaneously generate a blanket of tule fog on a moment's notice. Heck, for all I knew, they might. But I wasn't worried, and I caught her eye to let her know that.

She smiled weakly and turned back to Larken and my brother.

My long-lost cousin had started seeing a therapist, and already seemed far happier. It made my heart glad every time she smiled. She'd decided not to sell her thirty acres, but she wasn't ready to spend much time there, either.

So she and Larken had figured out a compromise. Joyous would give Larken a long-term lease for a pittance. Larken could use the money she got from her grandfather for off-grid systems like solar and wind power that could be moved if she ever wanted to relocate, and she and Colby were already making plans to build a straw-bale house to live in.

Like I said: crunchy.

And yes: Colby was on board.

Oh, he'd still have his Westfalia, and he'd probably still take off sometimes. But he and Larken had found a way to compromise as well.

Life was good.

RECIPES
AND
AROMATHERAPY

Astrid's Lavender Shortbread Cookies

Sweet but not too sweet, these cookies are pretty and delicate enough for a shower or wedding. They also pair well with a sharp cheddar for a snack or dessert course. Dried lavender buds can be found in many tea shops and are readily available online. If you use fresh from your garden, throw in an extra tablespoon. Other options are savory flowers from sage or thyme, or tiny pansies. You can substitute another ¼ cup of all-purpose flour for the ground nut flour but the texture won't be quite as nice and crumbly.

Makes 24 cookies

2 cups flour
¼ cup almond, walnut, or coconut flour
¼ teaspoon salt
1 tablespoon dried lavender buds OR 2 tablespoons fresh
1 cup unsalted butter (room temperature)
½ cup sugar
½ teaspoon vanilla extract

Combine flours, lavender buds, and salt in a food processor, pulsing a few times to combine. Don't over mix. Add butter, sugar and vanilla and process until a ball forms. Transfer dough to a 14-by-20-inch sheet of parchment paper that has been lightly floured. The dough will be a bit sticky. Form it into a log about eighteen inches long and two inches in diameter. Roll the parchment to encase the log and refrigerate for 2 hours or more. At this stage, you can also wrap it in plastic and freeze it for up to a month.

Preheat the oven to 375 degrees F and line a baking sheet with more parchment paper. Slice the shortbread roll into

¼-inch slices and place them on the baking sheet about an inch apart. Bake for 20 minutes or until golden around the edges. Cool thoroughly on a wire rack and store in an air-tight container for up to a week.

Maria's Favorite
Peppermint Foot Polish

The menthol in peppermint oil creates a cooling sensation when you use this refreshing scrub to exfoliate dry feet. Peppermint is also known to improve blood circulation, and has antifungal properties. Epsom salt has a lot of magnesium, a mineral that promotes relaxation. Sugar contains glycolic acid, an alpha hydroxy acid that assists in exfoliation. The suggested oils are low fragrance, so won't interfere with the heady scent of the peppermint.

½ cup Epsom salt
½ white sugar
½ cup almond or avocado oil
20 drops peppermint essential oil

Combine all ingredients in a mixing bowl and transfer to a glass jar with a lid for storage. To use, soak feet in a basin of water or the bath for five to ten minutes to soften skin. Scoop out some of the scrub with your hand and apply to feet, rubbing it in with your fingers (or a nail brush). Rinse thoroughly.

If you love Bailey Cattrell's
Enchanted Garden Mystery series,
read on for a sample of the first book in
Bailey Cates's *New York Times* bestselling
Magical Bakery Mystery series!

BROWNIES
AND BROOMSTICKS

is available from Obsidian
wherever books are sold.

THIS was a grand adventure, I told myself. The ideal situation at the ideal time. It was also one of the scariest things I'd ever done.

So when I rounded the corner to find my aunt and uncle's baby blue Thunderbird convertible snugged up to the curb in front of my new home, I was both surprised and relieved.

Aunt Lucy knelt beside the porch steps, trowel in hand, patting the soil around a plant. She looked up and waved a gloved hand when I pulled into the driveway of the compact brick house, which had once been the carriage house of a larger home. I opened the door and stepped into the humid April heat.

"Katie's here—right on time!" Lucy called over her shoulder and hurried across the lawn to throw her arms around me. The aroma of patchouli drifted from her hair as I returned her hug.

"How did you know I'd get in today?" I leaned my tush against the hood of my Volkswagen Beetle, then pushed away when the hot metal seared my skin through my denim shorts. "I wasn't planning to leave Akron until tomorrow."

I'd decided to leave early so I'd have a couple of extra days to acclimate. Savannah, Georgia, was about as different from Ohio as you could get. During my brief visits I'd fallen in love with the elaborate beauty of the city, the excesses of her past—and present—and the food. Everything from high-end cuisine to traditional Low Country dishes.

"Oh, honey, of course you'd start early," Lucy said. "We knew you'd want to get here as soon as possible. Let's get you inside the house and pour something cool into you. We brought supper over, too—crab cakes, barbecued beans with rice, and some nice peppery coleslaw."

I sighed in anticipation. Did I mention the food?

Her luxurious mop of gray-streaked blond hair swung over her shoulder as she turned toward the house. "How was the drive?"

"Long." I inhaled the warm air. "But pleasant enough. The Bug was a real trouper, pulling that little trailer all that way. I had plenty of time to think." Especially as I drove through the miles and miles of South Carolina marshland. That was when the enormity of my decisions during the past two months had really begun to weigh on me.

She whirled around to examine my face. "Well, you don't look any the worse for wear, so you must have been thinking happy thoughts."

"Mostly," I said and left it at that.

My mother's sister exuded good cheer, always on the lookout for a silver lining and the best in others. A bit of a hippie, Lucy had slid seamlessly into the New Age movement twenty years before. Only a few lines augmented the corners of her blue eyes. Her brown hemp skirt and light cotton blouse hung gracefully on her short but very slim frame. She was a laid-back natural beauty rather than a Southern belle. Then again, Aunt Lucy had grown up in Dayton.

"Come on in here, you two," Uncle Ben called from the shadows of the front porch.

A magnolia tree shaded that corner of the house, and copper-colored azaleas marched along the iron railing in a riot of blooms. A dozen iridescent dragonflies glided through air that smelled heavy and green. Lucy smiled when one of them zoomed over and landed on my wrist. I lifted my hand, admiring the shiny blue-green wings, and it launched back into the air to join its friends.

I waved to my uncle. "Let me grab a few things."

Reaching into the backseat, I retrieved my sleeping bag and oversize tote. When I stepped back and pushed the door shut with my foot, I saw a little black dog gazing up at me from the pavement.

"Well, hello," I said. "Where did you come from?"

He grinned a doggy grin and wagged his tail.

"You'd better get on home now."

More grinning. More wagging.

"He looks like some kind of terrier. I don't see a collar," I said to Lucy. "But he seems well cared for. Must live close by."

She looked down at the little dog and cocked her head. "I wonder."

And then, as if he had heard a whistle, he ran off. Lucy shrugged and moved toward the house.

By the steps, I paused to examine the rosemary topiary Lucy had been planting when I arrived. The resinous herb had been trained into the shape of a star. "Very pretty. I might move it around to the herb garden I'm planning in back."

"Oh, no, dear. I'm sure you'll want to leave it right where it is. A rosemary plant by the front door is . . . traditional."

I frowned. Maybe it was a Southern thing.

Lucy breezed by me and into the house. On the porch, my uncle's smiling brown eyes lit up behind rimless glasses. He grabbed me for a quick hug. His soft ginger beard, grown since he'd retired from his job as Savannah's fire chief, tickled my neck.

He took the sleeping bag from me and gestured me inside. "Looks like you're planning on a poor night's sleep."

Shrugging, I crossed the threshold. "It'll have to do until I get a bed." Explaining that I typically slept only one hour a night would only make me sound like a freak of nature.

I'd given away everything I owned except for clothes, my favorite cooking gear, and a few things of sentimental value. So now I had a beautiful little house with next to no furniture in it—only the two matching armoires I'd scored at an estate sale. But that was part of this grand undertaking. The future felt clean and hopeful. A life waiting to be built again from the ground up.

We followed Lucy through the living room and into

the kitchen on the left. The savory aroma of golden crab cakes and spicy beans and rice that rose from the take-out bag on the counter hit me like a cartoon anvil. My aunt and uncle had timed things just right, especially considering they'd only guessed at my arrival. But Lucy had always been good at guessing that kind of thing. So had I, for that matter. Maybe it was a family trait.

Trying to ignore the sound of my stomach growling, I gestured at the small table and two folding chairs. "What's this?" A wee white vase held delicate spires of French lavender, sprigs of borage with its blue star-shaped blooms, yellow calendula, and orange-streaked nasturtiums.

Ben laughed. "Not much, obviously. Someplace for you to eat, read the paper—whatever. 'Til you find something else."

Lucy handed me a cold sweating glass of sweet tea. "We stocked a few basics in the fridge and cupboard, too."

"That's so thoughtful. It feels like I'm coming home."

My aunt and uncle exchanged a conspiratorial look.

"What?" I asked.

Lucy jerked her head. "Come on." She sailed out of the kitchen, and I had no choice but to follow her through the postage-stamp living room and down the short hallway. Our footsteps on the worn wooden floors echoed off soft peach walls that reached all the way up to the small open loft above. Dark brown shutters that fit with the original design of the carriage house folded back from the two front windows. The built-in bookshelves cried out to be filled.

"The vibrations in here are positively lovely," she said. "And how fortunate that someone was clever enough to place the bedroom in the appropriate ba-gua."

"Ba-what?"

She put her hand on the doorframe, and her eyes widened. "Ba-gua. I thought you knew. It's feng shui. Oh, honey, I have a book you need to read."

I laughed. Though incorporating feng shui into my furnishing choices certainly couldn't hurt.

Then I looked over Lucy's shoulder and saw the bed. "Oh." My fingers crept to my mouth. "It's beautiful."

A queen-size headboard rested against the west wall, the dark iron filigree swooping and curling in outline against the expanse of Williamsburg blue paint on the walls. A swatch of sunshine cut through the window, spotlighting the patchwork coverlet and matching pillow shams. A reading lamp perched on a small table next to it.

"I've always wanted a headboard like that," I breathed. "How did you know?" Never mind the irony of my sleep disorder.

"We're so glad you came down to help us with the bakery," Ben said in a soft voice. "We just wanted to make you feel at home."

As I tried not to sniffle, he put his arm around my shoulders. Lucy slipped hers around my waist.

"Thank you," I managed to say. "It's perfect."

LUCY and Ben helped me unload the small rented trailer, and after they left I unpacked everything and put it away. Clothes were in one of the armoires, a few favorite books leaned together on the bookshelf in the living room, and pots and pans filled the cupboards. Now it was a little after three in the morning, and I lay in my new bed, watching the moonlight crawl across the ceiling. The silhouette of a magnolia branch bobbed gently in response to a slight breeze. Fireflies danced outside the window.

Change is inevitable, they say. *Struggle is optional.*

Your life's path deviates from what you intend. Whether you like it or not. Whether you fight it or not. Whether your heart breaks or not.

After pastry school in Cincinnati, I'd snagged a job as assistant manager at a bakery in Akron. It turned out "assistant manager" meant long hours, hard work, no creative input, and anemic paychecks for three long years.

But I didn't care. I was in love. I'd thought Andrew was, too—especially after he asked me to marry him.

Change is inevitable . . .

But in a way I was lucky. A month after Andrew called off the wedding, my uncle Ben turned sixty-two and retired. No way was he going to spend his time puttering around the house, so he and Lucy brainstormed and came up with the idea to open the Honeybee Bakery. Thing was, they needed someone with expertise: me.

The timing of Lucy and Ben's new business venture couldn't have been better. I wanted a job where I could actually use my culinary creativity and business know-how. I needed to get away from my old neighborhood, where I ran into my former fiancé nearly every day. The daily reminders were hard to take.

So when Lucy called, I jumped at the chance. The money I'd scrimped and saved to contribute to the down payment on the new home where Andrew and I were supposed to start our life together instead went toward my house in Savannah. It was my way of committing wholeheartedly to the move south.

See, some people can carry through a plan of action. I was one of them. My former fiancé was not.

Jerk.

Lucy's orange tabby cat had inspired the name of our new venture. Friendly, accessible, and promising sweet goodness, the Honeybee Bakery would open in another week. Ben had found a charming space between a knitting shop and a bookstore in historic downtown Savannah, and I'd flown back and forth from Akron to find and buy my house and work with my aunt to develop recipes while Ben oversaw the renovation of the storefront.

I rolled over and plumped the feather pillow. The mattress was just right: not too soft and not too hard. But unlike Goldilocks, I couldn't seem to get comfortable. I flopped onto my back again. Strange dreams began to flutter along the edges of my consciousness as I drifted in and out. Finally, at five o'clock, I rose and dressed in shorts, a T-shirt, and my trusty trail runners. I needed to blow the mental cobwebs out.

That meant a run.

Despite sleeping only a fraction of what most people did, I wasn't often tired. For a while I'd wondered if I was manic. However, that usually came with its opposite, and despite its recent popularity, depression wasn't my thing. It was just that *not* running made me feel a little crazy. Too much energy, too many sparks going off in my brain.

I'd found the former carriage house in Midtown—not quite downtown but not as far out as Southside suburbia, and still possessing the true flavor of the city. After stretching, I set off to explore the neighborhood. Dogwoods bloomed along the side streets, punctuating the massive live oaks dripping with moss. I spotted two other runners in the dim predawn light. They waved, as did I. The smell of sausage teased from one house, the voices of children from another. Otherwise, all was quiet except for the sounds of birdsong, footfalls, and my own breathing.

Back home, I showered and donned a floral skort, tank top, and sandals. After returning the rented trailer, I drove downtown on Abercorn Street, wending my way around the one-way parklike squares in the historic district as I neared my destination. Walkers strode purposefully, some pushing strollers, some arm in arm. A ponytailed man lugged an easel toward the riverfront. Camera-wielding tourists intermixed with suited professionals, everyone getting an early start. The air winging in through my car window already held heat as I turned left onto Broughton just after Oglethorpe Square and looked for a parking spot.

The
Enchanted Garden
Mysteries

by Bailey Cattrell

The Enchanted Garden behind Elliana Allbright's perfume shop draws people of all ages with its fragrant flowers and lush greenery. But when the magical serenity is interrupted by crime, it's up to Ellie to step in to solve the mystery before everything withers around her.

Find more books by Bailey Cattrell
by visiting prh.com/nextread

"Cattrell...casts a spell over readers with this charming mystery filled with likable characters and funny dialogue."—**Kings River Life Magazine**

"Bailey Cattrell has planted all the seeds to get this series off to a blooming start."
—*Escape with Dollycas into a Good Book*

baileycattrell.com
🐦 WriterBailey

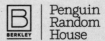